"You will never want for anything as long as you are my wife."

Leah couldn't find words to express how she felt. It was a lot to take in. She'd gone from having no plans or future to having a man offer her marriage and a daughter. She loved Molly, and yet she still couldn't get out the word *yes*.

Molly burst through the kitchen door and ran to Leah. The little girl grabbed her free hand and tugged for Leah to follow her.

Leah gently pulled her back and said, "Go tell Mrs. Frontz that I'll be there in a few minutes." It was only after the little girl hurried away that she remembered Molly couldn't or wouldn't speak. How was she going to tell Mrs. Frontz what she'd said?

She turned her attention back to Jake. He still held her hand firmly in his. "What about friendship, Jake? Can you allow yourself to be my friend?"

He squeezed her hand gently and warmth filled his voice. "I will give you friendship and respect, and I believe we will get along fine, Leah. Just don't ask for my heart..."

Books by Rhonda Gibson

Love Inspired Historical

The Marshal's Promise
Groom by Arrangement
Taming the Texas Rancher
His Chosen Bride
A Pony Express Christmas

RHONDA GIBSON

lives in New Mexico with her husband, James. She has two children and two beautiful grandchildren. Reading is something she has enjoyed her whole life, and writing stemmed from that love. When she isn't writing or reading, she enjoys gardening, beading and playing with her dog, Sheba. She speaks at conferences and local writing groups. You can visit her at www.rhondagibson.net, where she enjoys chatting with readers and friends online. Rhonda hopes her writing will entertain, encourage and bring others closer to God.

A Pony Express Christmas

RHONDA GIBSON

⟨H⟩ **HARLEQUIN**® LOVE INSPIRED® HISTORICAL

Recycling programs for this product may not exist in your area.

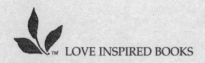

LOVE INSPIRED BOOKS

ISBN-13: 978-0-373-28288-3

A Pony Express Christmas

Copyright © 2014 by Rhonda Gibson

www.Harlequin.com

Printed in U.S.A.

I will not leave you as orphans; I will come to you.
—*John* 14:18

A very special thanks goes to Jean Williamson for all the wonderful resources that she provided to make this book possible. Thanks to Jean Kincaid, Kim Mort and Christina Rich. To James for your love and support, and above all, to my Lord and Savior.

Chapter One

❧

South Platte, Colorado
Winter 1860

"Rider! Coming in fast!"

Leah Hollister didn't have time to worry about her luggage tossed carelessly to the ground by the stagecoach driver, or the fact that the coach's rapid exit had drenched her feet in wet, cold snow. She heard horse's hooves pounding the ground, bearing down on her and the four-year-old child whose hand she gripped tightly within her own.

"Move, lady!" Panic filled the male voice that called out.

Leah scooped up the little girl and fled across the icy snow toward the porch of the large log cabin closest to her. Reaching it, she turned in time to see a young man on a horse speed past, leaping over her luggage with ease and heading toward a barn that was located on the far side of the house. Aware of the danger she'd just escaped, Leah's hands started to shake.

Two men were in front of the barn. One of them

sat on a compact, sorrel-colored horse. The other man stood off to the side, watching the transfer between the riders, just as Leah was doing.

The first rider handed a flat leather saddle bag to a man astride a mustang. As soon as the second rider had the bag, he laid low over his horse's neck and was gone almost as fast as the first young man had ridden in.

Leah stared after the rider until he could no longer be seen. She shivered as a blast of icy wind hit her uncovered face. Where was he going in such a hurry? Her gaze moved back to the barn and stable. The two other men had disappeared, presumably inside.

Molly buried her face in Leah's neck and shivered. She tried to burrow her slight body closer. One small gloved hand tangled in the opening of Leah's coat, allowing more cold air in, while the other clung to her worn rag doll.

Taking a deep breath, Leah walked back to their luggage, which still sat in the middle of the yard. Her tired brain tried to register what had just happened. Why had those riders been in such a hurry? What was in that bag that was so important? She'd never seen anything like it, but then, she hadn't seen much of life outside of an orphanage. Even the stagecoach ride had been exciting to a girl who'd been so completely sheltered. It dawned on her that perhaps the stage stop was also a pony express stop as well.

Her body trembled from cold as well as fright as she set Molly down and reached for the closest bag. The child's feet went in different directions on the slick, packed snow and Leah grabbed for her, helping her to stand upright again.

"You're okay," she comforted, but to her dismay, her voice wavered. Leah swallowed hard then leaned forward, determined to get her luggage and move them inside, out of the cold and out of danger's way. As she reached for the handle, her weight shifted and she did a little dance trying to regain her balance, but she couldn't stop the movement of her feet or the slickness of the ice underneath them. Leah's boots slipped out from under her and she fell, face forward, into her suitcases.

She groaned. This day had just gone from bad to worse. Tiredness lay on her shoulders like a mountain of snow on a small hilltop.

A man extended a hand to help her up. "Are you all right?"

"I'm fine." Leah pretended not to see his outstretched hand and used the nearest bag to push herself up from the ground. The toe of her boot caught in the hem of her dress. She groaned as she heard the tearing of fabric. Working to untangle her foot with as much dignity as she could muster, Leah pushed herself upright once more and dusted the snow from the front of her dark green traveling dress. "I believe so." She felt Molly's hand bunch up in her skirts.

The sharp voice softened as he offered, "Here, let me help you carry these inside the station."

For the first time, Leah looked at the owner of the deep voice. He scooped up two of the larger bags and stood tall before her. She estimated him to be about six feet, maybe an inch taller. He wore what looked like a buckskin coat and a brown, floppy hat. Dark brown boots covered his feet. She couldn't help but notice he also wore some sort of gun on his narrow hip.

Her breath caught in her throat when she glanced up to find a pair of soft, coffee-colored eyes watching her. Eyes that earlier had been wide with concern now seemed full of unhidden laughter. Even so, she liked his eyes and the deepness of his voice.

Embarrassed, Leah looked away; she pulled her short, threadbare coat around her. "Thank you for your help, Mr.—?"

"Just Jake, ma'am."

"Jake." The cold November wind pulled at her straight, mousy-brown hair, reminding her that she was no beauty and that she was soon to be a married woman. She raised her head. "I'm ready." He nodded and then strolled to the front porch.

A tiny hand tugged at her skirts once more. Leah reached down and picked up the little girl. Molly tucked a gloved thumb between her plump lips and laid her head on Leah's shoulder. She knew Molly was tired from their trip. Warmth for the little girl filled her heart as Leah patted her back.

Jake returned and picked up the other two bags. His gaze searched hers, a quizzical look in their depths. "You really should get inside, ma'am." Once more he turned to walk to the porch.

Leah nodded but didn't move forward. She focused her attention down the snow-covered road toward the town laid out before her. South Platte, Colorado, a small town that was about ten miles from Julesburg, Colorado. From what she could see through the falling snow, South Platte had a general store, a restaurant, a blacksmith shop, a livery, a church, and from the sound of the piano coming through an open door, a saloon.

Leah frowned. Did she really want to be here? She sighed. What other choice did she have? She had promised to deliver Molly to her uncle, Jake Bridges, and to marry Mr. Thomas Harris.

Her gaze jerked to the wide shoulders and back of the man carrying her luggage. Could that Jake be Molly's uncle, Jake Bridges?

For the first time she focused on the house that served as the stagecoach stop and also functioned as a pony express home station. A large log house stretched out before her. Sheds, various outbuildings and the barn surrounded the log house. Even though it was early, a full month before Christmas, the house had red and green fabric twisted into a form of garland on the second-story railing. A Christmas wreath hung on the door.

To one side of the house, a small grove of trees was the only vegetation in sight. The sound of running water had her looking over her shoulder at a river that was mostly frozen over. It wasn't close to the house, so she felt sure Molly would be safe.

The little girl shivered in her arms. Leah pulled Molly closer, realizing that every day she spent with her would make it harder for both of them when the time came to part. Leah would soon move out to the Harris ranch, and Molly would move into her uncle Jake's home, wherever that might be.

"Are you coming?" The man named Jake opened the door to the ranch-style building. His gaze ran over her and the little girl before he turned and stepped inside.

His deep voice pulled her from the stupor she'd been in and Leah nodded. If he truly was Jake Bridges, then Leah knew she'd have to get word to Thomas Harris of her arrival. Or perhaps she could hire Jake to take her out to the Harris ranch.

Thomas Harris's name whispered through her tired mind as she sat the child back down and scooped up the last remaining bag, Molly's bag. She really didn't know Mr. Harris, other than what she had read in the two letters he'd sent. They'd never met or exchanged pictures. The thought of marrying a complete stranger both scared her and offered a strange sense of comfort. Being Thomas Harris's wife would give her a permanent home. Something Leah had wanted all her young life.

Molly's little hand tangled into her skirt once more, reminding her that she had to take care of the child before she even contemplated her own life. Molly had been Leah's constant companion for over three months.

Knowing cholera was sweeping Sweetwater, Texas, at a rapid pace, Molly's father had brought her to the orphanage for safekeeping. The children and people who worked there very seldom came into contact with the town folks and he'd felt sure that Molly would be safe from the sickness that was sweeping the area. Then, when it became clear that both Molly's parents had taken ill, Mrs. Wilkins, the headmistress of the orphanage, had placed the little girl in Leah's care.

Molly's story was a sad one, for sure. Her mother had been the first to become sick. The poor woman died after several long days and then Molly's father had taken ill. He'd struggled against death, knowing he'd be leaving the little girl behind. It was only after he'd written a letter to his brother and then extracted the promise from Leah that she'd take Molly to his brother in Julesburg, Colorado, that he'd finally given up his battle. Fortunately, Molly would grow up knowing her parents had loved her, unlike Leah, whose parents had abandoned her on the orphanage doorstep when she was less than a year old.

Leah craved a home, and Molly's arrival in her life had made her realize how much. Shortly after John Bridges's death, Leah had answered Thomas Harris's ad for a mail-order bride. She'd learned from the ad that the Harris ranch was located in the same general area where Jake Bridges lived. She'd hoped to be close to the child and still be able to have a husband and a home.

Leah looked down at Molly. She still wanted to make sure the child was settled before she continued with her own life. No child should ever be left alone in this world.

Leah stepped up onto the porch. Making sure Molly was safe had become of utmost importance. If this Jake was her uncle, then Molly and Leah's time together would soon be over. Leah felt a tug at her heart and it wasn't comfortable. She was going to miss the little girl.

Jake reappeared and took the bag from her. His gaze darted to Molly before he went back into the house. Had she seen a flicker of recognition on his face? Surely not. Even if Molly was Jake Bridges's niece, Molly's father had said his brother had never met the little girl.

He dropped the bag inside the door and then held it

open for Leah and Molly to enter. Warm air stung Leah's chilled face. She looked about the spacious room. One half was a sitting area and the other looked like a dining room. The smell of coffee teased her tired senses as a door opened on the other side of a long kitchen table and a heavyset woman entered.

Seeing the two of them standing in the doorway, the woman rushed across to Leah and grabbed her hand, pulling her farther into the house. Her warm hands felt wonderful against Leah's ice-cold one. "Come on in, child. You must be chilled to the bone."

Leah allowed the woman to guide her toward the table. She noticed that the young rider who'd almost run them down was already seated. He held a steaming mug in his hands.

"I'll go get you a cup of coffee. That will warm you up and then you can tell us all about yourself." The woman left the room before Leah could respond.

"We weren't expecting anyone to arrive on the stage today." Jake pulled out a seat for her before he sat down.

The young rider added, "I'm surprised the stage came this far out with the snow falling and another storm on the way."

Both men stared at her as if waiting for her to speak. Leah didn't know what to say. Did she want to confide in total strangers?

How did she tell them that she and Thomas had agreed to meet in South Platte and then get married in Julesburg, Colorado? That Thomas had promised her a fine home and lots of room to raise flowers during the spring and summer months.

He'd sent stagecoach tickets and money for both

her and Molly to travel to the pony express station in South Platte. Leah remembered feeling blessed that her future husband was a generous man. She'd followed his written instructions and taken the very next stage out as winter had already hit Colorado and there would be no further chances for her to arrive before summer.

However certain she had been about the plans she'd made, discussing her personal business with strangers went against the grain and she found herself reluctant to divulge any private information. Did she really want to share all that? She took a deep, fortifying breath.

The older woman returned and placed a steaming mug down in front of Leah. "Here, drink this. It will make you feel better in no time." She was a short, plump woman with bright blue eyes. "I'll have your cider out in a few moments, Jake. Would the little one like a cup of hot apple cider, too?"

Molly nodded. Her doe-like eyes studied everyone about the table. Then she ducked her head and hid her face behind Leah.

"That would be lovely. Thank you." Leah patted Molly on the back.

The woman smiled and hurried back into what Leah assumed was the kitchen. For some odd reason, Leah had figured Jake to be a coffee-drinking man but it was obvious that the older woman knew he'd want apple cider.

Uncomfortable silence filled the room. Leah leaned down and unbuttoned Molly's coat. She pulled the little stocking hat from the girl's head. Soft blond curls floated about her angelic face. No one spoke as Leah removed the gloves from Molly's hands. She looked into the little girl's warm brown eyes. "Better?"

Molly nodded and tucked her thumb into her mouth once more. At four years old, she should have already stopped sucking her thumb, but with both her parents gone, Leah didn't have the heart to take away that single comfort from the little girl. She pulled Molly up onto her lap.

Leah picked up the hot cup and took a sip. She was surprised that the coffee tasted so rich and full. She'd been traveling for days, and most of the places the stage had stopped had served weak coffee with hardly any flavor. She almost sighed out loud as its warmth slowly filled her chest and stomach.

The woman returned with a metal pot that she set on the table and two more steaming mugs. The smaller one she placed in front of Molly. "Here you go, little one. This should help warm you up." A gentle smile graced her lips as she looked at Molly.

The sweet fragrance of apples drifted from the cup. Leah noted it was only about half full and didn't steam like her coffee or Jake's larger drink. She picked up the cider and handed it to Molly. It was warm to the touch, not hot. "Thank you." She offered a wobbly smile.

The older woman dropped into a chair at the head of the table. "You're welcome. I'm Agnes Frontz. Me and my husband, Charles, run this pony express station. He's at the general store picking up supplies but will be back in time for supper." She pointed to one of the two men. "This here is Will. He's one of the pony express riders that lives here when he's not working."

The rider tilted his head in her direction. He looked

no more than sixteen years old. His blue eyes sparkled in her direction as if he knew something she didn't.

Agnes moved on to the big man. "And I believe you've already met our stock tender, Jake Bridges."

Her heart sank. Leah looked at the big man. Light blond hair and brown eyes the same shade as Molly's looked back at her. She'd planned to find Molly's uncle but had hoped to delay her separation from the little girl for as long as possible.

Oh, Lord, please give me the strength to leave Molly in the care of her uncle.

Jake nodded at Leah before lifting the sweet cider to his lips and drinking deeply from the cup. He held her deep crystal-blue eyes over the rim. She had to be one of the prettiest women he'd seen in a long time. What was she doing out here in the middle of nowhere?

Her voice shook as she said, "It's nice to meet you all. My name is Leah Hollister."

"What brings you to our neck of the woods?" Mrs. Frontz asked.

Leah raised her head and looked Mrs. Frontz in the eyes. "Thomas Harris and I are to be married."

Mrs. Frontz poured more coffee from the metal pot into Will's cup. "Is he coming for you dear? With the weather it might take a while, but you're welcome to stay here and wait for him, if you'd like."

Jake watched Leah's lids slip down over her eyes as she shifted in her seat.

"I've some unfinished business before I let him know I've arrived." Her gaze rose to Jake's face, as if her business had something to do with him, before lowering once more. "But I'm sure Mr. Harris will be happy to pay for my room and board when he arrives."

The little girl slurped her drink and giggled. She was a cute thing but didn't look much like her mother. Jake wondered how long Mrs. Hollister had been a widow.

His first impression of her had been that she had good looks but no brains. Who else but a clueless city girl would stop in the middle of the yard like that and look about like a lost lamb? Hadn't Mr. Edwards, the stage coach driver, told her that this was a pony express station? That riders came in fast and hard?

Mrs. Frontz stood and picked up the coffeepot. "Don't you worry none about that. I'm sure the Harris men will take care of everything." For a moment she stared at Leah, the coffeepot extended away from her body, a questioning look in her eyes. Jake saw Leah's shoulders stiffen almost as if she dreaded giving the answers Mrs. Frontz required. She barely hid her surprise when Mrs. Frontz turned to the kitchen, calling back over her shoulder, "Boys, gather up the lady's bags and carry them up to one of the guest rooms."

Jake and Will pushed back their chairs to do as they were told.

Leah's soft voice stopped them. "I can take them." She set the little girl down and was on her feet in an instant.

"Oh, no, you won't." Mrs. Frontz set a bowl of steaming stew on the table and took Leah's arm. "You are going to sit right here and warm up while I feed you both. Then we'll send you off to your beds."

Jake hid his smile as he watched Leah do as she was told. Agnes Frontz was a hardworking woman who always got her way. She cooked and cleaned up after the riders and expected them to obey her every word.

She wasn't hard on them, but she did like to mother them. It looked as if Leah Hollister was about to receive the same treatment.

Jake picked up two of the bags he'd brought in earlier. The first time he'd seen the cases, with Mrs. Hollister standing in the middle of them, it had scared ten years off his life. He'd called to her that the rider was coming, and for a split second Jake had thought she was deaf or something. She'd stood as still as a statue before her sense had kicked in and she'd grabbed up the child and raced for the cabin.

Her soft voice stopped him at the foot of the stairs. "Mr. Bridges?" He heard a catch in her throat.

Jake turned. "Yes?"

Her words came out in a rush. "I'd like to speak with you alone."

His head shot up and a light eyebrow cocked upward. She returned his gaze, a determined glint in the eyes that stared unblinkingly back at him. Her hand gently stroked the little girl's hair.

"I'm not sure alone is a very good idea," Mrs. Frontz announced.

Jake nodded and handed the bags to Will, who juggled them but continued up the stairs. He looked to the older woman. Jake knew Mrs. Frontz meant well, but from the determined look on Mrs. Hollister's face, Jake felt he needed to hear her out. "We'll be over by the fireplace, Mrs. Frontz. If you don't mind taking care of the child for a moment, I'm interested in Miss

Hollister's business with me." He walked toward the big overstuffed chair that sat beside the fireplace.

Mrs. Hollister looked to Mrs. Frontz, who simply shrugged her approval. Leah placed her napkin on the table. "Thank you for watching Molly. I promise this won't take long."

Jake leaned against the rocks of the fireplace and waited. He couldn't help but be curious. What could she possibly want to talk to him about? They were strangers.

Her soft skirts swished across the wood floors. Leah Hollister was a beautiful woman. She held herself with regal grace as she approached him but her sea-blue eyes betrayed the unease she felt. She was probably the most eye-catching woman he'd ever seen. How long would she be staying?

For a moment he allowed himself to imagine what marrying a woman like her would be like. He pushed the thought away. Jake had no business thinking about women, period. He'd decided a long time ago to keep his distance from them. It wasn't that he didn't like the fairer sex, but he'd learned from past experience that they couldn't be trusted.

Today should have been his wedding anniversary. Instead his brother, John, was celebrating his own marriage. Five years ago, his brother and Jake's fiancée, Sally, had ripped his heart out. The betrayal had been almost more than he could bear. An hour before they were to meet at the church for Sally and Jake's wedding, Sally had arrived at the Bridges' farm. She had stood with her head down, not looking him in the eyes, while his older brother wrapped a protective arm around her shoulders and confessed that they'd married that morning in the wee hours of dawn.

Hurt by his brother's betrayal and the loss of Sally's love, Jake had taken the bag he'd packed for his honeymoon and left. Since his parents had already moved on to be with the Lord, he knew John and Sally would take over the small farm. There was no place for him there any longer. He'd not looked back, except once a year to reflect on the pain his heart had endured and to vow never to allow another woman into it again.

Maybe he was a fool, but Jake had taken the time to write his brother and tell him where he'd landed over the years. Jake had asked that they not write back unless he was truly needed and John had abided by his request.

Jake had determined in his heart that he'd never fall in love again. It hurt too much when the one you loved betrayed you.

Once she was seated, Leah spoke, pulling him from his sad thoughts. "Please, Mr. Bridges, sit down. I really don't want to crane my neck to speak to you."

She seemed to have the upper hand in the conversation, so Jake did as she asked. He sat down on the footstool with his back turned away from the dining table where Mrs. Frontz and Molly waited. He could hear the older woman speaking to the child. Jake turned his attention to Leah. "All right, I'm sitting. What is it you have to say to me?"

Leah dug into the pocket of her dress and pulled out an envelope. He watched her swallow as she looked down at the cream-colored paper. "I think it would be best if I just give this to you. Then you can ask me any questions you'd like."

He nodded his agreement and took the packet. Dread filled him as he turned it over. *To: Jake Bridges. From: John Bridges* was written across the front of the envelope.

What could his brother have to say that hadn't been said the day he'd left? He'd claimed to love Sally and couldn't live without her. He'd begged Jake to understand and asked him to reconsider leaving. But none of that mattered. John and Sally had betrayed him and he couldn't face them, not yet, maybe never.

But why had John sent a letter with a complete stranger? He looked up at Leah Hollister. He saw sorrow in her eyes and a deeper sense of dread filled him as he slid his finger under the sealed flap and opened the envelope.

He forced his gaze from her eyes and focused on the letter.

Dear Jake,
By the time you get this letter I will be dead. Sally passed away last night and the illness that took her has now consumed me, as well. I am writing this letter in hopes that you have forgiven us by now and that you will not hold our daughter, Molly, accountable for the harm that we did to you. Please take care of my daughter and love her as if she were your own.
John

More lines had been added below John's signature but Jake couldn't bring himself to read them, not yet. He stood and walked to the fireplace. He was thankful Miss Hollister didn't say anything as he passed her.

As surely as if someone had closed their hand about his throat, he felt the air squeeze from his lungs. Time had passed and with it the life of his brother. Never would Jake be able to make amends. He felt hot tears burn the backs of his eyes at what he'd lost and what his stubborn pride had cost him.

That same pride forced him to read the elegantly printed lines below his brother's. He flicked the paper open once more and continued reading.

Mr. Bridges,
Your brother passed away a few weeks ago. I am sorry for your loss. We will be sending his daughter to you since there is no room for another child at the orphanage and you are her only remaining relative that we can locate. It is our fondest hope that Molly will find her voice and happiness with you. Mr. Johnson, the bank president, has requested you contact him in regard to your farm.
Mrs. Wilkins, Sweetwater, Texas.

Jake swallowed the lump in his throat. He'd lost his brother and was about to become guardian to a niece that he'd met for the first time moments ago. If he understood the letter correctly, Molly also didn't speak. His throat felt dry, his eyes stung. His heart broke again.

He stood and leaned his forehead against the cool rocks of the fireplace and grieved. *Lord, what am I going to do? I have no room for a child. No place to keep her. I'm not sure I can do this.*

Chapter Two

Leah stood and placed her hand on Jake's shoulder. "I'm very sorry, Mr. Bridges, to have to bring you this sad news." She didn't know what else to say. His shoulder felt warm under her hand. The muscles tensed beneath her touch.

"Jake."

What did he mean? Leah dropped her hand from his shoulder. "Excuse me?"

He raised his head. Warm, brown, tear-filled eyes looked into hers. "Please call me Jake."

Shock at seeing the raw pain in his gaze took Leah's breath away but she managed to nod.

He squared his shoulders. "Thank you for bringing me the letter," he said. He looked over her head and across the room to where Molly sat at the table playing with her doll. "And for bringing her to me."

Again Leah nodded, not trusting her voice to escape around the knot in her throat.

"I hate to ask but…" His voice trailed off.

Leah swallowed. "You may ask me anything, Mr.—" she paused as she remembered his request

"—Jake." She kept her voice low, not sure she wanted Mrs. Frontz to hear her using his Christian name.

"Can the child stay with you until she gets to know me better and I can figure out a place for her to stay?" Sorrow filled his deep voice. His eyes returned to her face and pleaded with her to give him this time.

"I need to let Mr. Harris know I'm here," Leah answered. "But, until he comes for me, I will take care of Molly."

He nodded his acceptance of her terms. "Thank you." With those words, Jake took one last look at Molly and left the house.

Leah watched him go. She felt his sorrow deeply. The door had shut behind him before she turned her attention back to the other two people in the room. Leah didn't want to speak with Mrs. Frontz right now. Human nature would have the woman questioning her and it wasn't her place to tell Mrs. Frontz about Jake's loss.

"Why don't you drink your coffee?" Mrs. Frontz offered, indicating with her hand that Leah should return to the table.

Leah looked to Molly. The little girl had finished her apple cider and simply sat watching the adults. If she could talk, Leah wondered what she'd say.

Not wanting to reveal Molly's true identity until Jake was ready, Leah declined Mrs. Frontz's invitation with a shake of her head. "Thank you for the coffee, Mrs. Frontz, but if Molly is finished, I'd like to rest for a little while."

Molly hurried to her side. The little girl placed her hand within Leah's as if offering her support.

Mrs. Frontz nodded but the disappointment in her

face remained. Was she disappointed because she wanted to get to know Leah better? Or that Leah wouldn't be sticking around to answer her questions regarding Jake?

"Will placed your bags in the first room to your left at the top of the stairs." Mrs. Frontz pushed her chair back and gathered up the cups.

Leah smiled. "Thank you." At the other woman's nod, she took Molly's hand and climbed the stairs. What would she and the little girl do once they were behind closed doors? Leah sighed as she opened the door to their room. It was chilly and the quilt looked warm and cozy on the top of the bed. A nap sounded good to Leah but she didn't think she could sleep, knowing that Jake was somewhere hurting over the loss of his brother.

Molly entered the bed chamber, laid her doll on the quilt and crossed to the window. She clapped her little hands and pointed past the frost-covered glass. Snow drifted lazily to the ground. The little girl dug in her pockets and pulled out her hat and gloves. She ran toward the door and waited.

A quick glance about the room told Leah it was clean and had been well tended, but she'd look more closely later. "And where do you think you are going, young lady?" Leah asked, reaching for her coat.

Molly pointed back to the window.

"I see." Leah crossed the room to help the little girl get the hat and gloves on her head and hands. A smile graced the child's face as she tried to see out the window. It was as if Molly was afraid the snow would stop falling and she'd miss her chance to play in it.

Once she had Molly dressed and her own coat,

gloves and hat on, Leah laid a finger over her lips. "Let's be real quiet as we go outside. We don't want to disturb Mrs. Frontz, do we?"

Molly nodded her head in agreement. Leah knew it was cowardly to sneak out of the house but she just wasn't ready to face the woman's questions again. Also, she wanted to spend a little more time with Molly, alone, having fun and not facing the future. Cowardly, maybe, but at least for a little while she'd be happy.

The little girl tugged on her arm, drawing her attention. Leah scooped the child up and opened the door. She looked both right and left. Not seeing anyone she closed the door behind them and hurried to the stairs. The main rooms were empty and they managed to escape out the front without Mrs. Frontz seeing them.

Leah sighed as she lowered the child to the ground. Now what? They couldn't stand in the front yard, because who knew when one of those pony express riders would come swooping in. She grabbed Molly's hand and headed to the side of the house, away from the barn and the possibility of being seen from the kitchen.

It was quiet on this side of the house. Apple trees formed a small orchard and Leah smiled. Snow was already piling up against the house and Molly danced around trying to catch snowflakes on her tongue.

"How about we build a snowman?"

Molly rushed back to her and nodded.

They worked together as the snow fell swiftly. The call of "Rider coming in fast!" carried to them but neither paid any mind.

Leah knew they were far enough away from the front of the house that they didn't need to worry about the rider. The snow was a wet snow and packed well. It continued to come down and both she and Molly were wet. They stepped back to study their snowman. Molly pointed to the smallest snowball on top of the other two. She then pointed to her eyes, nose and mouth. Her small head cocked sideways as she looked up at Leah.

"Yes, he needs a face," Leah agreed.

The little girl nodded and then pointed to her own hat-covered head. Now where would she find a hat? Leah wondered. "I agree. He needs a hat."

Leah recognized Jake's voice before she turned around to see him leaning against the house.

"That's a nice-looking snowman you have there, Molly."

She nodded and pointed again at the place where its face should be. As if she thought that wasn't enough, Molly also pointed at her face.

Jake's chuckle warmed Leah's insides. How long had he been standing there? His eyes still held a hint of sorrow but she saw affection for Molly in them, too. That was good. Leah had been afraid he'd tell her he couldn't or wouldn't take his niece.

She watched as he walked forward with two stones and placed them where the snowman's eyes should be. Molly tapped her nose with a gloved finger.

He nodded. "Yep, still needs a nose." He took Molly's gloved hand and walked over to the trees where he broke off a small stick and returned. Jake held it out for Molly to take and then lifted her to put it into place.

When he returned her to the ground, Molly looked up at him and grinned. Did she realize that Jake was her uncle? Did he resemble her father enough for the little girl to put the two together? Leah didn't know.

Molly's brown eyes turned on her and she pointed to her lips.

"I'm not sure what we can use for his mouth," Leah confessed, looking about. The ground was covered in snow. Maybe they could dig and find a few stones to create the lips.

The little girl frowned. Suddenly her eyes lit up and she ran for the house.

Leah started to follow her but Jake's warm hand on her arm stopped her.

"She's just going into the house."

She turned to face him. "How can you be so sure?"

Jake laughed. "Didn't you see the look on her face? She thought of something she has and went to get it."

"Oh." Leah rubbed her cold hands together. Earlier she'd been too busy to notice the cold but now with Molly gone, and aware she was alone with a stranger, Leah began to feel uneasy. With the thin gloves and even thinner coat she was beginning to feel chilled to the bone, too.

"I hope Mrs. Frontz didn't give you a hard time after I left," Jake said, blowing on his own gloves to warm his hands.

Leah felt a moment of embarrassment. "No, I didn't give her the chance. Molly and I went up to our room after you left and then we sneaked outside while she was in the kitchen."

"I'm sorry. I should have stayed and explained to

her what was happening." Sorrow filled his warm eyes again.

Leah reached out and touched his arm. "It's all right. She didn't come right out and ask me what we'd discussed. I wouldn't have told her if she had. She'll understand soon enough." She didn't need to tell him that it was his responsibility to tell his employers about Molly, not hers.

Jake nodded. "Yes, I plan on telling everyone this evening before supper. But, I'd like to talk to Molly about it first."

"That would be best."

He seemed pleased at her response. "I hope you don't mind but I've asked Mrs. Frontz if we can have lunch in private."

Leah turned big eyes on him. "I'm not sure that is such a good idea." She rushed on before he could stop her. "I know you mean well but I want to be with you both when you tell Molly who you are. Right now, I'm the only person she trusts. I'm not comfortable sending her off alone with you. She might think I've abandoned her and I can't have that."

Leah heard the conviction in her voice and realized she'd not let Molly face her future alone. She squared her shoulders and waited for Jake to argue.

A grin filled his face. "I'm glad you care so much about her."

"I do." Leah's stomach growled just as Molly came running around the corner.

He leaned close to her and his warm breath caressed her cheek. "It sounds like it's a good thing I asked for an early lunch for three."

Jake turned from her to see what the little girl was

waving in the air. Leah tilted her head and looked around him to see, too. Her heart sank. Molly had found Leah's favorite pink ribbon.

Jake bent at the waist to take it from her. His gaze moved to Leah's face and he turned back to Molly. "Is this your pretty ribbon?" he asked.

She shook her head and pointed to Leah.

"Did you ask if we can use it?"

Again, Molly shook her head. Her eyes beseeched Leah.

Jake stood to his full height. For a moment Leah was worried he was going to scold the little girl. Jake surprised her by saying, "Well, I think it's too pretty for a snowman. After lunch we'll see what else we can find." He handed the ribbon back to Molly. "Perhaps you should give this back to Miss Hollister."

Molly did as she was told but didn't look too pleased.

"Thank you, Molly." Leah took the ribbon and then knelt down in front of the little girl. "From now on, you must ask me before you go through my things and take what you want." Once the little girl had nodded sadly, Leah stood.

"Who's hungry?" Jake asked.

Molly jumped up and down. She crossed to Jake and took his hand. Leah followed. It was obvious that Molly was already accepting Jake. The little girl wouldn't need her here much longer.

Heat filled Jake's face as he saw his room through Leah and Molly's eyes. It was a tack room within the barn. Bridles, saddles and other riding equipment stood against the walls or hung on the walls. A bed, small wood stove and a little wooden table were all that stood in the room. A shirt hung on a makeshift clothesline but other than that, the room was tidy.

Curiosity laced Molly's expression while mild amusement seemed to fill Leah's. He set the picnic basket on the table. "I know it's not much, but stock tenders don't normally require much."

In all honesty, he'd been surprised that Mrs. Frontz had agreed to let him bring Leah and Molly to his room. But, with some fast talking he'd convinced her that Molly would make the perfect chaperon and that they needed privacy to explain to Molly that he was her uncle, an uncle she'd never met.

Leah's voice pulled him back to the present. "It's very nice." Leah took off Molly's wet gloves and coat.

He almost snorted his amusement at her politeness but decided she wouldn't take the action well. Instead, he pulled a chair up to the table. "I'm sorry. I only have the two chairs. You ladies may have them."

Molly scrambled onto the closest one and smiled up at him. Her brown eyes, so much like his brother's, tore into his heart.

"Molly and I can share." Leah scooped the little girl up and sat down. The little girl squirmed in her lap and smiled across at him.

Jake opened the basket. He wasn't sure how to tell Molly that he was her uncle. Bitterness clawed at the back of his throat. What right did he have to raise his niece? He'd cut her parents out of his life five years ago. Sadness filled him because, without meaning to, he'd also cut this sweet little girl from his life.

He placed sliced bread and ham wrapped in a towel on the table, followed by a jar of pickles and sugar cookies. He also pulled out three plates and a fork for the pickles. It wasn't a large lunch but it was all that Mrs. Frontz had had time to pull together for them. Lastly he placed a jar of milk and three glasses on the table.

"This looks wonderful." Leah made a quick sandwich from the bread and ham. She placed it on one of the plates while he opened the pickle jar.

As they worked together to prepare the simple meal, Molly watched. Jake felt as if her big eyes followed his every move. Was this what it felt like to be a parent?

Once they each had a sandwich sitting in front of them, Jake sat down and blessed the food. It had been a while since he'd said grace because Mr. Frontz normally said the blessing. He kept it simple and said a quick amen.

Molly reached for the sugar cookie on her plate.

In a soft voice, Leah reminded her, "You have to eat half your sandwich and drink half your milk and then you can have the cookie."

The little girl looked to Jake. Was she asking him to intervene? What harm would it do if she ate the cookie first? His gaze moved up to Leah's. The look on her face warned him that now wasn't the time to dispute her words.

He grinned at Molly. "Eat up. If I finish my sandwich first I might be tempted to eat your cookie, too." Jake took a big bite from his sandwich.

A twinkle filled Leah's eyes as Molly grabbed her own ham and bread and began to eat at a fast pace. "Remember, ladies thoroughly chew their food before they swallow," Leah reminded the little girl.

Molly nodded and her eyes danced with pleasure as she ate and drank her milk. Leah picked at her sandwich and looked about the room.

Leah seemed to know exactly what the little girl needed to know to grow up into a young woman with manners and healthy eating habits. How was he going to be both mother and father to the child? To take his mind from the scary thought, Jake glanced around his room.

He was thankful he'd stopped long enough this morning to make the cot up. "I hope you don't mind eating here. Other than the main dining hall there was no other place, and I wanted to talk to Molly before I spoke to Mr. and Mrs. Frontz."

"This is fine," Leah assured him.

Molly's stopped chewing and looked at him. He read the question in her eyes. She wanted to know why he'd want to talk to her.

He put his sandwich down and placed his elbows on the table, one on each side of his plate. Molly continued to stare at him. She cocked her head to the side and waited.

Jake took a deep breath and then exhaled slowly. *Lord, please help me say the right thing.* "Molly, did your daddy ever tell you he had a brother?"

The little girl shook her head.

John and Sally had never told Molly about him. What had he expected? He'd abandoned his family. Only, where did he go from here?

Jake continued to hold her gaze. She looked so much like Sally, with her corn-silk hair, heart-shaped face and rosy cheeks. The only difference was her eyes. She had John's expressive brown eyes.

Seeing John's eyes looking back at him tore into his very soul. Over the years he'd missed his brother and realized that his memories of Sally were fading, but he'd never forgotten his brother.

Molly slid off Leah's lap and came around the table. Jake turned so that he could still face her. The little girl reached her arms upward and he pulled her onto his lap. She stretched her small hand up and touched Jake's hair and then ran her fingers over his lashes.

He closed them so she wouldn't poke him in the eye. Was she searching for similarities between him and his brother? Or was she simply curious about him? When he felt her hand on his head again, he looked into her face.

Leah said in a soft, encouraging voice, "Go ahead and tell her."

Molly looked from him to Leah and back to him again. She placed her hand on his heart and leaned her head against his shoulder.

"I'm your Uncle Jake, Molly. I'm your daddy's brother."

She raised her head and smiled at him. Had she already guessed? "Your daddy sent me a letter and in it he said you can live with me now. Would you like that?"

Molly nodded and then pointed to Leah.

Was she asking if Leah could live with them, too? Jake looked to the young woman. Her cheeks were turning a lovely shade of pink. It wasn't his place to tell Molly that her friend would soon be leaving to marry Mr. Harris.

Jake found himself holding his breath as he waited

to see what Leah would say. Molly climbed down from his lap. She hurried back to Leah and waited to be picked up. Molly was small for her age and weighed very little.

"Molly, you will be staying here with your uncle Jake, and I will continue on to meet my new husband. Remember? I told you that I was coming out here to get married."

Tears filled Molly's eyes. She wrapped her arms around Leah's neck and hid her face. Leah's sorrow-filled gaze searched out Jake's. He wanted to help them but didn't know how. His experience with heartache hadn't prepared him for raising a child who had lost so much already. Or helping a young woman who seemed to be looking at him for reassurance— or something else that he knew he'd never be able to give her.

Leah gently pulled Molly back. "I'm not leaving right now, little one. We have a few days to be together. Let's not be sad during the rest of our time together. All right?"

Molly wiped the tears from her cheeks and offered Leah a wobbly smile. She patted Leah's face as if to say, *I'm all right*. Her sad eyes seemed to say that it wasn't fair and that she felt as if she were losing her best friend.

Later that evening, cold air swept through the room, announcing that Jake had entered the parlor. Leah glanced his way and then faced Mr. Frontz once more. With her hands planted firmly on her hips, she protested, "I don't understand why a pony express rider can't take me on his next run and drop me off at the Harris ranch."

The old man shook his head. "Send him a letter. I won't risk sending you out to him."

Exasperation and weariness filled her. "But I've already told you. I sent a letter last week and haven't received an answer." Fear crept up her spine, sending chills down her back. The letter should have gotten to him days ago. Why hadn't he come? Had Thomas changed his mind?

Two pony express riders, Cole and Timothy, sat on the settee, snickering. Leah scowled at them. Didn't they realize this wasn't funny? This was about her future. Her new home. The older man snorted and she turned her glare back on him.

Molly tugged her small fingers free of Leah's and hurried to Jake. The little girl grabbed his hand. Her big brown eyes took in the scene that was unfolding before them. His seemed to be doing the same.

Leah and Molly had kept their distance from each other. Truth be told, Leah had pretty much isolated herself from everyone because she didn't want to see the questions in their eyes. But, even so, she'd sensed he wanted no part of being around her. He'd come inside and play with Molly or take her out to the barn to ride the horse but he'd said very few words to Leah over the past week.

Mr. Frontz's firm voice drew her attention once more. "Pony express riders don't deliver women, they deliver mail." Mr. Frontz turned his back and stoked the fire in the fireplace.

Leah took a deep breath and slowly released it, then spoke her thoughts. "Well, I am a mail-order bride.

Thomas Harris has paid my way to your stagecoach stop and I'm sure he will pay any cost you want to charge to deliver me to his ranch."

The old man hooted with laughter. "Honey, even if he could afford it, I'm sure Mr. Harris wouldn't pay for you to be delivered like the U.S. mail."

"Not at five dollars a half ounce," Cole muttered loud enough for everyone in the room to hear.

"I'll wager that gal weighs about one hundred and twenty pounds, give or take a pound." Timothy snickered back.

Leah glanced at the two young men. Each wore a wide grin and had laughing eyes. But that didn't stop her. She stood a little taller and glared at each of them. "I'll have you know, I only weigh one ten. Not that that is any of your business." She turned back to Mr. Frontz feeling foolish for arguing with the boys like a child.

Mr. Frontz looked Leah straight in the eyes. "Look, it's not just your weight, it's also not safe. These boys have to ride fast and they face all kinds of dangers while out on the trail. That's why they get paid twenty-five dollars a week to be riders." He dropped the poker into the wrought-iron holder on the hearth. "Plus, that weather out there has turned for the worst and would have you shivering so much you'd throw the horse and rider off balance."

Leah wasn't ready to give up. She raised her chin and declared, "I'm willing to face the dangers, Mr. Frontz."

"Well," the old man smothered a yawn with his hand and said, "I'm not willing to have you face danger and I don't believe these young men are, either."

He yawned again, this time not bothering to hide the fact that he was tired, sleepy and finished with their conversation. "The subject is closed for discussion, Miss Hollister."

Leah marched after him. He pointed at the riders behind her. "If I can talk one of them into taking me, would you forbid it?" She dared him to say yes.

"Not at all. You are welcome to ask away, but I'm telling you—" he nodded at the group behind her "—and them, no one is taking you anyplace."

The express riders stood at once, as if they'd received some unspoken code. They hurried from the house like chickens with their heads chopped off, scattering in all directions.

Dejected, Leah plopped down in the chair beside the fireplace. Molly released Jake's hand and hurried to her side. The little girl wrapped her arms around Leah's neck, offering comfort in the only way she knew how.

Ike, another young rider, stepped from the shadows. "Miss Hollister, did you say Thomas Harris?"

She looked up hopefully and nodded. "Would you be interested in taking me to him, Ike?"

The young man shook his head sadly. "No, ma'am, and it pains me to tell you but I think I know why he hasn't rit you back."

Confused, Leah asked, "Why not?"

Ike's words rushed from him like water over river rocks. "When I was in Julesburg yesterday I heard that Mr. Harris died. He got caught in that last storm and froze out by his pond."

Leah gasped. Sorrow and despair hit her at the same time. Thomas had seemed so nice in his letters. It was a shame that he'd died. But what was she going to do now? Where would she go? Not back to Texas since there was nothing and no one there for her. Then the thought hit her. She tried to stand but dread weakened her knees so that she couldn't rise from the chair. How on earth was she going to pay for the nights she'd stayed here and the food she'd eaten?

Jake moved to stand beside her. He placed a firm hand beneath her elbow. Was this his way of offering comfort? Why would he do so?

"Is this information from a reliable person, Ike?" Jake asked, bringing her thoughts into focus once more.

"Yep," Ike said as Leah watched his Adam's apple bob up and down as he swallowed hard before continuing. "The sheriff was talking to the undertaker."

With Jake's support, Leah got to her feet, picking Molly up. Her voice was strained as she said, "Thank you for letting me know, Ike. If you will excuse me, gentlemen, Molly and I will retire now." She walked to the stairs with her head held high, refusing to let them see that her world had just crumbled at her feet and that she had no idea how to make it all right again.

Chapter Three

The next morning, Jake sat at the dining table facing his employers, Mr. and Mrs. Frontz. It was still early and everyone else rested in their warm beds, something Jake hadn't done comfortably since Miss Hollister and his niece had arrived.

Mrs. Frontz yawned, then said, "Thanks for making the coffee this morning, Jake, but I wish you'd get on with whatever needs to be said. I have breakfast to cook."

He lowered his drink. "All right, then, I'll get to the point. Miss Hollister learned last night that her fiancé has passed away." Jake watched both of them nod and focus their gazes on the cups in front of them. He couldn't help but wonder how long they'd known about the demise of Mr. Harris. He shook his head and continued because that simple fact really didn't matter right now. "That means she will be leaving soon." Again he watched them nod.

"What does that have to do with us, son?" Mr. Frontz asked, raising his head and meeting Jake's eyes.

The older man called everyone son, so Jake didn't

take any notice. "Well, if Miss Hollister leaves, I assume full responsibility for Molly's care. So I guess I'm trying to tell you I'll be leaving soon, too. I can't raise a girl in the tack room off the barn."

Mrs. Frontz's face saddened. "Where will you go?"

"Back to Texas. I guess the family spread is mine now."

He didn't want to move back to Texas. Too many memories were there for both him and Molly. How would she feel going back to the place where her parents had died? But it was his only choice.

He didn't tell them he had no idea what he was going to do on that small piece of land. He'd hoped to make enough money to start a horse ranch, but now, with a child to raise, Jake just wasn't sure what he'd do. And he still had the problem of how to care for the child once he did have a work plan.

"Now, boy, you aren't making any sense," Mr. Frontz grumbled. "You're going to leave a good job here to go to Texas. For what? So the girl will have a place to live? What's wrong with living here?"

"Yeah, what's wrong with living here?" Mrs. Frontz echoed, fully awake now.

"I told you, I can't raise her in the tack room. At least back in Texas, I have a cabin." Jake didn't like it any more than they did but what other choice did he have?

Mr. Frontz studied him over his coffee cup. He took a drink and then plopped it down on the table. "So are you saying that if you had a roof over your heads, then you'd stick around?"

Jake nodded. "I reckon so." He loved working for the pony express and taking care of the horses. Most of them were mustangs and half-wild but he did love them. There were a few, like the one he allowed Molly to ride, that were tame. All of them were intelligent.

They sat in silence for several long minutes before Mrs. Frontz spoke. "You know, Charles. He could move into the old homestead. It needs a little work but it's livable."

Mr. Frontz nodded. "Yep, I could get the boys to clean the place today and have it ready to move into by this evening." He picked up his coffee once more.

"I'm sure I could round up some sheets and other things you'll need to make it a fine home for the little girl," Mrs. Frontz added in a hopeful voice.

Jake shook his head. "I'm not sure that's such a good idea. The other men aren't going to like that I have a nice home to live in when all they get is a room that they must share with each other."

"You leave the boys to me. Besides, the cabin's not that much bigger than their room." Mr. Frontz pushed his chair back. He dropped a big, callused hand on Jake's shoulder. "I'm glad you're staying. I didn't look forward to replacing such a good stock tender." He shoved his hat on his balding head and stomped to the back porch.

Jake studied the grounds in the bottom of his cup. That was one problem taken care of, but he had others to deal with.

Mrs. Frontz laid her hand on his. "Something else is bothering you. I can tell. Want to talk about it?"

He looked into her bright blue eyes. "I'm just thinking that if Miss Hollister leaves I'll need to hire someone to watch Molly." Jake sighed, his choices in babysitters were majorly limited here in South Platte.

Other than Mrs. Frontz, there were only a handful of women and most of them were past their prime and unhealthy. The others were too young and looking for a husband. Jake Bridges had no intention of letting any of them look at him as husband material.

"I'll be happy to watch her for you," Mrs. Frontz volunteered.

No, Jake knew he couldn't ask her to take on Molly's care. Her slumped shoulders spoke of how tired the older woman was. She already cooked and cleaned from sunup to sundown. He couldn't imagine her trying to keep up with an active four-year-old child, too. "That's nice of you to offer but I'll think of something. She's a handful and you already have plenty to take care of with the riders."

She nodded and stood. "Yeah. Speaking of the boys, they'll be down soon needing breakfast. Who's up first today?"

Jake grinned ruefully. He noticed she hadn't argued with him about Molly's care. "Ike."

"I'll make sure he gets an extra helpin' this morning." She muttered to herself as she pushed through the kitchen door.

Well, having a house to live in would be a big help but what was he to do about Molly's care? Jake knew he couldn't take her to the barn with him every day or have her follow him about the place while he made repairs. She needed a woman's care. A soft whisper filtered through his mind. She needed Leah Hollister.

What would Leah do now that Thomas Harris was no longer available to offer her marriage? Would she return to Texas? To what? Why had she left in the first place? There were so many things he didn't know about her. But he did know that she cared for Molly. She'd also shown no special interest in him or the other young men.

Would she be willing to marry him to assure herself that Molly would have a home? As far as he knew, Leah and Thomas hadn't really known each other before she agreed to be his bride. Perhaps she'd consider replacing Thomas with himself.

It sounded crazy as Jake ran the thoughts through his mind but a marriage of convenience might be what both of them needed. He sighed and took a sip of his now-cold coffee. Of course, he'd have to tell her that he couldn't offer her a real marriage, only friendship and a home. Would that be enough to keep Leah here with Molly?

Long before he could actually see her, the sound of her skirts swishing against the hardwood floors alerted him to Leah's arrival.

Molly entered the room seconds before Leah. His niece looked sweet this morning with her hair up in two braids like pigtails. Her cheeks were pink, as if she'd just endured a good scrubbing. She swung the rag doll by one arm. He reminded himself he would have to rearrange his entire life to accommodate Molly and prayed Leah would go along with him for the same reason.

Leah came to an abrupt stop when she saw Jake sitting at the table. A quick glance about the room revealed that he was the only one there. Molly waved as she skipped past him and headed for the kitchen.

"Good morning."

The richness of his voice flowed over her like

melted butter over hot potatoes. She offered him a smile and replied, "Good morning."

Leah pressed on to the kitchen to talk to Mrs. Frontz about working to pay for her room and board. She'd lain awake most of the night and had come to the conclusion that this was the only way to pay back what she owed. She wasn't good at cooking, but Leah did know how to clean. Maybe Mrs. Frontz would teach her how to cook and then she could help out in both the kitchen and with the housework.

"Do you have a few minutes to spare this morning? I'd like to talk about last night and I have something I need to ask you." Jake's deep voice interrupted her line of thought.

Leah turned to face him. He cradled his coffee cup between his two large hands. Rich brown eyes surveyed her face. Wasn't it bad enough that he'd witnessed her reception of last night's bad news? Did he really want to talk about it now?

"I should probably go help Mrs. Frontz with breakfast." Her hand flapped toward the kitchen of its own accord. She hoped he'd not noticed her lack of helping in the past.

"Please. I promise I won't take long and I'd like to talk without Molly's little ears hearing." He gestured for her to sit across from him.

He seemed determined, so Leah thought she might as well get it over with and sat down.

"Thank you." He rubbed the checkered tablecloth absently as if having difficulty forming his next words. "I'm sorry to hear about Thomas Harris. I understand he was a good man." Jake paused and took a sip from his cup.

Honestly, Leah didn't know if Thomas was a good man or not. They'd only known each other through the sparse letters they'd shared. She nodded, hoping Jake would continue.

"Correct me if I'm wrong, but you'd never met, is that right?"

Leah sighed. "That's right." What was his point? Was he going to suggest that since she had no marriage prospects she wasn't fit to watch Molly any longer? Did having one's fiancé die make her unfit? The irrational thoughts raced through her mind.

"So there is no chance you were in love or anything like that?" Jake leaned his arms on the table and stared into her eyes.

Feeling uncomfortable, Leah answered. "No, we weren't in love. Mr. Harris needed a wife to help out on the ranch. His mother is getting up in years and she hinted that if he should marry, his wife could take over the cooking, cleaning and such." Leah didn't mention the grandchildren Mrs. Harris had wanted and now would never have since Thomas was an only child. She wondered what would happen to Thomas's mother now that he was gone.

"So would you say it was a marriage of convenience for both of you?" Jake pressed, never taking his gaze from her face.

Leah felt heat crawl up her neck into her cheeks. This wasn't a conversation any woman wanted to have with a man she'd met only a few days ago. "Mr. Bridges, would you please just tell me where we are going with this conversation?"

He nodded. "After you answer my question."

"Fine. Yes, it was more of a marriage of convenience, but I would have made him a fine wife."

Jake leaned back in his chair. "Good." He continued to study her long and hard.

She pushed up out of her chair. "Well, if that is all you wanted."

"Wait."

Why she did as he said, Leah didn't know but she found herself back on the hard wood seat. "Why?"

Jake leaned forward once more. "I want to offer you the same deal as Harris."

"What?" The one word squeaked from Leah's throat. Was he offering to marry her? Was this God's answer to her prayer? It was so sudden.

He reached across the table and snagged one of her hands. Leah wasn't sure if he was trying to be endearing or simply holding her hand to keep her from leaving the room.

"I don't understand. What exactly are you proposing?"

"Well, I can't promise you love but I can promise you a home." He raked his fingers through his hair with his free hand. "Molly needs a mother and I have to work. So if you and I were to marry, she'd have someone to take care of her and you'd both have a home."

Home.

The word sank into Leah's heart. Hadn't she always wanted a home? Just last night she'd pleaded with God and asked for a home. She didn't ask for love. No one could or would love her, and if they claimed to, she'd always wonder what their motives were. After all, her own parents had given her away and they were the people she'd expected to love her forever.

Love wasn't something she could rely on, her whole life she'd relied on herself, not her parents and not a man. No, as long as love wasn't involved, Leah felt sure she'd be all right. She raised her eyes and studied Jake. He wasn't offering love, or even pretending to offer love, but he was offering her what she'd always wanted. A home.

"Look, I know it's not much, but it's all I can give you. I'm not a man who is going to fall in love with you. But I can offer you a house, food and a life with a little girl who needs you more than you'll ever know." His eyes pleaded with her to understand what he was proposing. "You will never want for anything as long as you are my wife."

Leah couldn't find words to express how she felt. It was a lot to take in. She'd gone from having no plans or future, to having a man offer her marriage and a daughter. She loved Molly, and yet she still couldn't get out the word *yes*.

Molly burst out of the kitchen door and ran to Leah. The little girl grabbed her free hand and tugged for Leah to follow her to the kitchen.

Leah gently pulled her back and said, "Go tell Mrs. Frontz that I'll be there in a few minutes." It was only after the little girl hurried away that she remembered Molly couldn't or wouldn't speak. How was she going to tell Mrs. Frontz what she'd said?

Leah turned her attention back to Jake. He still held her hand firmly in his. "What about friendship, Jake? Can you allow yourself to be my friend? My best friend?" Leah didn't need love but she did need friendship.

He squeezed her hand gently and warmth filled his

voice. "I will give you friendship and respect, and I believe we will get along fine, Leah. Just don't ask for my heart, my love or more than hand-holding." He rubbed his thumb across the back of her hand before releasing it.

His words both shocked and comforted her. Leah inhaled deeply. As she exhaled Leah whispered, "Then I'll marry you, Jake."

"Thank you." He got up and came around the table.

Leah stood also, unsure what he planned to do. Just moments before he'd said she should expect no more than hand-holding from this union. She turned to face him. Did he plan to seal their engagement with a kiss? Her heart quickened. Her first kiss from a man—her soon-to-be husband.

Jake took both of her hands in his, leaned down until their foreheads were touching and in a warm, low, gravelly voice whispered, "I promise, I'll be the best husband I know how to be now, and with time I'll hopefully get better at it."

Electricity snapped between them. Leah felt as if every hair on her head stood on end. It took her voice away once more. She nodded against his head.

He released her hands and straightened to his full height. "Now that that's settled, I better get back to work."

Leah watched him go through the door to the kitchen and heard the back door close. She took a deep breath punctuated with several even gasps. Her heart thumped madly. Her mind was a crazy mixture of hope and fear. The one clear thought she latched on to was that she was a soon-to-be bride once more.

What did the future hold for her? Leah rested a

hand against her chest in a feeble attempt to stop its erratic pounding. Momentary panic gnawed away at the new hope she'd just experienced. Had she jumped out of the frying pan and into the fire?

"Lord, I hope I haven't just made the biggest mistake of my life." Leah realized she'd said the prayer aloud and quickly looked about. Fortunately she stood alone in the room. The words hung in the air, as if taunting her as she headed to the kitchen. Was this the biggest mistake of her life? What if she married Jake, then her true love came along? Was there such a thing? She shook the fanciful thoughts from her mind. No one else had ever loved her, so she effectively squashed such fairy-tale images. She felt an acute sense of loss. Would she forever be unlovable? And even if she did find love, would she be able to trust that it was true? Could she count on another person not to abandon her?

The heavy smell of bacon and eggs greeted her as she entered the overheated kitchen. Mrs. Frontz stood beside the stove dishing up breakfast. She glanced over her shoulder. "Good morning, Leah. I hope you had a good night's sleep."

Leah didn't want to lie to her hostess, so she simply answered with, "Good morning."

For the first time since her arrival, Leah took a good look about the kitchen. It wasn't very big. Pots hung from hooks over the stove. A cabinet held other dishes. Molly sat at a makeshift table, made from two large barrels with a board stretched over the top, munching on a buttered biscuit. Her doll was propped up against another large bowl filled with biscuits.

"I hope you don't mind that I gave the small fry a biscuit," Mrs. Frontz said as she tipped scrambled eggs into a large bowl.

"Not at all. Is there anything I can do to help?"

The woman smiled over her shoulder at her. "Nope, I'm used to doing things my way. Breakfast will be ready in a few minutes. Why don't you go sit at the table? The men will be arriving any minute." If she found it curious that Leah was in her kitchen, Mrs. Frontz didn't let on.

Leah frowned. After the previous night's events, the last place she wanted to be was alone at the table with Mr. Frontz and the pony express riders. Besides, she couldn't bring herself to eat breakfast again, at least, not without making arrangements for payment for the meals she'd already eaten.

Mrs. Frontz turned toward her. "Is something on your mind this morning?" she asked, picking up the cooked eggs and a platter of bacon.

"Yes. I was wondering if you could use some help around here." Leah pressed on before the older woman could protest. "I have recently learned that my fiancé has passed away and I now find myself in debt to you and Mr. Frontz for my previous meals and my room."

Mrs. Frontz motioned for Leah to pick up the bowl full of biscuits that sat on the table in front of Molly. "Yes, I heard about that, but I don't want you to feel indebted to us." She pushed through the kitchen door and walked to the table where she spaced the food out on the table.

"I can't stay here and not work for my keep," Leah protested, handing her the bowl.

The older woman wiped her palms on her apron. "So, your intentions are to stay here?"

Leah nodded. She felt like a schoolgirl under Mrs. Frontz's steady gaze. It was if the older woman tried to read her mind, learn her plans and then judge her based on what she'd learned.

"For how long?"

Jake hadn't mentioned when they would be married and Leah wasn't sure if he'd want her to work, once they were. It just hadn't come up but she didn't think he'd care. "I'm not sure but I'm willing to work and pay you back."

Mrs. Frontz nodded and returned to the kitchen. Leah hesitated, uncertain if she should follow her or not. She knew there were still plates to set out and coffee to pour. After several moments, Leah followed her.

As soon as she entered the kitchen Mrs. Frontz asked, "So what are you willing to do?"

Leah walked over and picked up plates to take back to the table. "Whatever you need done. Although, I must admit I don't know how to cook. Growing up in an orphanage I didn't learn. But, I can clean, make beds and fetch whatever you may need."

The older woman smiled at her. "That sounds lovely. These old bones seem to get stiffer and more tired every year. I could use the help and I'd also be willing to teach you how to cook. Someday, you'll get married and we don't want your man to starve now, do we?" A teasing glint filled her eyes.

Leah thought of Jake and how hard he worked with the horses. The last thing she wanted was for him to starve. "No, ma'am, we don't."

"Well, now that that's settled, you have got to stop calling me ma'am and Mrs. Frontz. My name is Agnes and all my friends call me by my name." She scooped up clean coffee mugs and the coffeepot and headed back to the dining table.

Leah's confidence spiraled upward. How quickly things could change. She'd woken this morning uncertain of her future. Now she was to get married and had made a new friend, both events taking place before breakfast. That had to be a good sign. What could possibly go wrong?

Jake entered the house and inhaled the wonderful fragrance of breakfast. Mrs. Frontz was the best cook in the small town and he realized he would miss her meals once he and Leah were married. All morning he'd been thinking about what married life would be like and just couldn't fathom it. Neither did he understand the feeling of elation that took him through chores and remained with him at this very moment. He couldn't afford to be distracted by romantic notions. He rejected such ideas as absurd.

Everyone took their places at the table and Mr. Frontz said grace. As soon as the amen was spoken, he looked about the table and announced, "We're going to do things a little different today, boys."

That got their attention. Forks no longer clattered against serving bowls and plates. Jake's heart jumped in his chest. Surely Leah hadn't told anyone of their engagement. His gaze sought out hers. Her eyes met his with a quizzical gleam in their depths, as if she wondered the same thing as he.

"Mrs. Frontz and I decided this morning that we

want Jake to have the old homestead as his and Molly's new home. The girl needs a strong roof over her head and room to grow. You men will be helping me and Jake clean the place up for them today instead of whatever you had planned."

All eyes turned to Jake. He had expected them to be angry, but instead, smiles filled their faces. Now was as good a time as any to announce to everyone that he intended to marry Leah and supply a mother for Molly. "I want to let everyone know that I asked Leah to marry me this morning and she's agreed."

Everyone turned to look at Leah. A light pink filled her cheeks as she nodded. He smiled at her as the men began hooting and slapping him on the back. Mrs. Frontz laid her hand on Leah's and smiled.

Mr. Frontz's deep voice broke through all the noise. "Well, that's an even better reason for us to get started on cleaning up the old homestead." He nodded in Leah's direction.

Jake marveled at the joy his friends expressed. They ate and chatted about the upcoming wedding. Leah didn't say much. She simply smiled. Molly hugged Leah and he watched as Leah whispered something in the little girl's ear. Molly smiled happily and then began eating her breakfast.

Half an hour later, Mr. Frontz pushed back his chair. "Come on, boys. Let's see if the fireplace still works at the homestead."

Will, Cole and Ike followed him to the front door where they gathered coats and gloves and left.

Mrs. Frontz excused herself and asked Molly to carry her plate into the kitchen. Jake appreciated the fact that everyone gave him and Leah a few moments alone.

He walked to her side of the table and knelt down beside her chair. She turned to face him. "I hope you don't mind that I announced our upcoming wedding like that."

She gave him a smile. Her hand came up and she brushed the hair off his forehead. "No. We were going to have to tell them later, anyway."

He enjoyed the sensation of her warm fingers on his brow, almost too much, and pulled away. Jake stood. "Good, I'm glad."

Leah rose and began gathering dirty dishes from the table. "I have offered to help Agnes out around here. I hope you don't mind."

"Of course I don't. She needs the help. It was nice of you to offer." Jake walked to the front door and pulled on his own coat and gloves. "I'll see you later." He stopped and looked at her.

Cheeks flaming now, Leah said, "Have a good day." She didn't make eye contact with him but simply continued gathering the dishes. He wondered if she'd embarrassed herself by sweeping the hair out of his eyes.

"You, too." Jake felt the blast of cold as he opened the door and stepped out onto the porch. Storm clouds hung low in the sky, promising snow.

He reached up and touched the spot where Leah's fingers had grazed his forehead. Had he made a mistake asking someone he'd just met to marry him? What if she expected to someday fall in love? Jake dropped his hand. He ducked his head against the cold wind and walked toward the old homestead.

As he went, Jake silently prayed. *Please Lord, don't let her fall in love with me or try to make me fall in love with her. You and I both know that can never happen. I can't allow my heart to be broken again.*

Chapter Four

"Have you set a date yet as to when the wedding will take place?" Agnes asked as Leah walked into the kitchen carrying the breakfast dishes. She handed Leah an apron to wear.

Leah tied the apron around her waist and shook her head. "No, we haven't really talked much about it."

"A spring wedding would be nice." Agnes began grating slivers of soap into the tub of hot water.

"I would kind of like to have a Christmas wedding. When I was ten years old, a couple got snowed in and had to stay at the orphanage. They wanted to get married at Christmas and the headmistress let them have the wedding there. The bride wore a white dress and had red flowers with big petals. We got to decorate the dining hall with strings of cranberries and popcorn. I thought it was the most beautiful wedding I'd ever seen." Leah felt heat fill her face.

Agnes *tsked* as she placed coffee cups in the now-soapy water. "That does sound lovely but I'm not sure that's possible. Parson John isn't due to come back this way until the early part of the year."

Leah picked up a dish cloth and began drying the cups as Agnes handed them to her. "Parson John?"

"He's our traveling preacher. We see him about every three months or so."

"Oh." Disappointment squeezed Leah's chest. If the preacher wasn't due to return for several months, then she wouldn't be having a Christmas wedding.

Agnes handed her a plate. "Don't fret, child. It's not that long, and that will give us plenty of time to plan the wedding."

Leah nodded. "Are there any other preachers in the area?"

"Nope."

"Normally Parson John would be here during the holidays, but his sister is sick and he wanted to spend time with her and her family, so he left town last week to be with them."

The two women continued cleaning the kitchen. Agnes showed Leah where to place the plates, silverware, pots and pans. Just as they finished, the sound of the stagecoach pulling into the front yard drew their attention.

A beautiful rosewood mantel clock that sat on a shelf above the sink gonged out the time. Leah realized it was already ten o'clock.

Agnes set the coffeepot back on the stove and grabbed several cups. "Leah, look out the front window and see how many passengers are on the stage."

Leah hurried to do as she was told. The stagecoach driver was already down and placing a small stool in front of the door. She felt a stirring of excitement. The stool could only mean a woman would embark. The men never used a stool to step down on. The driver didn't look like the same man who had delivered her a week earlier. Expecting to see a woman descend the steps, Leah was surprised when the door to the stage opened and a small man stepped out, a bowler hat perched on his head. He wore a business suit and shiny black boots. She waited a minute longer to see who else might disembark. Seeing no one, she hurried back to the kitchen. "Looks like just one gentleman," she said.

Agnes pulled an apple pie from the pie safe and sliced two pieces. She poured steaming hot coffee into two mugs.

Leah watched her work with the skill of a practiced hand. "Do you think they will stay for pie and coffee?"

"The stagecoach driver, Mr. Porter, hardly ever leaves without a slice and a hot drink."

Leah searched her memory for the name of the stagecoach driver that had dropped her off and came away empty. "Why didn't the man who dropped me here stay for pie and coffee?" she asked.

Agnes pulled a tin of dried beans down and carried them to the table where Molly sat. She dumped them out in front of the child before answering Leah. "I suppose Mr. Edwards didn't want to get trapped by the snow. But, to be honest, he hardly ever comes inside. He drinks something stronger than my hot coffee or tea. Mr. Edwards just drops folks off and hightails it back to Julesburg." She walked to the cupboard and found a big pot. "He's probably at the Beni ranch now enjoying the wilder side of life."

Leah remembered Julesburg. They'd passed through the town without stopping but what she'd seen out the stagecoach window hadn't impressed her much. It was small and dirty, and loud music and shouts could be heard coming from the large sod house that sat beside a small trading post. She was thankful Thomas had told her to come to South Platte and wait for him here.

Agnes placed the pot next to Molly. "Think you can go through those beans and put the good ones in my pot?" she asked the little girl.

Molly smiled and nodded. She stood up on her stool and began sorting beans.

"That's a good girl," Agnes said, grinning at the child. "We'll make a fine cook out of you in no time."

Leah didn't recall a ranch being in or near Julesburg. "The Beni ranch?"

Agnes turned to Leah. "That's Jules Beni's place. He's the pony express station master in Julesburg."

"Oh, I didn't realize that there could be two home stations so close together." Then again, Leah realized she knew very little about the pony express.

"Julesburg is the main pony express home station in these parts. We're considered the swing station. Jake and some of the boys didn't care for the rowdy town, so when Mr. Slade, the division superintendent for the pony express, asked if we'd be willing to house some of the boys and a stock tender, we agreed. And here we are." Agnes took a wet cloth and returned to the dining area. She vigorously wiped the table clean.

A few moments later she called out to Leah. "Would you mind bringing those plates and coffee cups to the dinner table?"

Leah did as she was asked, happy to feel as if she was contributing a little toward her keep. She watched the men enter the house and take seats at the table. Agnes placed a cup and plate in front of the passenger and gave each man a fork. Leah served Mr. Porter his pie and coffee.

"Thank you, Mrs. Frontz," Mr. Porter said, picking up his fork and digging into his pie. Around a mouth full of crust and fruit he asked, "And who might this lovely lady be?"

Agnes put her hands on her hips. "Now, you behave yourself, Porter. That's Miss Hollister, soon to be Jake's bride."

Mr. Porter gulped down his pie and smiled. Both his front teeth were missing. "I'll see that I do, Mrs. Frontz." He turned to the gentleman who sat across the table from him. "Ladies, I'd like for you to meet Mr. Isaac Dalton."

"It's nice to meet you." Agnes and Leah spoke in unison.

"The pleasure is mine."

Mr. Dalton wasn't a tall man. As a matter of fact, in comparison to Jake, Leah found him to be short. He was small boned and looked like he belonged in an office out East rather than here in rugged Colorado. Leah checked her thoughts. What was she doing, comparing a complete stranger to her future husband?

Agnes slipped into one of the chairs. "Are you staying the night, Mr. Porter, or heading to Denver?"

"Mr. Dalton and I have discussed it and with the storm coming in, we've decided to head on out. I take it you have no other passengers staying right now?"

She shook her head. "No, Miss Hollister and sweet little Molly are our only boarders at the moment."

Leah felt an anxious tension shiver down her spine.

She turned to find Mr. Dalton studying her. She felt uncomfortable under his green gaze. "Speaking of Molly, I should go check on her. If you gentlemen will excuse me." Leah didn't wait for their answer. She hurried into the kitchen.

Standing on the other side of the door, she heard Mr. Dalton say, "She seems awfully young to have a daughter."

Agnes ignored his statement and asked a question of her own, "What do you do, Mr. Dalton?"

"I am taking a position at the bank in Denver," he replied.

Leah thought she heard a great deal of pride in his voice. Everything about Mr. Dalton screamed "businessman." She pushed away from the door and went to help Molly sort beans. There was something about the man that made her feel uneasy. He was nothing like Jake.

How could she think such a thing? Leah realized she knew very little about Jake. She tried to picture him in business attire. A smile touched her lips. She'd soon see him in both, Leah thought. At their wedding surely he would dress in a suit and shiny boots. Or would he? Truth be told, she had no idea what her future husband might or might not wear to their wedding. She just prayed he'd take off the gun belt for their special day.

Leah picked at the beans. Maybe it was a good thing the preacher was out of town. She knew nothing about Jake Bridges, other than he was a stock tender for the pony express.

A flicker of uneasiness swept through her. Did anyone really know him? How long had the Frontzs known him? Hadn't Thomas said in one of his letters that the pony express had just started up in April?

She looked to Molly who seemed focused on picking rocks and blackened beans from the pile. Had her feelings for the little girl gotten her into a bigger mess than she'd already been in? A tiny flicker of panic began to take root in her thoughts.

Leah bowed her head and silently prayed. *Lord, if I've made a mistake, please help me to get out of my promise to marry Jake. And if it's not a mistake, please help me feel your assurance and help me to get to know him better. Amen.*

Jake dug into lunch with a feeling of accomplishment. He and the others had worked on the cabin all morning. So far, they had cleaned out the chimney, reinforced the windows and the door, swept the floors and removed cobwebs that had developed in what seemed like every corner of the house. Then they'd mixed hay, dirt, water and rocks to pack the cracks in the log walls.

His gaze moved to the stagecoach passenger, Mr. Dalton. The man's eyes followed Leah's every move, much the way a hungry cat watches a sparrow hop from branch to branch. At the moment she was carefully cutting Molly's meat into tiny pieces. Jake wondered if he should start sitting closer to her and the little girl. After all, they would soon be a family.

Mr. Frontz took a sip of hot coffee and then said, "Mr. Dalton, Agnes tells me you're a banker."

Mr. Dalton wiped his mouth. "Yes, sir. I'm looking forward to beginning work at Clark, Gruber and Co." He, too, pushed his plate back and picked up his mug.

Jake thought of the money he had stashed in his room. He'd considered putting it in the bank, but in all honesty, he just didn't trust them. He'd heard of banks being robbed and folks losing everything.

"That's that two-story building they built back in July, right?" Will asked from his position at the table.

"I don't rightly know what it looks like. This will be my first trip to Denver," Mr. Dalton confessed as his gaze slid back across the table to land on Leah, who gently wiped Molly's face.

Jake cleared his throat. "Leah, if you and Molly are finished eating maybe you'd like to come down to the stables with me and check on the horses." He hadn't planned on taking them, but he also didn't want her in the same room with a wealthy banker, either.

Leah looked up at Jake and grinned. "I think we're about done, aren't we, Molly?"

Molly nodded and pushed out of her chair.

Leah looked to Agnes. "I'll be back in a few minutes to help clean up the kitchen and this mess."

Agnes waved her away. "Don't worry about the dishes, they'll be here when you come back."

Leah offered Jake a small, shy smile. "We'll go get our coats and be right back." She pushed Molly along in front of her toward the stairs.

"Would you like a slice of pie while you wait?" Mrs. Frontz asked Jake.

"No, thanks." Jake pushed away from the table. "Lunch was wonderful. Thank you, Mrs. Frontz."

Agnes smiled. "It was my pleasure."

"I'd like another slice of that pie, Mrs. Frontz, and then Mr. Dalton and I will need to be on our way. I'd like to beat the storm into Denver." Mr. Porter held out his plate for her to put the pie on.

She took his plate. "You're welcome to stay overnight," Agnes said, cutting out a large section of the apple pie.

Jake silently prayed the stagecoach would be on its way. He didn't much care for Mr. Dalton, even though he'd just met the man. He moved to the door and pulled on his own coat and gloves.

"Thank you, but I'm sure Mr. Dalton is in a hurry to get to work. Besides, with the storm coming in I really don't want to get snowed in here."

Mr. Dalton's eyes moved to the top of the stairs, where Leah had disappeared. For a moment, Jake thought he'd argue with the stagecoach driver. He turned back to the table and said, "He's right. I appreciate the hospitality, but the sooner I get to Denver the sooner I start my new job."

Jake felt himself exhale. The sound of little feet pounding down the stairs alerted him to Molly's return. He looked to the little girl and grinned. She ran to him and jumped. Instinctively Jake caught her up and swung her around. He marveled that she didn't squeal with joy.

"She sure is a lively kid, isn't she?" Disapproval dripped from Mr. Dalton's voice.

Jake turned to glare at the man only to find him staring up at the stairs and watching Leah descend. Her skirt swished as she crossed to him.

"She is very lively, but we love that about her, don't we?" Leah replied, looking Jake in the eye. Or was she looking at Molly?

He lowered Molly to the floor. "Yes, we do." He tweaked Molly's nose but held Leah's gaze.

Leah turned and opened the door. Molly ran past her and bounded off the end of the porch.

Jake placed his hand on the small of Leah's back as she crossed the threshold. He hoped that Mr. Dalton would notice and realize that Leah wasn't available, to him or any other man. He didn't understand his possessive feelings and told himself that, if she was to be his wife, he wasn't sharing her with anyone but Molly. He closed the door behind them.

"Mr. Porter is an interesting man, isn't he?" Leah asked as she followed Molly off the edge of the porch.

"How so?" Jake hadn't ever really thought about him.

She glanced at him. "His life seems very adventurous."

Again Jake felt at a loss. "Really?"

"Well, he was telling Mr. Dalton and me about the time the Indians chased him to Denver. They seemed to think he had something they wanted, but since he didn't stop and ask them what, he said he'll probably never know why they were chasing him. And, when I asked if that happened a lot, he said yes, and that he's even been held up by new settlers, too." Her eyes shone with excitement.

Jake nodded and tucked his hands deep into his coat pockets. He noticed that Leah shivered in her thin coat. Would she object to him buying her a new one? Maybe he'd surprise her with an early Christmas present. She couldn't object to that, could she?

"But he told me if I thought that was exciting, I should have some of the boys tell me about their adventures as pony express riders. Do you think the boys would share their stories with me about their rides?" She looked up and saw Molly try to pull the doors to the barn open. "Molly! Wait for us," Leah said.

The little girl turned to face them. She waved her mitten-covered hand in a way that said, *come on!*

"We're coming," Leah called back to her.

Jake smiled at the way she could seem so young one moment and yet act so motherly the next. "I'm sure the boys would be happy to share their adventures." He pulled the barn door open and grabbed Molly's hand before allowing her to run inside. "Molly, no running in the barn and remember to watch where you step."

From the corner of his eye he caught the smile that trembled on Leah's lips. Jake turned to face her, took one of her hands in his and teased, "Leah, no running in the barn and watch where you step." He glanced down at her scuffed boots. "We wouldn't want to soil those lovely slippers, now, would we?"

She laughed and gave him a gentle push. "I'm freezing. Let us in. We'll remember the rules." Leah looked down at Molly who was smiling from ear to ear. "Won't we, Miss Molly?"

The little girl bobbed her head.

Behind them, Jake heard the front door of the cabin open. He hurriedly ushered them inside the barn. Just before he closed the door, he glanced over his shoulder to see who had left the house. Mr. Porter and Mr. Dalton stomped down the front steps and hurried to the stagecoach.

Good. With Dalton leaving, Leah could go back to

moving about the house without a stranger gawking at her. What did he care? He didn't. Did he?

Exhaustion filled every bone in her body. Leah slipped into the dining room chair and sighed. How did Mrs. Frontz, a woman twice her age, do this every day? Cook, clean, cook some more, clean some more, it was an endless cycle. Leah had helped out at the orphanage but she hadn't cleaned up after four pony express riders and visitors who arrived on the stagecoach.

The highlight of her day had been when she'd been in the warm barn with Molly and Jake. Molly had been beside herself with excitement. Jake seemed to relish the child's enthusiasm and lifted her up so she could pet the horses. Not once had Molly acted afraid; in fact, Leah could see they would have to teach Molly the dangers of getting under the horses' hooves. She needed to have a bit of fear if she was going to be around the big animals. Leah enjoyed the brief tour of the barn and seeing the various mustangs.

Jake set Molly upon the back of one of the tamer horses. The little girl giggled and pulled her red ribbon from her hair. Molly leaned forward and tied it to the bridle.

When the three of them stepped outside, Leah noticed that someone had placed a sprig of mistletoe and a Christmas wreath over the doorway. A smile touched her face when Jake leaned over and kissed her on the cheek. For a moment, it felt as though they were a family celebrating the Christmas season.

Thirty minutes later, Leah went back to the kitchen

to clean up, just so that she and Agnes could start dinner.

After the kitchen was cleaned, the beans put on to boil with a big chunk of ham hock and corn bread set to baking for dinner, Agnes showed her the other two guest rooms and asked if Leah would mind helping out with their cleanup. She agreed.

So, they dusted and swept the two guest rooms. Agnes showed Leah where she kept the clean linen and explained that when guests were staying, the rooms had to be freshened up every day. They didn't need to change the bedding every day, but the rooms would need to be dusted, swept and all the trash thrown out.

Then they swept the hall and dusted the staircase banister. Agnes hurried back downstairs to finish up dinner and since Leah didn't know what to do as far as meal preparation went, she set the table and poured coffee into mugs.

She smiled as she remembered filling Molly's and Jake's with hot apple cider. The knowledge that soon she'd be taking care of them both gave her a warm, fuzzy feeling deep in her chest. The sound of the men entering the house pulled her from those thoughts.

Chairs scraped against the wood floor as the men noisily took their seats. Leah looked up to catch Jake smiling across the table at her. Molly sat beside him, waiting for them to serve the meal. She lifted her cider cup to her lips and drank deeply of the sweet liquid.

Mr. Frontz made quick work of saying grace and then everyone was clanging dishes as they served themselves. Leah watched Jake take care of Molly's plate along with his own. They'd spent most of the day together and it looked as though Molly intended to keep him busy for the rest of the evening, too.

"Pass that plate of corn bread," Agnes said, giving Leah's arm a little nudge.

"Oh, I'm sorry. My mind was elsewhere." Leah picked up the plate and handed it to her new friend.

Agnes grinned. "I could see that."

Heat filled Leah's cheeks. Had the other woman noticed she'd been staring across at Jake and Molly? What did it matter? Surely Agnes knew that she'd only been concerned with Molly's care. Leah dipped beans and ham into her bowl and passed the pot to Agnes.

"How did the housecleaning go, boys?" Mr. Frontz asked.

Ike answered in his soft manner. "I think it went well." He shot a smile over at Leah. "It still needs a woman's touch, but it's livable now."

Mr. Frontz's next question was more of a statement than a question. "Jake, how about tomorrow you take Miss Hollister to see her future home?"

Jake nodded his agreement while chewing on a big hunk of corn bread. Molly tugged on his sleeve, and when he looked down at her she pointed to herself. Leah watched his Adam's apple bob as he swallowed and then said, "Sure, Molly, you can come, too."

The men began talking about horses and things that needed to be done about the station. Agnes caught her attention by saying, "Leah, we'll see what we have in the way of furniture. I'm sure between the two of us, we'll find plenty of stuff to decorate the old homestead. It's not that big."

Decorate? Leah had no idea where to start with

decorating a house. She'd never had a home, and Thomas's was supposed to have come already furnished. "I've never decorated a house before. Will you help me?"

Agnes laughed. "I can't say I'm any good at it but we'll sure give it our best. How does that sound?" She patted Leah's hand.

"Between cooking, decorating and learning how to be a mother, I think I have a lot to learn," Leah said, just loud enough for Agnes to hear. She looked around the table to make sure none of the men had heard her.

"I'll teach you how to cook. As for being a mother, well, Charlie and I were never blessed in that department but I'll sure do all I can to help you." She nodded her head sharply. "And that's a promise." Agnes's eyes shone with unshed tears.

Leah's heart went out to her. She would never be a true mother, either, and felt at that moment a kinship to the older woman. Jake had made it clear—theirs was to be a marriage in name only. Leah covered their hands with her other one. "I'll try to be a good student, so I'm going to hold you to that promise." She released the older woman's hands. To soften the mood, she grinned in what she hoped was a mischievous manner at Agnes and continued, "Because I need all the help I can get."

When she glanced across at Jake he tipped his head slightly toward her. Admiration shone in his brown eyes. Had he heard their conversation? Or just seen the looks on their faces and knew they were bonding? Leah didn't know but she prayed that he wouldn't marry her and then up and move her away from Agnes before she could fulfill her promise.

Chapter Five

Leah had surreptitiously watched Jake as he'd eaten his meal. Unlike the riders, and even Mr. Frantz, Jake's manners had been that of a gentleman. That was good. A gentleman would make a nice, thoughtful husband, right? And he'd taken care of Molly, too. He had wiped her little face when she needed it and carried on a conversation on the little girl's level even though she didn't respond with more than a nod or smile.

Oh, mercy. Leah sighed heavily, causing Jake to eye her questioningly. She smiled and shook her head. They stared at each other across the silence. Did he know the uncertainty roiling around in her head? His eyes darkened as he held her gaze. Her pulse accelerated and her breath seemed to have solidified in her throat. She gave a nervous little cough.

Wham! The front door slammed open and crashed back against the wall. The men leaped to their feet. Leah's gaze flew to Molly, whose eyes were round with fright. Her lower lip caught between her teeth and she twisted her hands in her dress.

Jake's hand seemed to automatically reach for the little girl and he pushed her partially behind him, shielding her from the view at the door. His eyes widened and his other hand reached for the gun at his belt. Leah turned to see the commotion.

Two men covered in icy snow fell into the room. She recognized Mr. Porter immediately and gasped. He held Mr. Dalton upright against his own body with one arm around his waist. Dried or frozen blood smeared the left side of Mr. Porter's face.

Everyone acted at once.

Jake rushed to the door and looked outside. He closed the door swiftly against the blowing snow and ice that begged to enter the warmth of the room.

Mr. Frontz and the young riders helped Mr. Porter with Mr. Dalton. "What happened?" Mr. Frontz asked.

The boys half dragged, half carried the man's limp body to the couch. His coat fell open and Leah saw his white shirt was covered in blood. Her stomach lurched. What had happened? She felt a small hand clutch her skirt and looked to find Molly standing beside her chair. Big eyes looked up into her own.

"We were ambushed." Mr. Porter's voice held fury and fear.

"Indians?" Mr. Frontz asked, leading the stagecoach driver to a chair at the table.

"In this weather I couldn't make out any skin color." Porter slid into the chair Mr. Frontz held for him.

Agnes hurried around the table to the couch. "Leah, go heat some water. Molly, go get the clean rags from the upstairs closet."

Leah and Molly ran to do as they were told. Leah

took deep breaths as she poured water into a small pot. She put it on the stove to heat and then poured Mr. Porter a cup of hot coffee.

She carried the cup back into the main room.

"What did they look like?" Mr. Frontz's worried eyes met his wife's.

Mr. Porter shook his head as if to clear it. "They hit us so fast I didn't have time to really get a look at them. I heard shots, and the next thing I knew I was flying through the air. Must have hit my head because everything went black after that."

Jake spoke from his position by the front door. "Did they follow you?"

Mr. Porter took the cup Leah offered him, his hands shaking. "No, they were long gone by the time I came to."

Mrs. Frontz eased Mr. Dalton out of his coat and shirt. Molly ran to her, holding out the rags. The little girl stood staring down at the gaping wound in the man's shoulder.

"Molly, come help me with the water," Leah called, to get the child's attention.

Molly didn't move.

Jake walked to Molly and gently picked her up. "Come on, sweetheart. Let's go help Leah in the kitchen."

Molly buried her face in her uncle's neck. His long legs carried her past Leah, who held the kitchen door open. He gently sat Molly down on the stool she'd occupied earlier. "Are you all right?" Jake knelt down in front of her and swept the hair off Molly's forehead.

She nodded. Big tears filled her eyes.

"He's going to be all right, you know. Mrs. Frontz

and Leah are going to take good care of him. Aren't you, Leah?" Jake turned to look at her. His eyes pleaded with her to help him comfort the little girl.

Leah moved to stand beside him. She dropped her hand to his warm shoulder. "We sure are. How would you like to finish your dinner in here with your dolly?"

Molly nodded her consent and picked up her doll. She hugged it close and stared at the two adults in front of her.

Leah removed her hand from Jake's warm shoulder and turned to see if the water was boiling. It wasn't, but she thought it might be hot enough to clean the man's wounds. She used the dipper and scooped water into a clean bowl.

"That's my girl," Jake said. He extended his hand for the bowl. "I'll take the water to Agnes if you want to get her settled in here."

She handed it to him. "Thank you."

His hand brushed her cheek and he lowered his voice. "Are you all right?" he asked.

"Yes, I'm fine. Just a little startled, is all." Leah tilted her head slightly, leaning into the calluses of his palm.

They scratched as he pulled away. "Good." He walked out the door leaving her feeling bereft. There was no other way Leah could describe it.

Remembering that Molly was in the room, she turned to face the little girl. "I'll be right back with your beans and corn bread."

Molly clutched her doll and whispered in her ear. Leah wished the child would talk to her. She scooped up another clean bowl for Mr. Porter's dinner and carried it to the table.

Two express riders were already back in their seats eating the rest of their meal. Leah placed the bowl in front of Mr. Porter and grabbed a clean spoon from her own place to give to him. "Please eat something, Mr. Porter. It will make you feel better."

"She's right, Dan. You can't help him now. Let the missus take care of him. You'll need your strength when we go get the coach." Mr. Frontz sat back down in his spot and nodded to Leah. She saw pride in his eyes and wondered if it were meant for her.

Before she headed back to the kitchen, Leah walked over to where Mrs. Frontz and Jake were tending the bullet wound in Mr. Dalton's left shoulder. "Is there anything I can do to help?" she asked, and once more her stomach rolled.

Agnes's gaze darted up to her. "We'll need to rip up one of the older sheets to make him a bandage. Would you mind seeing to that for me?"

"Not at all, I'll take Molly her dinner and then go get the sheet." Leah turned to leave.

Ike stood a few feet away, watching. "Miss Hollister, I can take care of the girl, if you'll allow it," he offered in his soft voice.

She looked to Jake, who nodded his acceptance. "Thank you, Ike. That would be most kind. Would you mind eating with her?"

"I'd be happy to." He walked toward the table scooping up the two bowls. "Will, would you carry mine and Miss Molly's drinks to the kitchen for me? I'm going to have dinner with her this evening."

"Sure," Will said around a mouthful of beans and

bread. He grabbed the remainder of what Ike and Molly would need for their meal then followed Ike through the kitchen door. Satisfied that the young men could handle the rest of dinner, Leah hurried up the stairs. At the top she took several deep breaths to calm her nerves.

Leah hoped Agnes wouldn't need her to help clean the bloody wound. She'd seen the bullet hole in Mr. Dalton's shoulder. Her stomach did a sort of fish flop at the thought. She inhaled deeply and told herself that if Agnes needed her, she'd do her best not to get sick at the sight of blood.

She found what she needed and then returned quickly with the sheet. Leah handed it to Jake, who stood a few feet away, watching Agnes wash Mr. Dalton's wound. The sight was ugly, to say the least. Leah looked away. "I'll go get a room ready for him." Leah silently prayed Agnes would dismiss her.

At the older woman's nod, Leah hurried to the kitchen door and looked in on Ike and Molly. He glanced over his shoulder at her.

"I'll be back as soon as we get Mr. Dalton in his room," she said, hoping Ike wouldn't think she was checking up on him.

He nodded, and said, "I was just telling Miss Molly a story. As soon as she's done eating, if it's all right with you, I'd like to take her out to the barn so we can comb down Ole Bessie."

"Ole Bessie?" Leah asked.

Ike grinned. "Yeah, she's Mrs. Frontz's old mare. I take care of her, and tonight I could sure use some help."

Relief filled Leah. She'd been afraid Ike and Molly

would eat in silence, that a young man would not understand the need to fill the silence so Molly would be reassured. Her respect for him grew and she smiled her thanks. "I think that's a good idea. Thank you."

He tipped an imaginary hat.

Molly jumped down and ran to hug her. Then she ran back to Ike and grabbed his hand. He stuffed corn bread in his mouth but allowed her to pull him to the back porch.

"Make sure she's bundled up good," Leah called after them. She picked up Molly's doll and smiled.

Ike answered, "I will."

"Where you going?" Jake spoke right behind Leah and she jumped with a hand on her heart.

"You scared me."

He placed an arm around her shoulder, but looked questioningly at Ike.

"We're going to rub down ole Bessie." Ike seemed to wait for instructions from Jake or for permission.

Comprehension dawned on Jake's face and he nodded as he saw Molly's hand clutched in Ike's. "Good idea." He ran a hand over his face. "Take a couple of the guys with you. Better to be safe."

Leah drew in a sharp breath. She hadn't even thought of the danger surrounding them. It felt good to have someone watching out for her and Molly. She felt an urgency to confide in him, to share her feelings. She turned grateful eyes to Jake. He studied her face, feature by feature, and she never spoke the words. But Leah knew from what passed between them that he understood more than she could ever have told him.

She reentered the main room and moved with

haste and purpose toward the stairs. As she passed the couch, she heard Agnes say, "Let's move him to the table. That bullet has to come out."

Leah stopped and turned. The men were already clearing off the table and carrying things to the kitchen. Thankful to escape, she hurried up the stairs. Once there, she wasn't sure what to do. She and Agnes had already swept, dusted and changed the sheets on the beds. She didn't know which room Agnes wanted him in.

Leah did know that she didn't want to head back downstairs. The last thing she wanted to witness was a man getting a bullet dug out of his shoulder. She bowed her head and took a moment to silently pray for Mr. Dalton and Agnes.

She finished and raised her head. There were only four rooms on this floor. The one she and Molly occupied, the library and two other guest rooms. Leah heard Mr. Dalton groan loudly and, not wishing to hear more, hurried to the last room down the hall.

It was the farthest from the room she shared with Molly. She told herself he would be more comfortable several doors down from a little girl's room. Molly tended to run and jump about a lot, and he'd need his rest.

The truth of the matter was that she couldn't bear to hear him in pain. She closed the door behind her and looked around. It was a nice room that appeared almost identical to hers. Chills ran up her arms. Even with the door left open all day, the rooms still remained cold. She reopened the door to let the heat from downstairs rise.

She moved to the bed and pulled back the covers. Next, Leah fluffed the pillows. Her gaze moved about the room once more, but everything seemed to be in order. She checked the water pitcher and saw that it was empty. Since she'd put fresh water in the pitcher in her own room earlier, Leah hurried to retrieve it. On her way out the door, she tossed Molly's doll onto the bed.

Another look about the empty bedroom proved there wasn't much more she could do. Taking a deep breath, Leah headed back down the stairs. She approached the table slowly and felt the blood siphon from her face.

Agnes was placing a big white cloth over the wound and said, "The bullet is in deep, it might even be in the bone. We've decided to wait until Doc can take it out." She handed Leah the bowl, now filled with bright red water.

Leah tried to not look at it. Her stomach felt queasy again. She prayed she wouldn't get sick and hated this weakness of not being able to stomach the sight of blood.

Jake took the bowl from her shaking hands. "I'll take care of this." He gave her shoulder a gentle squeeze. "You all right?"

"Yes, thank you." She took a deep breath while laying a hand over her upset stomach. "I'm just not good in these situations."

He patted her shoulder and turned to dispose of the water. "Is Molly back?"

Leah followed him to the kitchen. "No, she's still out in the barn."

"Good. I for sure didn't want her to hear the noise

Dalton was making. That bullet is buried pretty deep." He walked out the back door.

She eased onto Molly's stool, feeling faint. Poor Mr. Dalton. Leah could only imagine the pain a bullet would cause.

Jake returned with the empty bowl. "We better go help Agnes get him upstairs, and then Mr. Frontz wants to go get the stagecoach. It's going to take all us men to get it back."

"Mr. Porter is going, too?"

He shook his head. "He has to."

"But he's hurt."

Jake nodded. "Yes, but he's the only one who knows where the coach is." Jake must have seen the concern on her face because he pressed on. "He's not hurt that badly. I cleaned his head wound. Thankfully the bullet only grazed his temple. His head hurts, but he'll live."

Leah sighed. "Well, I hate that you are all going out in the storm."

He stopped and gave her an encouraging smile. "We'll be fine, you'll see."

She nodded, still not liking the thought.

They entered the main room, where Agnes carefully finished up Mr. Dalton's dressing. "We need to get him upstairs. Which room did you prepare?" she asked Leah.

"The one with the green quilt on the bed."

Cold air filled the room as Will entered the front door. "We're about ready to leave, Jake."

"Help me get Mr. Dalton up to bed and then we'll join the others." Jake moved to the wounded man's head while Will hurried to grab his legs.

As they carried him up the stairs, Agnes fussed about like a mother hen. "Be careful, don't jostle him too much," she warned. "I don't want him to start bleeding again."

Leah hurried up the stairs in front of them. She held the door while the men carried Mr. Dalton to the bed and laid him down.

Agnes checked Mr. Dalton's shoulder. She *tsked* as she fussed with his pillow. "Jake, before you leave I'll need help getting him out of the remainder of these soiled clothes."

Leah backed out the door and shut it behind her. She heard Molly running up the stairs and was grateful that it was time to put the child to bed. Leah didn't know how much more of this day she could endure.

Molly's appearance caused her to smile. The little girl stood in front of her wearing a man's overcoat. A straw hat that covered her whole head flopped about as if she were a scarecrow in the wind. Leah expected the child to tell her everything she'd done while they were apart, but Molly peeked up at her from under the brim of the hat and beamed a smile. No words came to explain the joy on her face. Leah wondered if Molly would ever talk.

The doctor had said she'd hold her own council until she was ready, and until then just to be patient with her. That was easier said than done. Leah returned the little girl's smile. "Come along, Molly. Time for bed."

Molly came forward and grabbed Leah around the legs. The hat fell to the floor as she tilted her head to look up at Leah.

Ike came up behind Molly. He picked up the hat

and put it back on Molly's head with a grin. "I think she had fun."

"I think so, too, thank you." Leah hugged Molly against her leg. "She appears very happy."

"Do you know where Jake is? Mr. Frontz is ready to go."

Leah pointed to the bedroom. "He and Will are helping Agnes get Mr. Dalton into bed. But Jake has already said that as soon as they are done they will be right down."

Ike nodded. "Thanks. I'll let Mr. Frontz know." He turned and took the stairs back down two at a time.

Molly released Leah's leg and hurried into their room. She pulled off the borrowed coat and hat, tossing them on the bed. Leah followed her and shut the door. The little girl's skirt spun about her as she danced around the room before scooping up her doll.

Leah watched her romp with the doll for several moments before calling a halt to her fun. "Time to settle down, Molly." She picked up Molly's nightgown and held it up for the little girl to see that she wasn't teasing.

After she got her undressed and into her nightgown, Leah put Molly to bed and kissed her forehead. Molly held her rag doll up for a goodnight kiss, too. While she waited for Molly to fall asleep, Leah sat by the window and read from her Bible.

She turned to the book of Ruth and began at chapter one. As she read, her thoughts swirled. To Leah, Ruth's life story seemed quite different from her own, and yet in some places they were exactly the same. Ruth ended up marrying a man she'd just met, simply so she could survive and not have to return to her homeland. Leah felt as if she were in a similar predicament. Ruth wanted a new spouse so that she could take care of her mother-in-law; Leah was marrying Jake so that Molly would have a secure home. Ruth and Boaz ended up falling in love. It was there that Leah stopped the comparison and closed her Bible. But, try as she might, she couldn't help but feel a bottomless peace and satisfaction at the turn of events in her life. She wondered briefly if Ruth had experienced the same emotion.

Steady breathing told her that Molly was finally asleep. Leah pulled the covers up to the little girl's chin as her mind chased her private daydream. Would she and Jake fall in love? What would it feel like to know the love of a good man? Leah pushed the thought from her mind. If her own parents hadn't loved her, how could Jake?

The desire to go to bed pulled at her, but in good conscience Leah couldn't go just yet. She needed to check on Agnes and Mr. Dalton. The older woman was probably just as tired as Leah felt. Plus, she wanted to know when the men returned with the stagecoach.

She slipped out the bedroom door and walked the short distance to Mr. Dalton's room. The door was ajar so Leah stepped inside. Agnes sat beside his bed. Lamplight illuminated her face. In sleep the older woman looked much younger.

As if sensing her presence, Agnes jerked awake. She sat up and looked at Leah for several moments as if trying to remember where she was.

Leah whispered, "I'm sorry. I didn't mean to wake you."

Agnes brushed the hair off her forehead and looked to Mr. Dalton, who appeared to sleep peacefully. "That's all right." She felt his forehead and sighed. "Good. He doesn't have a fever."

"Would you like for me to sit with him for a while?" Leah asked, stepping closer to Agnes and the bed. She looked down on Mr. Dalton. He was a little pale but otherwise looked fine.

The older woman shook her head. "No, child. That wouldn't be decent and you have to watch over Molly. I'll be fine until the men get home and then I'm sure me and the boys can come up with a schedule of sorts so that we can all get some rest." She walked over to the window and looked out.

Leah followed her. Snow blew against the house and the wind howled at the window. She hadn't noticed it before, but now felt a shiver sweep over her at the sound. "I wonder how much longer they'll be gone."

"Hopefully not much longer," Agnes whispered back. "Charlie took all the men so that they could make quick work of righting the coach and getting it back here."

They stared out at the falling snow for several minutes. Agnes searched the yard and surrounding area with her eyes. Leah could tell she was worried about the men, too.

Agnes turned from the window. "Why don't you go get some sleep? I'll be fine until the men return." She patted Leah's arm. "That youngin will be up bright and early, and will want you up, too." She walked past Leah and returned to her chair beside the bed.

"All right. If you need me, don't hesitate to wake me." At Agnes's nod, Leah slipped out of the room.

Leah went to the kitchen and got a fresh water pitcher for her room. She'd hate for the child to wake up and want a drink.

The house creaked as she descended the stairs. Leah hurried to the kitchen, found the pitcher and filled it with fresh water. Looking about she realized that the kitchen hadn't been cleaned and rolled her sleeves up. The last thing Agnes needed was to come in in the morning and have to clean up dirty dishes.

As she worked, Leah realized the men would be freezing and a hot cup of coffee would make them all feel better before going to their beds. She set the coffee to brewing and continued to work.

An hour later, the kitchen was clean, mugs sat on the table waiting to be filled when the men arrived, and the kitchen smelled of freshly brewed coffee. The sound of the front door opening and boots stomping on the front porch had her racing to the main room.

Her heart did a little skip when she saw Jake enter the house. His hands and face were red, but the smile in his eyes and on his lips assured her he was fine.

"I've made coffee," she said in the way of greeting.

They all looked tired but happy to hear that she had something hot and ready for them to drink. Leah hurried to the kitchen and grabbed the pot. She poured each man a mugfull.

Jake took his. "Thank you, Leah."

"I'm sorry. I don't know what Agnes did with the cider, so I didn't make you any." She felt a flush come to her cheeks.

He touched her cheek in a gesture of reassurance.

"The coffee is fine. Thank you for making it." Jake wrapped his hands about the mug and drank deeply.

His hand had felt chilled against her skin, and yet Leah felt warm inside. Her cheek still retained the cold from where his hand had briefly touched her face. She felt her cheeks flame and decided to focus on the job at hand, seeing to all the men's comfort and not just Jake's.

As she refilled Mr. Frontz's cup, he asked, "Is Agnes still up there?" His gaze moved to the top of the stairs.

Leah nodded.

He turned to the men. "Who goes out next?"

Ike raised his hand.

"Son, you go on to bed." He looked at the other young men. "I need volunteers to sit up with Mr. Dalton."

They all raised their hands.

"Good, we'll each take a shift. Will, you go on up and relieve Mrs. Frontz. Timothy, in an hour you relieve him. Cole, you're next. I'll take over after Cole if you'll step in after me, Jake."

Everyone nodded.

Mr. Porter stepped up. "What about me? I'll take a turn like the rest of you."

Mr. Frontz clapped a hand on the other man's shoulder. "Yes, you will. Jake's shift will be finished at five. You can take over from him."

Mr. Porter nodded.

"Now that that's settled, I suggest you all get to bed." Mr. Frontz watched as each young man headed out of the house through the kitchen. He turned and headed up the stairs, Will close behind.

Leah assumed Mr. Frontz would collect Agnes and then head on up to their rooms on the third floor. She picked up the mugs and cups and took them back to the kitchen. She dropped them into the pan of soapy water. Her back hurt, but she wasn't about to leave the kitchen with dirty dishes in the sink.

"You wash and I'll dry."

Leah jumped. She hadn't realized that Jake had followed her to the washtub. "No, you're tired and need your rest."

"So are you. If we work together, we can both get our rest."

His deep voice pulled her gaze to his. He was serious. Did he really care that she was tired, too? She suddenly felt wide awake.

Jake picked up a dish towel and waited for Leah to start handing the cups to him. He'd seen the surprised look on her face. Was she truly unspoiled? Hadn't anyone ever offered to help her with chores before?

He realized he knew very little about the woman standing beside him. She handed him a cup without meeting his eyes.

Earlier in the barn, she'd listened as he'd talked about the horses and the care required to prepare them for their long rides with the pony express riders. She had kept her thoughts to herself, seeming content to listen to him. Was she used to keeping her own counsel? It felt strange, but Jake knew that if they were going to create a happy home for Molly, they were going to have to spend time together and communicate while doing so.

"Leah, what was your childhood like?" The

shocked expression on her face had him wishing he could take the spontaneous question back.

She cleared her throat. "I grew up in an orphanage. My parents dropped me off on the doorstep when I was somewhere between six months and a year old."

He heard the hurt and bitterness in her voice. "I see. But that doesn't really tell me what your childhood was like." Jake didn't know why he was pushing her, just knew that he had to get to know her better. After all, she would be raising his niece with him.

Leah blew a strand of hair out of her eyes and handed him a cup to dry. "It wasn't horrible. We had a very strict schedule. We rose each morning and made our beds, had breakfast, did our morning chores, went to lessons, ate lunch, went back to lessons, and then after dinner we did our evening chores. Only then were we allowed to read or play quietly." She handed him the last cup and picked up the tub to toss out the dirty water.

Jake set the mug down and reached for the washtub. "Here, let me do that." He was surprised when she handed it over with no fuss.

He dumped the water and returned to find her wiping down the counter. Jake set to putting the mugs back in the cabinet where they belonged.

"Why do you want to know about my childhood?" Leah asked, weariness dripping from her words.

Did she expect him to renege on his marriage offer? Her crystal-blue eyes studied him. It was if she were waiting for the other shoe to fall, as his grandmother would have said.

Jake walked to the table and pulled out a stool for Leah to sit on. When she sat, he answered, "We need to get to know one another. I simply thought talking about our childhoods would be a good starting place." He sat down in Molly's usual spot.

Leah looked down at her hands. "Oh, I see."

Did she really? Did Leah realize that with just that one question he'd learned how defensive and hurt she felt about growing up in an orphanage?

"What was your childhood like?" she asked.

He was surprised by the question, but realized that he shouldn't have been. "It was hard. My papa bought a small farm in the middle of nowhere. We worked that land from sunup to sundown and half the time ended up with nothing or very little to show for the work. Mama raised hens, so every Saturday afternoon she'd go to town and sell the eggs in exchange for flour, salt, coffee and sometimes sugar."

"So, you didn't have much fun, either." Leah picked at the scrap of material that covered the table.

"I wouldn't say that." He grinned as he thought of the good times he and his brother had enjoyed together as kids. "I learned how to hunt and fish, that was fun. And, in the summer, after the fish were caught, we'd swim in the water hole." Jake thought about the fun he and his brother had had, splashing each other and oftentimes their parents, too. "Sometimes, Mama and Papa would help Grams down to the watering hole and we'd have picnics on the shore."

"I thought you said life was hard," Leah's voice almost accused.

He watched a pink flush fill her cheeks as she heard her own tone. Jake reached across and captured one of her hands. The palms were lightly callused, but not nearly as much as his own. "Life is what you make of it, Leah. It can either be filled with hardships and you never feel happiness, or it can be filled with hardships and you make your own happiness. I believe that's what my parents did. Life was hard, but they found pleasure in the simple things and taught my brother and me to do the same."

Jake fell silent. In a way, he was talking to himself as well as her. It had been hard when his parents had died, but he and his brother had carried on with life. Now looking back, maybe he should have stayed around when John married Sally. What would life be like for him now, if he had? Sorrow at the lost years threatened to overtake him.

She tugged her hand free of his. "I suppose you are right."

Jake couldn't let her go without bringing her spirits up. "Tell me, Leah. What did you do to have fun when you were a kid?"

Leah's eyes searched his face. "Promise not to laugh?"

He drew an *X* over his chest with his finger. "Cross my heart."

A smile twitched her lips at his silly action. She took a deep breath and then blurted out, "We had books that we could look at and read. There was one full of pictures. Pictures of beautiful flowers and brightly colored birds. I think I read that book a million times and dreamed of the day I could plant a flower garden. I imagined that I'd have a home and could place those flowers about so that their beauty could be shared by everyone. And maybe, the beautiful birds would visit my yard, too." She smiled at the mental image and then dropped her eyes back to the table.

A piece of Jake's heart went out to her. Someday he'd make sure that she got that flower garden. Until then, Jake vowed to give her joy in some form or fashion for as long as he lived. Not because he loved her; he refused to open his heart up to such hurt again but because it was the right thing for him to do as her husband.

She cleared her throat and stood up. "Well, I need to get some rest. I'll see you at breakfast."

"Good night," he called to her as she hurried from the kitchen. Jake pushed away from the table and headed toward the barn. Icy-cold wind hit him in the face as he crossed the yard. Leah's childhood had been hard. He hoped that she'd find an easier life with him and Molly.

He opened the door to the tack room and began working on a saddle strap as he worried. Maybe Leah would be better off finding a man who would love her instead of marrying him, a man who would never give her his heart.

Chapter Six

The next morning, Jake took his time feeding and watering the horses. After a restless night, he wasn't ready to face Leah. She deserved better than he was offering. A loveless marriage wasn't something every little girl dreamed of. They dreamed of love, flowers and, in Leah's case, colorful birds.

He'd mulled their conversation over in his mind. Not once had she mentioned love, but what little girl wouldn't want to be loved? And since she'd grown up without her parents' love, surely Leah would expect her husband to love her. Wouldn't she?

Jake's stomach growled, reminding him he'd had very little for dinner. It was time to go in. Time to face her. He opened the barn door and headed across the yard. He was thankful the snow and wind had let up. The sun shone brightly and the earth glistened with a fresh blanket of snow.

He pushed the front door open. Warm air kissed his cheeks. He pulled his coat off and hung it on one of the many hooks beside the door. His hat and gloves were pushed into the coat pockets.

"About time you got in here," Mr. Frontz greeted from his place at the table.

Jake grinned as he crossed the room. "Was I holding you up?" he asked, slapping the older man on the back.

"Not me." Mr. Frontz stuffed what remained of his biscuit into his mouth.

Everyone around the table was munching as if it were their last meal. "Doesn't look like anyone else waited for me, either," Jake observed.

"Didn't say they did. Just said it's about time you got here." Mr. Frontz buttered another biscuit.

Jake took his place at the table. Molly sat across from him, beside Leah this morning. The little girl wore a pink dress and the ribbon that she'd wanted to put on the snowman a few days ago. "That's a mighty pretty ribbon you're wearing, Molly."

Molly looked across at him and beamed. She pointed at Leah as if to say the ribbon belonged to her.

Leah grinned down at the little girl. "Molly's borrowing it today."

The little girl nodded and then went back to her breakfast of scrambled eggs, sausage and biscuit.

Agnes asked, "What time are you two going to the homestead?"

Leah looked to him, also.

Jake answered, "I was thinking we might go after breakfast, if Leah still wants to."

Molly bounced about on her seat with excitement. He'd told her the day before that she could go with them and now wished he hadn't. After his restless night, Jake wasn't sure it was still a good idea for Leah to marry him. He wanted to talk to her, in private. But, he'd already agreed and wouldn't stop the child from going now.

Leah's soft voice pulled him from his thoughts. "Maybe after I help Agnes with the dishes."

Agnes flustered. "Nonsense! You did all of last night's dishes and made sure the men had something hot in their bellies before sending them to bed. You don't have to do dishes this morning, too."

"I don't have to, but I'm going to." Leah stared back at Mrs. Frontz, daring her to argue.

Jake focused on filling his plate with food while enjoying the women's standoff. Agnes pursed her lips and stared right back at her. Leah raised an eyebrow.

"Aw, Agnes, let the young woman help out if she wants to. What's it going to hurt?" Mr. Frontz asked, pushing away from the table.

The pony express riders seemed to be ignoring the events around them but Jake knew better. Ike grinned down at his breakfast, while Cole and Will stuffed their faces with food. Jake decided to mimic Cole and Will, and tucked into his own breakfast.

"Fine. But, I'll do the washing and you can do the drying," Agnes agreed.

Leah turned her attention to Jake. "Molly and I will be ready in about an hour."

The pony express riders pushed away from the table. "Thank you for the fine breakfast," Will said for all three of them as they stomped out of the house.

Jake heard Mr. Frontz giving them chores out on the front porch. The sound of boots clomping off the steps told him the men were gone. He resumed eating. How was he going to talk to Leah about the fairness of his marriage offer if Molly came with them to the house?

He looked up and found Leah staring at him. Her eyebrow quirked up at him, much as it had with Agnes a few moments earlier. Had he missed something she'd said? Was she expecting him to say something?

Leah waited for him to respond. When it was obvious he wasn't going to she asked, "Well, is that acceptable for you?"

He waved his fork in the air. "Oh, sure. I'm sorry. I just assumed you'd know it was all right with me."

"How would I know that? I don't know what your plans are for this morning." She began picking up plates and stacking them.

Molly got down from her chair and carried her dolly to the couch. Mrs. Frontz scooped food onto a clean dish and headed up the stairs. "If you two will excuse me, I'm going to take Mr. Dalton his breakfast."

Leah felt heat fill her cheeks. She'd forgotten all about the injured man. What was it about Jake that turned her brain to mush? Last night he'd wanted to talk about their childhoods. She'd hated telling him she'd grown up in the orphanage, and then when he'd lectured her on how to handle being alone all her life, she'd wanted to scream at him.

Thanks to him, she'd tossed and turned all night. Worry ate at her insides. What if he'd changed his mind about marrying her? Did he think she was too damaged to take care of Molly? That she wouldn't give Molly a happy childhood? Those questions and more had danced about her mind until she didn't think she could stand another moment of being idle and in bed.

Leah carried the dirty dishes to the kitchen and sat them on the counter. She picked up a damp rag and headed back to the table to wipe down the area where Mr. Frontz and the riders had eaten.

Jake stood as she entered the room. "I'll see you ladies in an hour. Do you want me to come inside and collect you? Or would you rather meet me out at the barn?" he asked.

"Maybe you should come get us. I don't want to interrupt your work," Leah answered as she picked up his dishes.

His brown eyes looked troubled. Leah couldn't help but worry that he was having second thoughts. How could she convince him that she would be a good mother for Molly? And wife for him?

As soon as the dishes were done, Leah called Molly to her. "Are you ready to go look at our soon-to-be home? We can wait outside for Jake, if you want to."

Molly grabbed her hand. A big smile graced the child's face. Leah followed as Molly tried taking two steps at a time going up the stairs for their coats, hats and gloves. Her tiny legs stretched till she almost lost her balance and fell back against Leah for support. They both laughed and Leah felt a lightening of her load. Could it be that the good Lord knew what she needed and had set her down right in the middle of it? She surely hoped so, and that is what she would cling to today. Hope.

Once they were outside, the sun shone and glistened on the snow but its rays warmed their faces, making the day seem warmer than it was. As they waited for Jake, Leah let Molly play in the fresh snow. The little girl started to build what looked like a small castle. Leah chuckled as Molly danced around it with glee.

Maybe Jake was right about hardships. Molly had lots to be sorrowful about, but instead she chose to play in the snow and dance.

"Has anyone ever told you that you have a pretty smile?" Jake asked as he crossed the yard.

At first Leah thought he was talking to her, but then she noticed his gaze was on Molly. The little girl ran to him and jumped into his waiting arms. He swung her around and then put her back down.

He turned to Leah. "Ready?"

The two of them looked at her. Matching smiles covered their faces. Leah had to admit they both had nice smiles. "Ready."

Holding Molly's hand, Jake led them around the house. He traveled a snow-covered path. It took them about five minutes to arrive at a small log building.

Leah had seen it from the side of the house and thought that it was a storage building. She could see the small chimney puffing out white clouds of smoke. A chimney she hadn't noticed before.

"I know it doesn't look like much, but I can promise that it will be warm and dry and all ours." He cast a worried glance over his shoulder at her.

"I'm sure it will be just fine," Leah replied, praying she was telling the truth.

Jake lifted Molly and stomped up the two small porch steps. He opened the door and stepped back down the steps to allow Leah to pass. "Ladies first."

Taking a deep breath, Leah entered the house. It

was one room with two windows. The fireplace was off to the left, and when she turned to the right, she saw a small bed. She could see where fresh mud and grass had been pushed between the logs to shut out the cold air. A back door was the only other thing of interest in the small room. And she'd been worried about how to decorate it. Leah almost laughed at the thought.

The sound of his boots on the steps reminded her that she still stood in the doorway. After being in the main house, Leah felt cramped as she walked farther into the room. Where would she cook? Where would all three of them sleep? Questions swirled through her mind in quick succession.

Jake closed the door behind himself and Molly. Putting Molly down, he said, "Can you cook over the fireplace?"

Cook over the fireplace? The question echoed through her mind. She didn't know how to do much more than boil eggs on the stove in the house. Cook on a fireplace? What did that even mean?

"I, ah—" Those were the only two words she could get out and one of them was a sound, not a word. "I—"

Jake laughed. "I'll take that as a no. Don't worry, Agnes and I will teach you."

Leah fought down the panic and turned her thoughts to another worrisome problem. "Where will we all sleep?"

Jake pointed to the bed. "I thought you and Molly could have the bed and I'll pull my cot in from the tool shed."

Was the room big enough for both? She eyed the

wall. "Maybe we can turn the bed against the back wall and put the cot on the other side?" It was more of a question than a statement.

Molly ran to the bed and bounced on the mattress. She smiled at them both.

"Molly likes it," Jake said, sounding a little depressed.

Leah turned to face him. She plastered what she hoped was a bright smile and said, "Oh, I like it, too. There are just things that need to be worked out." Like how to cook, where to sleep and where to put all their belongings. She didn't voice the last but they screamed through her mind, all the same.

"Good. I'm sure Agnes can help us figure out how to arrange things so we will have plenty of room." He didn't sound sure.

Trying to sound confident, Leah asked, "Will you help me move the bed? And then we can see if the cot will fit."

Jake nodded and walked to the small bed. "Hop down, little one."

As soon as Molly moved from the bed, Jake pulled it around to fit the wall. "Oh, that opens it up a little. Don't you think?" He turned to her with hope in his expression.

It was going to be tight but Leah couldn't crush his hopes. "Yes, and we'll use under the bed to store our clothes and shoes."

He nodded. "I could go get the cot, and Molly and I could start staying here tonight." Jake looked to the little girl.

She surprised them both by running to Leah and

shaking her head hard. Molly grabbed Leah's skirt and buried her face in the material.

Leah saw the hurt look cross Jake's face before he masked it. She bent down and pried Molly from her dress, remaining on eye level with her so she could clearly see the child's reactions. "Sweetie, are you afraid of your Uncle Jake?" Leah was pretty sure that wasn't the case, but she wanted to make it clear in Jake's mind that his niece didn't fear him.

Again Molly furiously shook her head. She leaned into Leah and wrapped her arms around Leah's neck.

Feeling as if she were going to be choked, Leah gently pulled away from the little girl. "Do you just want to stay with me until Uncle Jake and I get married?"

Jake knelt beside them. "You don't have to come live with me until you're ready," he told Molly.

His eyes held Leah's and she felt as if he were speaking to her, too.

Molly reached out and touched Jake's face. She smiled as her hand connected with the afternoon stubble. Releasing Leah, Molly leaned over and hugged Jake.

He started to speak, then hesitated, apparently torn by conflicting emotions. "I know this house is small. If you would rather move back to Texas where I have a small farm, I'll let the Frontzs know that we'll be leaving in the spring. That's the soonest I'd feel comfortable leaving with the weather the way it is."

Leah shook her head. "No, the house is fine." Squatting on the floor like this, all three of them together, kind of made her feel like part of a family.

Maybe a small house was what they needed to get to know each other better.

Molly pulled away from them and walked to the window.

Still kneeling beside her, Jake's gaze moved to the fireplace. "Are you sure? It won't be easy."

Leah felt as if she understood his emotions. A week ago, he'd been a bachelor doing what he wanted. Now he was faced with having a daughter and a wife to take care of, not something he'd planned to do at this stage in his life.

Maybe she assumed too much. But Leah didn't think so. She'd never had male influences in her life, but she wanted one now and couldn't think of anyone she'd rather have than Jake.

"Easy or not, we're in this together." Leah reached out and put her hand on his shoulder.

His returning grin set her heart to fluttering. Leah quickly jerked her hand away and stood up. As she turned to look at Molly, Leah mentally chanted, *I will not fall for his easy smile, I will not fall for his easy smile.*

Chapter Seven

That evening, Jake sat in the bedroom with Mr. Dalton, who lay sleeping on the bed in front of him. Jake rested his head in his hands and listened to the other man's steady breathing. He couldn't get Leah off his mind and it bothered him. Maybe he'd made a mistake in offering to marry her? Was he opening his heart? And if he did, would she crush it? How many times would those thoughts drift through his mind like a whisper on the wind?

Mr. Dalton groaned in his sleep. Jake looked up. He knew the other man was in quite a bit of pain. The doctor had arrived shortly after Leah and Molly had returned to the house. He'd worked for an hour getting the bullet out of the man's shoulder. As Agnes had thought, the bullet had lodged in the bones of Dalton's shoulder.

Jake eased to the edge of his chair and searched the man's face to make sure that he was still out. The doctor had left medicine to help Mr. Dalton sleep and Mrs. Frontz had given him a healthy dose to make sure that he did. A soft snore confirmed the medication was working.

Jake eased back. The sound of the dinner bell told him the others would soon be inside to eat. The swish of skirts on the stairs alerted him to the fact that he'd be eating in a few moments. He tilted his head to the side as Leah entered the room.

"I've brought you a bowl of stew and some corn bread." She carried a tray.

"Thank you." He took the tray and smiled up at her. He had to admit that Leah was very pretty. From her silky brown hair to her small boot-clad feet, she radiated beauty. Her face was soft and her light blue eyes expressive. Pink-tinted cheeks and rosebud lips completed her sweet look. What man wouldn't want her for a bride?

"How's he doing?" she asked, turning her attention to Mr. Dalton. She approached the bed and rested her palm on the other man's forehead. "Agnes asked me to make sure he isn't running a fever," Leah explained as she stood. "I'll be happy to report that he isn't."

Jake set the tray down on the bedside table. The rich fragrance of hot stew teased his nostrils. "That's good."

"It's a bit chilly up here. Would you like a blanket to wrap up in?" Leah asked, turning her attention to him once more.

Jake took a sip from the coffee mug that rested on the tray along with the food. Sweet apple cider coated his tongue. "No, I'm used to it being cool."

Leah nodded. "I guess it does get chilly out in the tack room."

He used the cup to warm his hands. "A little."

She studied him for several moments. "Jake, why don't you go ahead and move into the homestead? At least there you would have the fireplace to keep you warm at night."

Jake thought her cheeks might have turned a deeper shade of pink but in the fading light he couldn't be sure. "I just might do that."

"Good." Leah started toward the open door. "I best get back and help Agnes with Molly."

"Thank you for bringing up my meal."

Leah bobbed her head. "I'll be back in a bit to get your dishes. Do you need anything else?"

He wondered if she would have asked anyone that question or if she was prolonging her departure. "No, thank you." Jake looked down at the tray. "I think I have all I need."

"Then I'll see you later." She left the room.

Jake sat back down and pulled the tray to him. He blessed the food before taking a big bite of the corn bread. Sweetness coated his tongue and he pulled the bread back to look at it. What was the new flavor? Agnes's corn bread had never been sweet.

Had Leah made the corn bread tonight? He'd liked to have asked her. His sweet tooth beckoned him to eat the rest and he did with pleasure.

A few minutes later he heard someone hurrying up the stairs. The sound of her skirts swishing up the steps alerted him that his visitor was Leah.

She sounded breathless as she asked, "Have you tried the corn bread yet?"

"I did and it is wonderful. Did Agnes do something different to it today?" Jake didn't need to be told that

Leah had made it. Even with the low light he could tell that her cheeks were bright red.

"Yes. She let me make it and I messed it up."

Jake heard the despair in her voice. "How so?" He could honestly say that he enjoyed it. "I thought it was delicious."

Leah came farther into the room. Disbelief sounded in her voice. "Really?"

"Oh, yes." He held the tray out. "See. Mine's gone and I'd love another piece."

"Really? Jake, I accidently put sugar in it."

"Oh, that's what makes it taste so good. Do you think I can have more?" he asked, holding out the empty saucer that had held the bread.

She took the plate. "Sure, I'll be right back." Leah walked out of the room much slower than she'd entered.

As soon as he heard her feet on the stairs, Jake put the tray back on the table and then hurried out the bedroom door. He stopped at the top of the stairs and listened to the conversation below.

"This corn bread is good," Cole said.

Agnes laughed. "Leah made it."

"It's sweet," Timothy mused.

Leah's voice sounded up to him. "I'm sorry. I realized a few moments ago that I had accidently put sugar in the batter."

Mr. Frontz's booming laughter bounded up the stairs to Jake. "No reason to be sorry, Miss Hollister. This is wonderful. I can't think of a thing wrong with the corn bread tonight."

"See? I told you," Agnes said.

Jake returned to the bedroom. Had Leah come to

him first? Had she been worried that he would dislike the corn bread? Had she taken a bite and then hurried to his side? He didn't know what to think of his future bride. Could it be that she needed this marriage as badly as he? That she needed a helpmate— someone to feel needed by? Was she looking for a forever friend?

Leah climbed the stairs again. She'd been up and down them so many times today she'd lost track of the number. Taking a deep breath, she stopped at the top of the stairs. Weariness crept between her shoulder blades and into her hairline.

Jake stepped out of Dalton's room and came to stand beside her. "It's been a long day, hasn't it?" He turned and leaned against the banister.

"It has." She sighed and turned to look down the stairs.

Two of the pony express riders sat in front of the fireplace chatting in quiet voices. Cole had left half an hour earlier on his run and wouldn't be back for two days. Leah said a little prayer for his safety. She had planned to stay and listen to Will and Timothy talk about their recent rides, but tonight her body simply wanted to lie down and rest.

"I appreciate that you are helping Mrs. Frontz. She is getting older and I'm afraid that the work is taking its toll on her." Jake steepled his fingers over the edge of the railing.

Leah didn't tell him that she was trying to pay off her room and board. She didn't want Jake to feel indebted to the Frontzs for her care, since she was now marrying him instead of Thomas. She could pay off her own debt, and knowing that gave her a sense of accomplishment. Even if it did mean she had to work hard. "I enjoy working with her and she's teaching me how to cook."

"If I'm not mistaken, you taught her something to-night." He grinned across at her.

Leah tried to hide her smile. "I'm sure she already knew how to make sweet corn bread."

"I've never had it and I've been here a few months now," he said.

She tilted her head sideways to look at him. "Only a few months?"

"Yes, I was working in Julesburg at the home station there, but Mr. Slade decided that Mr. Frontz could run his swing station like a home station so I asked to be moved here." He turned around and glanced toward Dalton's door.

"So, how long have you been here?"

"Four months." He walked to the door and looked inside. Leah assumed he wanted to be sure his patient was still asleep.

When he returned to her she asked, "Why not stay in Julesburg?"

He looked back down at the riders and Mr. and Mrs. Frontz. "Julesburg is a rough town. Thieves, out-laws and other unsavory sorts live and come through there every day. I can't speak for the other men, but for me the decision was easy. I didn't want to associ-ate with that sort of people."

"So, would you say you are a God-fearing man, Jake?"

Jake turned to face her. "I am, and I expect my wife to be God-fearing also. Are you?"

She nodded. "Yes."

"Good." He returned to rail.

Leah was glad her future husband believed in the same God that she did. "Jake?"

"Umm."

"Did any pony express riders stay in Julesburg?"

"I'm afraid so. Some of them liked the life that Julesburg had to offer. Cole, Timothy, Ike, Will and I chose to live here." He stretched and yawned.

Leah impulsively yawned also. "Good night, Jake. I'm glad you came to South Platte." She turned and entered her room.

His soft voice followed her. "I am, too, Leah. Good night."

She closed the door and leaned against it. Molly had kicked the covers off and lay on top of them. Leah's heart went out to the young riders who had decided to stay in Julesburg. It surely didn't sound like a good place for young men.

The sound of boots alerted her that Mr. and Mrs. Frontz were heading upstairs. She listened as Mr. Frontz greeted Jake. "How's he doing?"

Jake's warm voiced flowed through the door. "He hasn't stirred."

"Good. Go catch a few winks. I'll stay with him tonight."

"If you want to get a few hours' sleep, I can stay with him."

"No, son, you've done your fair share tonight. Go get some shut-eye."

"All right, but before I go, I have a question."

Leah leaned her ear against the door. She held her breath as she listened. It probably wasn't right that she was eavesdropping, but for some reason she felt glued to the door.

"What's on your mind?"

"Well, I was wondering if you'd mind if I moved into the homestead tomorrow."

A rich laugh came from the older man. "It's yours. If you want to live in it now, go ahead. Mrs. Frontz and I gave it to you."

"Thank you, sir."

It sounded as if Mr. Frontz slapped Jake on the back. "Go on to bed with you, son. Morning will come mighty early for all of us."

The sound of boots stomping farther down the hall informed Leah that Mr. Frontz had walked away. She was about to push away from the door when Jake's soft voice stopped her. It sounded as if he were right up against the door on the other side.

"Sleep well, Leah."

She gasped. Had he known she was standing there listening? A warm chuckle was her answer and then his boots pounded back down the stairs.

The next morning Leah laid the dish towel on the sink and sighed. Jake hadn't come in for breakfast and she wondered what he was doing. She'd made a mess of breakfast, but the men and Agnes had been great about it.

Molly played a few feet away. She'd plaited the little girl's hair into braids this morning and tied them together at the ends. Solemn brown eyes looked up at her, as if she sensed Leah looking at her.

Before Leah could speak, Agnes walked through the door. "Mr. Dalton ate most of his breakfast."

"Even the bacon?"

Agnes laughed. "Yes, he said to assure you he liked it crispy."

Molly grinned up at them and then continued playing with her doll.

"If crispy means burned, I'm glad." Leah sighed. So far, her cooking skills left much to be desired. She'd scorched the bacon and oversalted the eggs.

"Now, don't be getting upset. We all had to learn. Some of us learned from our mothers early in life, others learned later." Agnes put Mr. Dalton's dirty dishes in the sink.

What would it have been like to grow up with a mother? Leah could only dream of such things. She looked down at Molly. If she were to marry Jake and become Molly's mother, she'd have to learn faster and better.

"Agnes, may I borrow Leah for a little while?"

Leah turned at Jake's voice. When had he come in? He stood behind the divided door, and she could only see the upper half of his body. His brown eyes searched her face. A grin split his lips. What did he want with her?

"Sure. Molly and I were about to go to the general store to see if Mr. Hamilton has any of that rock candy left."

Molly jumped to her feet.

"But first we have to finish the rest of these dishes."

The little girl's smile slipped from her face.

Agnes laughed at her expression. "Oh, come on now. We all have to learn to do dishes sometime. Today, you can dry."

The only dishes left were Mr. Dalton's plate, silverware and coffee mug, so Leah knew Molly wouldn't have much to do before she could go for her treat. Agnes held out one of the many aprons that she and Leah wore when doing chores.

Leah turned to look at Jake. "I'll need to grab my coat and gloves."

He nodded. "I'll wait."

As she hurried up the stairs to her room, Leah wondered again what Jake wanted with her. Was there a chore he needed help with? She grabbed her coat and headed back downstairs.

When she reentered the kitchen, Agnes was showing Molly how to make sure the cup she held was dry. "See, no water is left on it. Now, sit it over there and I'll wash the plate next." Agnes looked up at Leah. "Take your time. We're going to have egg sandwiches for lunch and I can take care of those when the small fry and I get back from the store."

Leah grinned at the endearing "small fry," as Agnes had dubbed Molly. "Thank you." Leah dug her gloves out of her coat pocket and slipped them on before joining Jake outside.

He stood beside the door, waiting as promised. Once they were out of hearing range, Jake said, "I hope you don't mind me pulling you away, but I want to get your opinion on something."

Leah waited for him to say what but he didn't elaborate further. She walked with him toward the homestead. The sun was shining but the temperature was bitterly cold. She pulled her coat closer to her body.

Without Molly with them they were able to walk faster and arrived pretty quickly at the cabin. Jake motioned for Leah to go in ahead of him. She opened the door and was pleasantly surprised.

Warmth welcomed her into the cabin. She looked about. The bare wooden floor now had a large round rug in the center of the room. A table sat beside the fireplace with three chairs. She recognized it as the one that had been in his room in the barn. On the opposite wall sat a cabinet that housed the few dishes that he'd also had in his old room.

Leah turned and saw that he'd brought in his cot and placed it on the front wall under the window. A smaller rug lay beside each of the beds. A dresser was between the beds against the wall. It had three drawers. She smiled—one for each of them.

He closed the door. "Do you like it?" Jake asked from behind her.

"It looks wonderful." He'd carried wood inside and a fire burned in the fireplace. She rubbed her arms, enjoying the warmth. "It seems so cozy."

Jake walked farther into the room and sat down at the table. "I asked you to come because I wanted to make sure that I'd placed things where you will like them and also wanted to be sure you liked the rugs."

"I do like them." She noticed for the first time they all matched. Each held different shades of browns and tans. The rugs added warmth to the room. "Wherever did you find them?"

He grinned. "Mrs. Frontz had them in storage. She said we could use them. I told her if you liked them, we might want to buy them from her."

Leah looked about her new home. The two windows were still bare, but other than that there wasn't a lot more that needed to be done to the place.

"I'm glad you suggested I ask to stay here. I think I'll be much more comfortable tonight." Jake shrugged out of his jacket.

He hung it on a nail beside the back door. "Do you think Molly will have enough room to play in here?"

"I believe so. She doesn't have many toys." Leah didn't mention that the child only had the doll to play with. Mrs. Frontz had let her play with a cup, spoon and small plate.

The little girl liked to pretend she was having tea, or at least that's what Leah thought she was playing. Molly still wasn't speaking, other than to whisper in the doll's ear.

"I'm whittling her a horse for Christmas. Do you think she'll like that?" He sounded unsure.

Leah gave him what she hoped was a reassuring smile. "I think she will love it." She'd also been thinking about what to give the little girl for Christmas. "I'm thinking about making her doll a couple of dresses." Leah sat down across from him at the table.

"She'll like that, too. Ike asked me this morning if him and the boys could give her something for Christmas." He traced the wood grain on the table with his finger. "She's going to miss her ma and pa." Sadness dripped from his voice.

"Yes, but I think she'll have a nice Christmas."

Leah hadn't talked to him about a Christmas wedding. She wondered if now would be a good time. She cleared her throat before asking. "Jake, do you know if there are any other preachers in or around this area that could marry us the day before Christmas?"

His head jerked up. "You want to get married on Christmas Eve?"

His big brown eyes bored into her.

"I do… But if you don't want to…" Her voice faltered. And the sting of tears burned her eyes.

Jake knew immediately that he'd said the wrong thing. Her eyes filled with moisture and he couldn't stop the constricting of his throat and heart. What was it about a woman's tears that made him feel so helpless?

He grabbed her hands. "Of course I do. You just took me by surprise. I didn't think you'd want to get married until the preacher got back." Jake rubbed his thumb across the back of her hand, hoping it would offer her some form of comfort.

"Okay." Her voice sounded croaky, like an old bull frog. She blushed.

"Good." He released her hands and rubbed his chin. "I'm not sure about a preacher, though."

She wiped at her left eye. "Agnes told me that the regular minister was out of town. I was hoping you could find another one."

Right now Jake would do anything to make her smile. "I could ride over to Julesburg and see if there is a visiting minister there," he offered, knowing in his heart that there wasn't.

He was rewarded with a tilt of her lips. "You would do that?"

"Of course. I'll check with Mr. Frontz and see if I can get off." He stood. "Ready to go back?"

She stood, also. "Thank you. I know it's silly, but I've always wanted a Christmas wedding. Are you sure you don't mind?"

Jake placed a hand in the small of her back.

Through her coat he could feel her backbone. Leah really was thin. He'd talked to the pony express boys and knew that living in an orphanage wasn't easy. Food was limited, as well as personal space.

The protectiveness he felt for her both shocked and scared him. He didn't want to care deeply for Leah. Was he feeling what other fiancés felt? He remembered feeling this way toward Molly's mother, but somehow this was different. No, this wasn't love. Love was an emotion that he certainly didn't want to feel.

They walked the short distance from the cabin. Leah turned to him and smiled. When they got to the main house, Leah stepped up on the porch and faced him. "Thank you, Jake. Having a Christmas wedding has always been one of my dreams." She tiptoed and kissed him on the cheek before turning to go inside.

One of her dreams? What other dreams did Leah harbor? "Leah?"

She stopped in the doorway and faced him. "Yes?"

"Would you and Molly like to go ice fishing this afternoon?" He hadn't planned on asking her, but Jake knew that he wanted to spend more time with Leah.

"That would be fun. After Molly's nap, we'll come out."

He nodded. Jake returned to the barn. He checked on the horses and began to muck out their stalls. What was it about Leah that made him feel so protective? She seemed to have an invisible wall up. It was as if she, too, were afraid to trust.

"Rider coming in fast!"

Jake heard the call and rushed to pull the mustang out of its stall. The gelding hurried along beside him, the horse's high spirit seeming to scream his desire to race in the wind. He stopped the horse and waited.

He recognized William Cody. Will jumped from his horse and took the reins from Jake. "Thanks, Jake. See you in a week or two!" he yelled as he raced away.

"Were you expecting Cody today?" Mr. Frontz asked as he came around the barn.

Jake shook his head. "Nope, but I had a horse ready." He pulled on the reins of the tired horse Will had left behind.

A knowing grin split Mr. Frontz's face. "I figured." He followed Jake into the barn. "How did Miss Hollister like the homestead?"

"She liked it." Now was as good a time as any to ask for time off. "I'd like to take an afternoon off and go to Julesburg." Jake removed the horse's saddle.

"Did you have a particular afternoon in mind?" Mr. Frontz asked.

Jake carried the saddle to the tack room. "I was thinking I'd go tomorrow. Leah wants a Christmas wedding."

Disbelief filled Mr. Frontz's voice and face as he asked. "In Julesburg?"

"No, I'll be looking for a minister there. I think Leah wants to get married here." Jake realized he really didn't know what more Leah wanted in regard to their upcoming marriage.

"Well, that's a relief." The older man picked up a currycomb and stepped into the mare's stall. "Are you taking her and Molly with you?"

The thought of taking his niece into the rough town sent a chill down Jake's back. "Julesburg is still too rough for ladies, so, no."

"That's a relief."

Jake turned his attention on his boss. "I'm not a greenhorn, you know."

Mr. Frontz continued working on the mare's coat for several moments before answering. "I know, and I admire that about you, but sometimes young men will do things for their future brides that they normally wouldn't consider doing. I'm just glad you are keeping your senses about you."

Jake didn't know whether to be insulted or flattered. Mr. Frontz seemed to be under the impression that Leah held some secret power over him, and Jake didn't like that idea one bit.

Chapter Eight

Leah bundled up Molly. The little girl jumped around with excitement. "Be still, Molly, or we aren't ever going to get outside."

Molly stood perfectly still. Her brown eyes danced as she waited for Leah to finish buttoning her coat up.

Why had she accepted his invitation to go fishing? Ice fishing, at that. She'd never been ice fishing. Leah didn't have the slightest idea how one went about fishing through the ice. Oh, she'd heard of it but had never done such a thing in her life.

The little girl became restless again. Leah understood the child's giddiness. They'd been cooped up in the house and Molly wanted to get outside and play. After working in the kitchen and doing her light cleanup of the rooms, Leah was ready, too.

She pulled a hat over Molly's head and stood. "I need to check on Mr. Dalton real quick. Why don't you go down and see if Agnes has a cookie for you?"

Molly turned and ran down the stairs. Leah sighed. No matter how many times she told that girl a lady walks down the stairs, Molly always ran. She had more energy, especially after nap time, than a kitten with a ball of string.

Leah pulled her gloves on as she walked to the banker's room. She peeked inside.

"Do come in, Miss Hollister," his weak voice called.

The room was darker than the rest of the house. "How are you feeling this afternoon?" Leah walked to the window and pulled back the curtains, allowing sunlight into the room.

"Feeling better now that you are here."

Leah was never sure if he was teasing or being polite or exactly what he meant when he said that. Did he say it to Agnes, too? Probably so. There was no reason to make more of his words. She turned to find him smiling. Leah had expected him to be pale and weak, but his face held all its color in the bright sunshine. "Molly and I are going out for a bit. Do you need anything?"

He motioned for her to come closer to the bed. "I'm a little thirsty."

Leah poured a glass of water and carried it to him, noting that he looked much stronger today. He pushed himself up and used the headboard to lean against. She handed him the glass.

His right hand shot out and grabbed her wrist. Water sloshed in the glass.

"What are you doing?" Leah demanded.

He removed the glass from her hand while still holding her wrist. A smile pulled his lips across. It wasn't a friendly smile. His eyes held a coldness that frightened her.

Leah tugged her arm back, hoping to dislodge his

hand from around her wrist. She was amazed at his strength. "Release me," she demanded. Heat radiated from his fingers, feeling as if they were hot bands holding her in place.

Should she scream for help? Leah didn't want to alarm Molly, but she couldn't stay hunched over the bed with him holding her captive. What was he doing?

"Are you about ready?"

She welcomed the sound of Jake's deep voice coming from behind her. It sounded rougher in her ears than normal. Her gaze swung up to Mr. Dalton's. His fingers slowly released her. Still holding her gaze, he took a deep drink from the glass she'd given him.

Her heart pounded in her chest.

He handed the glass back. "Thank you for the drink, Miss Hollister."

Leah's hand shook as she put the glass on the bedside table. She turned to Jake. "Yes, I'm ready." She had felt ill at ease around Mr. Dalton before; now she knew she had reason to feel that way.

Jake followed her from the room. He closed the door and reached out for her hand. It trembled in his light grasp. "Are you all right?"

Where Mr. Dalton's hand had been threatening and hard, Jake's felt warm and caring. "Yes. I'm fine." How could she explain what had just happened? Had he seen? What must he be thinking?

Jake was so angry he could spit nails. Instead, he put on what he hoped resembled a calm face. He hadn't liked Dalton before and he liked him even less now. Over the past couple of days, the men had quit sitting with the banker. It had fallen to Agnes and

Leah to see to his care. Now Jake regretted not being around more.

Dalton had some explaining to do regarding the way he'd just manhandled Leah but now wasn't the time for confrontations.

Leah's fingers shook in his hand. "Are you sure you're all right?" he asked.

She slowly pulled her hand away. "Yes, I think I'm a little overtired." Leah walked toward the stairs.

Jake followed. "Too tired to go ice fishing?"

"Oh, no. Molly is excited about going. I can't take that from her." She offered him a tight grin.

They continued down the stairs. Jake realized his face must be more expressive than he liked because when they got to the bottom of the stairs she said, "Jake, I'm fine. Really."

"Good." He wasn't sure what he was going to do about Dalton. Jake knew he'd need to tell Mr. Frontz what he'd witnessed. Maybe together they could decide what should be done about the banker.

Molly sat on the couch stringing buttons onto a long piece of yarn. She held it up for their inspection. The buttons were mainly brown and black.

"What are you going to do with that?" Jake asked, bending over to look closer at the buttons.

She held the string up to her neck and demonstrated that it was a necklace. Her brown eyes, so much like his brother's, shone back at him.

"That will be a pretty necklace." He stood up. "Are you ready to go fishing?"

Molly laid the string down and got off the couch. The little girl slipped her small hand into his and nodded.

Jake looked to Leah. She stood off to the side, watching them. Her gaze rested on Molly. Leah's eyes were soft and a motherly love shone through them.

She would make a good mother for Molly. Leah looked up and caught him watching her. Her cheeks turned pink and she ducked her head.

He tugged on Molly's hand. "Let's go, ladies. If we catch enough fish, we'll have them for dinner tonight."

Jake led them through the kitchen and out the back. He'd left two fishing poles beside the porch, as well as a large bucket with an ice auger inside and a bait bucket. He handed Leah the bait bucket with a grin. "Leah, do you know how to cook fish?" he asked as he continued on toward the frozen river.

"No, but I'm sure Agnes will be happy to teach us."

"Us?" Did she expect him to help cook the fish?

Leah looked to Molly and laughed. "Molly and me."

The pompom on Molly's hat bobbed as she nodded her head in agreement. Pulling her hand out of Jake's, she skipped ahead of them. When she came to the edge of the water, Molly stopped and looked back at him.

"Some of the boys beat us out here." Jake pointed to some holes in the ice.

Molly and Leah fought to keep their footing on the ice while Jake studied the surface of the river. Several holes had been dug and he could tell that the ice was over four inches thick. Jake decided to use a hole that had already been created.

A thin layer of ice had formed so he took the end of the ice auger and used it much like a hammer to break the surface. After skimming out as many of the ice chips as he could from the water, Jake placed heavy weights on the ends of the fishing lines.

"I'll give you the first fishing pole," he said to Leah as he baited the hook. Happy that the bait was secure, Jake handed her the pole.

Leah took the rod and lowered the weighted line into the water. "Why did you scoop out the smaller pieces of ice?" she asked.

"Those shards are so sharp they can cut the lines," he explained, slipping bait onto his hook.

Molly laid down on her belly and tried to see down into the water.

"Molly, don't get too close to the edge. That water is so cold it will freeze your nose off."

The little girl looked up with a mischievous grin.

Leah continued, "And if you stay on your belly like that, your belly button is going to freeze to the lake and, who knows, we may have to leave you out here till spring."

Jake hid his grin as his niece hurried to get up. Concern laced her features as she wiped at the moisture on her tummy. Then her gloved thumb went into her mouth as she stood next to Leah, looking down into the hole.

He finished baiting his own fishing pole and joined them. Their breath was frosty in the air. To take his mind off the cold, Jake asked, "Molly, do you know any fishing songs?"

The little girl shook her head. Her big brown eyes studied him. He saw the question in their depths. She wanted to know if he knew any songs. How did she suck on her thumb with a glove on it? "Doesn't that glove taste funny?" he asked.

Again, she shook her head.

Jake pretended to put his thumb in his mouth. He jerked it back. "Yuck! That tastes nasty!"

Both Molly and Leah laughed. Molly pulled her thumb out of her mouth and looked at it. Leah laughed again, bringing a smile to his face.

"Enough talk about nasty-tasting thumbs," he said. "I don't know any songs but I had an uncle once who made up a poem about fishing. Want to hear it?"

Both of them nodded.

Jake cleared his throat, raised his head and began to recite. "Fishy, fishy, in the sea, won't you come out and be a friend to me? I'll put you on my little hook. Then for supper you will cook." He smiled, revealing all his teeth.

Molly clapped her hands.

Leah looked at him with a comical expression to say the least.

Jake took a bow. "Thank you. If I ever take you hunting, I'll recite the one about the little deer."

"Oh, no, you don't. I think that one might be a little much for her." Leah laughed. "Not to mention me."

Over the next three hours, Leah caught six fish. Jake grinned as he tossed his third fish of the day into the bucket that had held his ice auger. The auger lay on the surface of the frozen river. He was glad that he hadn't had to use it the way it was intended. It took a lot of hard work to get a hole dug.

"Do you think nine fish are enough to feed everyone?" Leah asked. Her gaze moved to the edge of the river where Molly played.

Cold shivered down his spine. "Well, when we add

them to what the other guys caught, I think we'll have a nice fish fry."

Leah grinned. "Do you know who came fishing earlier?"

"Uh-huh. Ike and Cole were out here shortly after breakfast. I believe they took six back to Agnes." He began to gather their supplies. He all but clapped his hands. "We'll be having fish for dinner tonight."

Leah pulled her line from the water and then handed him the fishing pole. "This has been fun." She picked up the ice auger and, once he'd secured the fishing lines, took the two poles from him.

Her blue eyes sparkled up at him. Rosy cheeks spoke of just how cold it was. "I agree. We'll have to do it again."

Her voice turned soft. "I'd like that."

Jake grinned. "You know what is more fun?" he asked, picking up the bait and fish buckets.

"What?"

"Ice skating."

Leah looked about the frozen lake and all the holes that dotted its surface. "I don't think it would be safe to skate out here."

Jake laughed. "No, it wouldn't, but we could skate farther down."

Her gaze moved down the river. "Oh, I suppose we could."

"We could rope off a big section and make sure that Molly doesn't go past the ropes." Jake spoke his thoughts aloud. "It would be fun. We could build a small fire, make hot chocolate and maybe even cook something over the flames."

Horror filled her face.

"What's wrong?" Jake spun around looking for the danger that had placed such fear in her pretty features.

"I have trouble cooking on a real stove. I can't imagine cooking over an open fire."

Jake shook his head. "Woman, you scared years off my life," he jokingly accused, relieved there was no real danger present. "Besides, women cook over fire pits every day."

"I'm sorry, but this woman doesn't," she shot back.

Molly ran toward them. She looked into the fish bucket and clapped her hands.

He handed the little girl the bait bucket to carry. Then he casually wrapped an arm around Leah's shoulders. "I'll make you a deal. When we cook over open flames, I'll do the cooking."

An impish grin split her full lips. "Promise?"

Now what was she up to? Had he just tapped into her teasing nature? He'd play along. "Promise."

"Thank you, Jake." Pure mirth seeped through the words.

Jake pretended to growl and then asked, "What are you up to?"

Molly and Leah shared grins. The little girl covered her mouth and her eyes danced with laughter. Whatever Leah was up to, Molly understood it.

"Oh, nothing, really." Leah's mouth spread into a full-fledged smile. Her even white teeth shone. It was the first time he'd seen her this playful, and she seemed to be genuinely happy.

He dropped his arm from her shoulder and draped it around her waist, then set the fish pail down. Before she could protest, Jake pulled her against his side and proceeded to tickle her with his free hand.

Leah's laughter filled the air. "Stop! Stop!" But he paid no attention.

He inhaled her sweet fragrance.

"What is so funny?" he asked, tickling her more.

Molly jumped around them, flapping her arms. The little girl reminded him of a chicken with its head cut off. It amazed him that she didn't verbally join in the fun.

He stopped tickling Leah for a moment. "If you don't tell me quick what you are up to, I'm going to tickle you some more," he threatened her.

"All right, all right!" she squealed.

Reluctantly he released her. He missed the warmth against his side immediately. Her hair now hung around her shoulders in disarray, and her blue eyes danced with happiness. He merely stared, tongue-tied. Leah Hollister was the most beautiful woman he'd ever seen. But Jake had learned from Molly's mother that beauty didn't make the woman special or trustworthy. Fear of his heart being broken forced him to look past her outer beauty.

Leah tried to put on a serious face but her lips continued to twitch as she said, "Did you forget our house has a fireplace in it?"

He felt as if his mind was mottled. "So?"

"It's an open flame." Leah giggled.

Molly clapped her hands in joy.

Although his thoughts had just been somber, Jake couldn't help but feel the laughter boom within his chest and from his gaping mouth. She'd tricked him. Or had he volunteered? Yes, he'd said it. She'd just weaseled a promise out of him; a promise that he would do all the cooking over an open flame. What she didn't know is that it was a promise he'd freely give again.

They almost felt like a family as they made their way back to the station. Right here, right now, Jake knew he was happier than he'd been in a long time, and that both scared and pleased him. This kind of happiness could only lead to heartbreak. *His* heartbreak.

It was a little after lunch the next day when Jake rode into Julesburg. The village was named after Jules Beni, the hard-drinking, French-Canadian fur trapper who had established it in 1859 as a trading post.

Jake frowned as he observed the group of rugged shacks interspersed with saloons. During his short months away from the town, it had grown even more dangerous. Men of all types stood on the walkways watching him enter.

He recognized Theodore Rand, one of the pony express riders, and tipped his hat in the young man's direction. Theodore was a good man, but Jake had no desire to stay in this den of thieves any longer than he had to.

In front of the trading post that also served as the home station, Jake got off his horse and tied it to the hitching rail. He made his way inside.

Jim Moore, another express rider, motioned to him once he was inside. Jim sat at a small table off to the right. Jim was big for a pony express rider, at five feet, ten inches tall and weighing about one hundred and sixty pounds. Jake noted that Jim's back was to the wall, not the door. Men learned fast in Julesburg not to sit with their back to the entrance. It wasn't safe.

The two men studied each other. They'd developed a friendship when Jake lived at the home station. Jake knew Jim to be honest and trustworthy.

"What brings you to our little station?" Jim asked, indicating that Jake take a seat to his left where he would also be facing the door.

Jake noticed he and Jim were the only two in the trading post portion of the building. He eased into the chair. "You aren't going to believe this, but I'm looking for a preacher."

The sound of Jim's chair legs hitting the floor echoed through the quiet room. "Why? You havin' a funeral out at the Frontzs' place?"

The thought of getting married would seem like sudden death to some of the men of this rugged town. "Nope. More like a wedding."

Jim eased his chair back once more. "Who's the lucky gal?"

"Her name is Leah Hollister."

The express rider placed a piece of straw between his teeth. "And the gent?"

Jake cleared his throat before answering. "Me."

The straw moved from one side of Jim's mouth to the other. "You?"

"Yep. I find myself in need of a wife and she needs a husband. Made sense to get married and solve both our problems."

Jim laughed. "You don't see getting married as putting yourself in a world of different problems?" He swished the straw to the other side of his jaw.

Jake grinned. "I'll let you know."

"When's the big day?" Jim asked, setting his chair down once more.

"Leah wants a Christmas wedding, so sometime around Christmas." Jake looked about the trading post. It resembled the general store in South Platte but held different things, such as Indian rugs and pottery.

Jim stood and walked to the coffeepot. "Want a cup?" He held up a chipped mug that he'd pulled from a shelf over his head.

"Love some." Jake stood also and stretched. With no one else around he felt free to browse the store. "Where's Beni?" he asked, picking up a pair of boots and looking at the size. Too small. He replaced them.

Jim poured the thick brew. "Went over to the livery, said he'd be back in a bit. You know how that goes. He could be gone for the rest of the day. Things have been slow with the storms coming through. Now that they've slacked off some, I'm thinking business will pick up soon. Beni must think so, too, since he's been off at the livery a lot lately."

A sparkle caught Jake's attention by the counter. He walked to the glass case and looked inside. "I'm surprised Beni has a fancy case like this and that it hasn't been smashed up yet."

Jim laughed. "Yeah, his wife brought it in filled with those pretty trinkets. Don't expect it will last long. See something you like?" He came over and handed Jake the coffee.

A flower pin with clear stones sparkled up at him. Leah had once mentioned flowers. Maybe she'd like something like that for Christmas. "Is the case locked?"

"Sure is."

"How much do you think ole Beni will want for that flower pin?"

Jim slapped him on the back. "More than it's worth, I'm sure."

Jake nodded. His gaze landed on a woman's ready-made coat hanging against the wall. He walked over and pulled it off its hanger. The fabric was a soft blue. Would Leah like it? It looked as if it would fit her. A price tag hung from the sleeve. He whistled low. Instead of putting the coat back, he handed it to Jim.

"Can I buy this now?" he asked.

"Sure can. I'll make sure Beni gets his money," Jim said, holding out his hand.

Jake laughed. He knew his friend would give the money to Beni. Even if Jim had second thoughts about giving it to him, Beni would get it, one way or another. Fishing in his pocket, Jake pulled out some money and handed the price of the coat to his friend.

He nodded. "I need to be getting back. Could I ask a couple of favors from you?"

Weariness entered Jim's reply. "Depends on what they are."

"Nothing too hard." Jake looked at the cash still in his hand. "Would you find out from Beni what he wants for that pin?" He handed some money to Jim. "If it's more than that, pay the difference and I'll pay you back."

"All right." Jim stuffed the money into his front pocket. "What's the second request?" He leaned against the counter.

Jake grinned. "If that preacher or another preacher happens to come this way, would you send him to South Platte? The sooner the better."

Jim's stance relaxed. "That's it?"

Living in Julesburg wasn't easy. Men stole from

and killed each other on a regular basis. Jake hated that his friend felt the need to keep his guard up, even around old pals. He slapped Jim on the shoulder. "That's it."

Jim walked with him to the door. "I heard that the preacher might be coming back this way. I'll be sure and send him to South Platte for you, but are you sure you're ready to settle down?" he asked.

Jake nodded. The question echoed in his mind as he rode back to South Platte. Was he really ready to get married, settle down and have a family? Did he have a choice? With the care of Molly came great responsibility. Leah's pretty blue eyes came to mind. Jake reminded himself that he wasn't going to fall in love, not with Leah, not with anyone. Once more he mentally built an invisible wall around his heart to keep it from being broken.

Chapter Nine

A week later, Leah leaned forward and listened as Will began to tell them about his latest ride.

"I really thought I was a goner this time." He inched even closer to the edge of the soft cushions on the settee.

His eyes danced with excitement and the joy of having a good story to tell. Like all good storytellers, he let his statement hang in the air.

Unable to wait any longer, Leah asked, "What happened?" She felt like a little girl again, listening to stories of adventure. Leah was aware that everyone in the room wanted to know the answer to her question as much as she did.

"It was dusk, and I was going through one of the more dangerous areas. Usually I'm alert because of the Indians, outlaws and black bears that frequent around there. Anyway, I looked back over my shoulder," he said, "and saw them coming…as hard as they could ride after me, yellin' and shootin'."

Leah held her breath as she waited to hear more.

"Who were you running from this time, Indians or outlaws?" Ike asked in his soft tone.

"Bandits. I pushed Wild Boy as fast as his legs would go. We managed to stay out in front of them but their bullets whizzed about my head like angry mosquitos. It felt as if they would follow me all the way here, but after a few miles their horses must have tired because they fell back." Will took a deep breath.

"Why would bandits be chasing you, Will?" Leah asked when it became clear he had no more to add to his story.

He grunted as he sat back. "I suppose they thought I was carrying cash in the mailbags."

"Could be they just wanted his horse, too," Ike added.

Everyone in the room nodded their agreement. Agnes sat in one of the big chairs mending a shirt for her husband. Ike stood by the fireplace staring into the flames. Leah imagined he was reliving one of his own wild rides. Mr. Frontz held a book with a ragged cover in his hands.

The front door opened and Jake entered the house. "Evening, everyone."

Leah grinned. She'd been worried about him when he hadn't shown up for dinner.

"I saved a plate for you in the kitchen." Agnes put her sewing to the side and prepared to stand up.

Leah stopped her. "I'll get it for him. You rest." She hurried toward the kitchen, aware that her heart beat overtime.

The sound of a cowbell drifted down from the second floor. Leah glanced up the stairs. She wanted to ignore the sound, knowing it was Mr. Dalton summoning someone.

Agnes had given him the bell earlier, since they were both too busy to stay at his side all day. Leah had managed to stay away from the offensive man but poor Agnes had traveled the stairs many times. Leah sighed, knowing it was her turn to go up.

She heard Jake say, "Stay put, Agnes. I'll see what he needs." There was gruffness to his voice that she hadn't heard before. His boots pounded up the stairs.

Thankful she didn't have to attend to the man, Leah entered the kitchen. The rich smell of fresh bread greeted her. She and Agnes had baked all day. Leah enjoyed baking; something about kneading and working with dough gave her a sense of accomplishment.

Taking Jake's dinner from the warm oven, Leah wondered what Mr. Dalton wanted now. She felt he was well enough to be on his way, but Agnes had insisted he stay upstairs one more day. She'd heard him the night before moving about upstairs. Leah had locked her room, something she'd never felt compelled to do before.

Jake pushed through the kitchen door. "It smells wonderful in here." He walked to the table and sat down on one of the stools.

Leah carried his plate to him. She placed it on the table and asked, "What did Mr. Dalton want?"

"A drink of water."

She frowned. He could have gotten the water on his own. So why ask Jake for water?

Jake pulled the plate to him and picked up a slice of fresh bread. Just before taking a bite from it, he said,

"I think he was disappointed it was me that came at his summons."

"Oh?" Leah poured him a glass of apple cider.

He chewed and swallowed. "I think he's taken a shine to you."

She said the first thing that popped into her mind. "He's vile."

Jake nodded. "I agree."

He picked up his fork and dug into the roast beef and potatoes. "After tonight, he'll be gone."

Relief washed over her like water off a duck's back. "He's leaving, then?"

"Yep. I spoke with Mr. Frontz this morning and we've agreed that he'll be leaving in the morning." Jake drank deeply from the cider.

Leah sat down on Molly's stool. "I know it's unkind of me to say, but I'm glad he's leaving." She met Jake's gaze. Intense brown eyes looked back at her.

Jake sat his spoon down and leaned forward. "Leah, if any man ever treats you like he did yesterday morning, tell me."

So he did know. She'd felt certain he saw the way Mr. Dalton had grabbed her and pulled her toward him. Now she knew for sure that he had. Leah dropped her gaze and nodded her head, even though she doubted she'd bring up such a personal matter with him.

He grunted. "If you are to be my wife, you have to trust me to take care of you. I can't do that if I don't know what is going on. I want to hear you promise you'll tell me."

Leah sighed. He was right. Married couples

shouldn't keep secrets. She raised her head and met his gaze once more. "I promise."

A smile parted his lips. "Good. Now, would you like to know what I found out in Julesburg today?" He picked up his fork and turned to the roast beef.

What was it with men and their love of leaving a woman hanging with their words? He'd promised to check into finding another preacher to perform their wedding. Had he found one? She saw his lips twitch and realized he was deliberately not telling her. Leah gave in and asked, "What did you find out in Julesburg?"

Jake pushed his plate back and grinned. "Well, a preacher came through not too long ago. My friend said he thought the minister might be coming through again and has promised to send him our way, if he comes."

At first Leah was excited but then she realized he said "if." "What if he doesn't come back through?"

"Then we'll have to wait for Preacher John to come back." As soon as the words exited his lips, Jake knew he'd said the wrong thing. She caught her bottom lip between her teeth and looked away.

He admired her for trying to put up a brave front. "Yes, a spring wedding would be nice, too."

Why was Leah so set on a Christmas wedding? He picked up his dishes and took them to the wash bucket. Before turning around to face her, Jake finished off the glass of cider. "Well, don't give up hope. I'm trusting a preacher will show up before then."

Leah offered him a wobbly smile. "Me, too." She washed his plate and silverware, and rinsed them.

Jake picked up the dish towel and dried. "Tomorrow night I'd like to take some time and read to Molly from the Bible before she goes to bed. Pa read to us every evening before we retired and I thought I'd pick up where he left off." He put his plate and cup away. Jake was glad Leah didn't object. He hoped by reading to his niece they would grow closer.

He and Leah hadn't talked about where she was in her relationship with the Lord and he wasn't sure how to ask. Jake knew they shouldn't marry if she wasn't a believer.

"That's a good idea, Jake." Leah handed him the silverware. "I read every evening but hadn't thought to read the Bible to her. I should have."

If she read from the Bible, surely Leah was a believer. Jake worked up the courage and asked, "So, you are a believer?"

Leah nodded. "Oh, yes. I've been a Christian since I was eight years old." Her pride in her faith spoke volumes.

"I'm glad. Where do you think would be a good place to start reading to her from? She's only four, and I want her to understand what I'm reading." He dried the fork and knife, taking more time than was actually needed.

She tossed the dishwater out the back door. "I'd start in Genesis. Molly won't understand most of it but you will be giving her a foundation, and if you continue with the readings, she'll learn."

Jake hung the dish towel up and turned to face her. "We'd better get back in there before they come looking for us." He opened the door to let her pass before him. He inhaled her clean scent as she walked past. Had she always smelled so fresh and wholesome? He pushed the thought aside. It wouldn't do to allow any type of feelings to grow for Leah.

Saturday morning dawned bright and sunshiny. Leah awoke to Molly jumping on the bed beside her. "I'm up, you little monkey."

Molly ran to the closet. She climbed onto the box that she used to get her dresses down.

Leah knew the child was excited because Jake had promised to take her ice skating. According to him it was going to be an afternoon of fun. Leah had her doubts, since she didn't know how to skate. "Molly, we're not going to the river until after lunch."

Molly ignored her and pulled down her favorite blue dress.

"If you wear that one, you might tear it. Why don't you wear the brown one?"

The little girl shook her head. Over the past few days, Molly had become more stubborn and forceful in what she wanted to do.

Leah tossed the covers off and immediately felt the coolness of the room. "Let me rephrase that. Molly—" she allowed a sternness to enter her voice "—wear the brown one."

Again the four-year-old shook her head.

"All right, then, I guess you can stay with Agnes while we go skating." Leah walked around the child and pulled down her own brown dress. It had seen a lot of wear and if she happened to rip the hem, it could be easily repaired.

Molly stomped her foot and held up the blue dress.

"You can wear the blue, if you want to. But you will not be going skating in it. Either put on the brown dress or stay home." Leah turned her back on the little girl and pulled on her own clothes. She refused to argue with Molly.

She heard Molly return to the closet. Fighting the urge to look, Leah sat down at the dressing table and began to put her hair up. Since she was wearing her brown dress, Leah chose a blue ribbon to weave into her hair. Brown wasn't her favorite color, either, but it was sensible to wear on an outing that could result in damage.

Molly came to stand beside her.

Leah turned to her and saw that the little girl had put on the brown dress. Her bottom lip stuck out in a pout. "Since you are being a good girl and doing as I asked, I'll let you wear the pink ribbon today."

Molly nodded, but her expressive brown eyes spoke volumes regarding her unhappiness. She cradled her doll in her arms as Leah pulled her hair up in a ponytail.

They finished dressing and went downstairs. The doll's head bumped on each step. Molly seemed to have forgotten her misery over the dress and skipped to the kitchen.

Leah heard Agnes say, "Don't you look pretty this morning."

She pushed the kitchen door open and inhaled the sweet scent of baking ham. Her gaze moved to Agnes, who held Molly in her arms.

"I'm sorry we're running so late this morning," Leah apologized.

Agnes smiled. "You aren't late. Today is Saturday. We agreed that you get to sleep in today and I get to sleep in tomorrow."

"Yes, but I meant to come down sooner."

The older woman sat Molly down and waved her comment away. "I saved you both a plate of eggs and bacon. Go ahead and sit down while I get them for you."

Molly scrambled up on her stool. She smiled broadly as Agnes set the plate down in front of her.

"I declare, I think small fry is growing," she announced as soon as Leah had finished saying grace.

Molly tucked into her breakfast as if she hadn't eaten in weeks. She took a moment to grin up at Agnes.

Leah nodded. "I'm afraid so. I'm going to have to make her some new dresses at the rate she's shooting up." She wondered if she should mention to Jake that Molly needed two new dresses.

Agnes pulled a chair up and sat down, too. She cupped a mug of coffee between her palms. "What time are you heading out to the river?"

"Shortly after lunch. Why? Do you need me to do something for you?" Leah buttered a slice of bread and handed it to Molly.

"No. I was just thinking that if you and Jake don't mind, perhaps Charlie and I could join you. It's been ages since I've been ice skating." Agnes rolled the mug in her hands. Her gaze locked on the liquid within.

Leah reached across and laid her hand on Agnes's arm. "I think that's a great idea. The more the merrier."

Happiness filled the older woman's eyes. "I'm glad you feel that way. I thought maybe we could slice up this ham, some bread and maybe cheese and take that with us."

Molly clapped her hands and reached for another slice of bread. She held it up for Leah to butter.

"If you keep eating like this, I might have to get you bigger shoes, too. You are going to fill your little ones up with bread and butter," Leah teased her, handing back the bread. She returned her attention to Agnes. "I wish there was a place to sit out there. It's going to be cold on that ice, and I'll be honest, I'd rather watch than skate."

Agnes tapped her fingers against the cup. "I'll see what I can get the boys to come up with." She raised her gaze to look at Leah. A teasing grin touched her lips. "I'll dig out my skates and we can share them, I believe our feet are about the same size and then you can at least try it."

Leah laughed. "We'll see." She took a bite of bacon and eggs, then sighed. Agnes's meals always tasted better than her own.

Molly slipped off the stool, taking her doll with her. She went to a low cupboard and pulled out a pretty white tea set with pink flowers on it.

"Are you supposed to be playing with that?" Leah asked, worried the child would break it.

"I gave it to her yesterday to play with," Agnes answered as Molly nodded.

"What if she breaks it?" Leah asked, still concerned.

Agnes smiled at Molly. "She'll be careful."

Leah buttered a piece of bread. She felt uncomfortable letting Molly play with the tea set but didn't want to upset Agnes.

"The stage will be arriving a little before lunch. I thought I'd add some of that ham to the beans," Agnes mused as she nursed her coffee.

"Do you think we'll have any guests?" Leah dreaded having boarders. It had been a couple of days since Mr. Dalton had left. If he was any indication of how stage passengers behaved, she'd really rather not see anyone stay.

Agnes stood. "I'm not sure. We'll need to clean the rooms and put fresh sheets on the beds."

"I'll take care of that," Leah volunteered. She gathered up their dirty plates and carried them to the wash bucket.

"Good. That will give me a chance to mop the floors down here and dust." Agnes grabbed the dish towel and began drying the dishes that Leah washed.

Leah hated to think of Agnes pushing a heavy mop about the floor. Lately she'd noticed that the older woman stood with her hand on her back more times than not. "If you'll dust and sweep, I'll be happy to mop once I get things taken care of upstairs," she offered.

"Now see here, Leah Hollister. I'm not so old that I can't do my share of the work around here. I appreciate all that you've done, but if you keep doing all the hard work I'm going to get fat and sassy."

Molly looked up at Agnes's sharp tone.

"I'm sorry. I didn't mean to imply you were," she offered the woman a grin. "If you want to mop, I don't have a problem with that."

Agnes sighed. "I'm sorry, that came out sharper than I intended. You've been a big help to me and I appreciate it."

Leah hugged her. "No harm done. Besides, I wouldn't want you getting fat."

Agnes laughed. "Are you implying I'm sassy?"

"Nope. Not me. I think I'll head upstairs and get those rooms cleaned." Leah released her friend and turned to leave. "Molly, are you coming with me?"

Molly shook her head and pointed to her doll and tea set.

"Leave her. Small fry can help me, if I need help."

Leah nodded and then hurried up the stairs. There was a lot of work to be done and a short time to do it. The stage would be here soon and lunch would need to be ready to put on the table.

As she cleaned, her thoughts went to Jake. What was he doing this morning? She'd missed him at breakfast. Did he think about her as much as she thought about him?

She took a deep breath. Best not to worry about where he was or whether he was thinking about her. Leah didn't want to become dependent on Jake. There was always the possibility that he'd change his mind about marrying her. New thoughts of abandonment tore through her mind. Would he leave her standing in front of the preacher, alone?

Chapter Ten

The stagecoach was late. Jake just hoped that it hadn't run into any trouble. It was bad enough that Mr. Porter had been robbed a couple of weeks ago. With the Indians unhappy because new settlers were taking more and more of their land, and Julesburg attracting outlaws like flies on rotten fruit, traveling in these parts had become a dangerous business. He said a quick prayer for the stagecoach and any passengers it might have on it before tossing a small pair of skates over his shoulder and heading up to the house.

Jake opened the door to find Molly dancing about in her coat, gloves and scarf. Leah sat at the table dressed to match his niece. The only difference was the color of the ribbons in their hair. "Well, aren't you two just the prettiest ladies." Jake picked up Molly and swung her around.

"Thank you," Leah answered for both of them.

His gaze met and held hers. "Ready?"

A look of dread filled Leah's face. "Not really."

Jake asked himself what could possibly be wrong.

She'd seemed pleased at the idea a few days ago. "Have you changed your mind about going?"

"No, but I've never skated before. I'm just nervous about getting on the ice with them on." Leah picked up the blades that Agnes was sharing with her and stood up.

He gave her what he hoped was a reassuring smile. "If we get out to the river and you don't want to skate, you don't have to." Jake took the skates from her and placed them over his shoulder. Then he took both her hand and Molly's in his. "I don't want either of my girls to feel like they have to do anything that makes them nervous. We can have fun without getting on the ice."

Jake felt self-conscious as he realized he'd just called Leah his girl. That wasn't the way he thought of her at all, he told himself. She wasn't his. They weren't even married yet.

Was he letting her into his heart? Surely not! Caring for Leah too much could land him with a broken heart again. No, Leah wasn't his girl and she never would be. Sally had been his girl, or so he'd thought until she'd up and married his brother.

Was it fair to compare Leah to Sally? He mentally argued with himself. Yes, they were both women and women were hazardous to a man's heart.

To take his thoughts off Leah and women in general, Jake turned to Molly. "I found a pair of skates for you at the general store." He dropped Leah's hand and pulled the skates off his shoulder. "Here you go. What do you think of them?"

The little girl turned the skates about as if she were studying them so she could answer him. After several long moments, Molly gave him a big smile and hugged him about the waist.

He scooped his niece up into his arms and gave her a bear hug. "I'm glad you like them. Now let's go see if you can skate on them."

At her nod, Jake headed toward the river, aware that Leah followed close behind.

Leah sat on one of the many logs that someone had placed in a circle on the riverbank. A campfire blazed in the center. She marveled at how everyone had pulled together and created a fun place. Someone had roped off an area for skating and Jake had told Molly not to pass the ropes.

Jake held Molly's hands and stood behind her as the two of them skated on the frozen water. She'd still not gotten up the nerve to join them. The sound of his laughter and Molly's squeals told her that they were having fun.

She thought about him calling her his girl. Leah told herself it meant nothing; after all, he'd called Molly his girl, too. Still, her heart had done a little flip-flop.

Leah reminded herself that he couldn't really think of her in that manner. And she refused to hold the hope that he could. He needed her to watch Molly, nothing more. Would that be enough to keep him from leaving her? Leah didn't know. Would she ever be able to trust that he wouldn't leave her? What about after Molly was grown? Would Jake leave her then? Again Leah didn't know, it would be foolish on her part to expect anyone to love her forever considering her own parents hadn't loved her enough to keep her with them.

"It looks fun, doesn't it?" Ike asked.

Leah looked about to see that he had sat down on the log beside her. Ike picked up a stick and poked at the fire.

"Yes, but I'm afraid to try it," Leah confessed.

Ike looked up at her and studied her face before he asked, "Why?"

Leah picked up one of the skates and held it up for him to see. "These do not look safe to me."

Ike chuckled. "Good point. I've never been fond of them, either." He placed a few more small twigs on the fire.

She pulled her coat tighter around her. Leah continued to watch Jake and Molly. He spun his niece on the ice as if he'd skated all his life. Who knew? Maybe he had.

"Jake's a good skater. Molly's safe with him," Ike assured her.

Leah nodded. "I know. I've been watching them now for about thirty minutes. You'd think they'd both be tired, but they sure don't look like it."

"Nope, he can skate like that for hours."

She turned on the log to face him. "Jake comes out here and skates a lot?"

Ike nodded. "I think it helps him think." He grinned at her. "My ma was the same way. In the winter, she'd strap on the skates and go to our little pond. Sometimes she'd be gone for hours, but she'd come home refreshed and ready to take on the world." Sadness filled his eyes and he looked away.

Leah guessed Ike to be about sixteen years old. At

the moment, it appeared that sorrow weighed on his shoulders like a hump on an old woman's back. She asked, "What happened to your ma?"

He sighed. "She died when I was sixteen."

Sixteen? Had she died recently, then? Empathy overwhelmed her. She'd lost both her parents before she could even remember them. This young man had just recently lost his. "I'm sorry."

"Thank you, but it wasn't your fault. It was mine."

Shock washed over Leah. What did he mean, his fault? Before she could ask, Ike excused himself and walked away.

Leah turned her attention back to the skaters. Jake, Molly, Cole and Timothy moved along the ice. It looked as if they were gliding instead of skating.

She heard Cole yell, "Hey, Jake, want to race?"

"Now's not a good time," he called back, making a point to look down at Molly.

Timothy taunted him. "Aw, Cole, you know Jake isn't as fast as us, he's afraid he'll lose."

Leah wondered what Jake's response would be. He ignored them and continued to focus on keeping Molly upright.

"That's right. He's too old to keep up with us," Cole added.

It was playful banter and Leah laughed.

"They sure are having fun out there." Agnes joined her with a big basket.

"What's in the basket?" Leah asked.

"Ham, bread, pickles, cheese, dried apples and dried peaches." She set the basket down at her feet and rubbed her gloved hands together. "Did I hear those boys trying to challenge Jake to a race?"

Leah nodded. She returned to watching the skaters. "What did he say?"

"He told them now's not the time. And now he's ignoring them." She smiled as Jake swung Molly on the ice. She could see the little girl's big grin.

"Let me have those skates." Agnes held out her hand for the blades.

Leah watched as Agnes began strapping them on her feet. "You're going to go out there?" she asked in disbelief.

"Yep. I'm going to skate off to the side with Molly and watch that man of yours beat the ice off those boys in a race." Agnes chuckled at her own play on words.

Ike returned with more wood for the fire. "Anything to eat in that basket?" he asked.

"Sandwich makings, dried apples and dried peaches." Agnes set the last strap into place. "Be back shortly."

The way she walked to the edge of the river, it looked as if her ankles might snap. "Be careful," Leah called after her.

Once on the ice, Agnes had no trouble getting to Jake and Molly. She said something to Jake. He smiled and then sped off to join Cole and Timothy. Agnes took Molly's hand and they moved to the sidelines.

Jake and the young riders skated to one end of the marked-off area and looked to Agnes. She raised her hand high and then lowered it swiftly. With Jake in the middle of the other two, they sped off.

Cole was in the lead, then Timothy.

Jake cruised along behind them, looking at ease. He looked to where she sat and waved. Why wasn't he racing? The other two were way ahead and bumping elbows to keep each other from getting ahead.

At the same time, the young riders noticed that Jake wasn't with them. They both slowed and looked behind them.

Jake shot forward and passed them both.

Their mouths dropped open and then their minds clicked as they realized Jake was in the lead. With a flourish of action, the two young men pressed forward but they were too late.

They had agreed that whoever got to the opposite rope border first would win, establishing an imaginary line. Jake beat them to it. He spun on his skates, sending up a spray of ice.

Molly jumped up and down, clapping her hands.

Cole and Timothy groaned and hung their heads.

Leah realized that she had stood up and was squealing with happiness to see him win. He'd outsmarted the younger boys and won.

"I knew he'd win," Ike said around a mouthful of dried peaches.

Leah laughed, relieved that he didn't look as sad as he had earlier. "How did you know?"

He shrugged. "Jake always wins."

Ike began constructing a ham and cheese sandwich.

Leah sat back down. She realized once again that she knew very little about her future husband. One thing she did know was that, since he enjoyed being on the ice so much, he probably would like a break from babysitting Molly. She watched as he and Agnes played with the little girl.

If ice skating was a big part of Jake's life, then

Leah decided she needed to learn how to skate, too. "Ike? Do you have a pair of skates I can borrow?" she asked, still watching Agnes and Jake.

"Sure. I don't use them often but I do have a pair. I'll go get them." He left, munching on his sandwich.

Leah leaned forward and warmed her hands. Her heart began to pound in her chest as she thought about putting on the skates. The blades were so thin she worried she'd fall.

Cole and Timothy had a ball and were hitting it back and forth with sticks. Leah wasn't sure what they were playing, but they seemed to be keeping score as they yelled out points when the ball passed one of them.

"Here you are," Ike said, returning.

Leah took the skates and looked at them. The blades looked sharp and were curled at the toes. She assumed the curled metal would help her stop on the ice. Leather straps hung off to the sides.

"Let's get you closer to the river before you put them on." Ike picked up one of the logs and started forward. "You can sit on the wood while we get the straps on around your boots."

I can do this, Leah silently said to herself as she followed. *There's nothing to it. If Molly can do it, surely I can*. Still, her heart took up a tempo that frightened her even further.

Ike set the log down and motioned for her to sit. Leah did as he asked, breathing hard. He knelt in front of her and waited for Leah to hold up her foot so he could strap on a skate.

She watched as he wrapped the leather around her

boot and secured it. The sound of scraping against ice drew her eyes upward.

Jake stood behind Ike, grinning. "Decided to join us?"

Ike finished fastening the skates and stepped back. He offered her one of his hands. "Here, let me help you stand."

Leah's hand shook as she took his. Her legs felt like jelly as she stood. She knew she was going to fall and gripped Ike's hand tighter.

Jake stepped forward and took her other hand. The two men pulled her to the ice.

Ike handed her other hand to Jake. "She's all yours, old buddy." Laughter filled his words.

Leah began to wobble. She looked down at the skates, praying her skirt didn't fly up when she fell.

Jake ordered in a warm, firm voice, "Look up, Leah."

She did as he said, but looked over his shoulder at the hard ice of the river. Her legs trembled, her breath quickened and her heart threatened to leap from her throat.

"Now, focus on me. Don't take your eyes off my face. Understand?" Jake gently pulled her toward him.

Leah looked into his coffee-colored eyes. She saw assurance and the request to trust him. A blur of fabric spun past them. Leah jerked her head to the side to see who it was. Her legs began to go in two different directions. She gasped.

Jake pulled her against him to keep her from falling. His warm chest and arms supported her flailing body. "Leah."

The huskiness of his voice drew her gaze back

to his. She stood so close she could feel the warmth of his breath on her face. His hands locked securely around her arms and his compelling eyes riveted her to the spot.

His voice softened once more. "You are all right. Just focus and trust me. Let your body movements find the rhythm with mine."

His breath smelled of apple cider, clean and fresh. She allowed her body to relax while he held her upright. Her pulse skittered alarmingly. "See?" His voiced soothed, "You are fine."

Leah forced out the word, "Yes," her voice shakier than she would have liked.

"We can stand just like this until you're ready to move," he offered, easing the pressure from her arms.

Leah missed the warmth his body had radiated. She inhaled a deep breath.

"Bend your knees slightly, Leah, and lean toward me just a bit."

She followed Jake's instructions. Leah wanted to lose herself in his dark brown eyes, but this was no time to stand and stare. Especially when the corners crinkled as he smiled at her.

"That's good." He moved back again, pulling her along with him.

Leah gulped as her feet glided smoothly on the ice.

"Don't panic. I've got you." Jake's fingers slid down her arms to her wrists. "See? This isn't so bad, is it?"

Staring into his eyes wasn't bad at all. Falling on frozen ice, well, that would be very bad. "It's not all good," she answered.

His laughter caused her to smile, too.

Jake switched his grasp to her fingers, slowly linking their hands together. The he slid his hands down to her fingertips.

Leah wondered how he could move so gracefully on the ice. The man was skating backward, and that just seemed unnatural. "How do you do that?"

"Do what?"

"Go backward?"

Jake laughed once more. "I can't explain it but someday, after you've learned to go forward, I'll show you."

Leah noticed that her breathing wasn't as quick as it had been. Her heart wasn't struggling to leave her chest and her legs had firmed up. She grinned.

He continued to stare into her eyes. "Did you see me skating with Molly earlier?"

"Yes."

He rubbed his gloved thumb against hers. "Good." Jake tilted his head to the side. "Now, look over my shoulder and find something to focus on."

"Okay, but why?" Leah did as he said. She saw a tree on the bank and stared at it.

Slowly Jake untangled his fingers from hers. "I'm going to move behind you and skate with you like I did Molly."

Leah held her breath and tried to retain her balance without him helping her. She focused on the tree as he'd instructed. The sound of a loud plop broke her concentration.

A squeal of fright had her jerking her eyes from the tree, turning her head at a fast pace, and just as she realized it was Molly she'd heard, Leah's feet went out from under her and she, too, fell with a loud plop. She turned to check on Molly. If the little girl was hurt, Leah was determined to go to her. Even if it meant crawling on the ice to do so.

Agnes stood beside the little girl, helping her up. Leah sighed with relief. She looked up to find Jake standing beside her. His grin surprised her. He wasn't angry that she'd fallen?

"See? That wasn't so bad." He held out a hand and Leah let him help her up.

She laughed. "No, that wasn't bad at all." She didn't elaborate on the fact that her backside stung a little from the fall.

"Good. Now again. Focus on me."

She allowed him to pull her close, his big arms sliding around her waist as he stared into her eyes. No, this wasn't bad in any way, form or fashion. Uneasiness settled over her. Even without love, Leah felt sure she could gaze into this man's eyes forever. And those kinds of thoughts were dangerous to her heart.

It was late in the afternoon when they tromped back to the home station. Leah felt as if she'd worked all day. Her legs seemed weighted down but her heart seemed to have sprouted wings, giving her a light happiness that she hadn't felt in a long time.

Jake walked beside her with Molly on his shoulders. The little girl would rest well tonight. Her cheek lay on the top of his head and she'd closed her eyes.

The sound of the stagecoach arriving drew her head up. Leah watched as it came to a stop in front of the house. Unable to see if there were passengers aboard, she listened for the sound of extra voices.

They rounded the stagecoach just as a woman in

a new green traveling dress stepped down. Leah admired the way she seemed to glide down the steps, her hand tucked daintily in Mr. Edwards's big hand.

Jake stopped walking.

Leah turned to him and saw that his eyes had grown round and his jaw had dropped. His face paled as if he'd just seen a ghost.

"Nellie?"

A light, tinkling laugh floated to them. "You remembered." The stranger stepped from the stage and waited until they reached her side. Then her arms wrapped around him in a tight hug.

Nellie's blond curls fell over her shoulders as she gazed up at him. Leah couldn't believe how green the woman's eyes were. They looked like emeralds and sparkled with happiness. Who was this woman and what did she want with Jake?

The stagecoach tilted as another person got off. He was a tall man with a top hat and waistcoat. His brown hair and dancing blue gaze landed on Leah.

"Come along inside everyone. There is a hot supper waiting for all of us," Agnes said, stepping around the group.

Leah turned to Jake. "I'll take Molly." Her voice sounded tight in her own ears. She raised her arms for the little girl to slip into.

Jake nodded and handed the child over. His eyes never left Nellie's face. "What are you doing in Colorado?" he asked.

She'd never heard his voice sound so husky. Leah lowered Molly to the ground. "Come on, sweetie. Let's go help Agnes." Leah pulled the child behind her.

Molly pulled her hand from Leah's. She turned and

stared at Jake and Nellie. Her lower lip trembled and tears filled her eyes. "Mama?"

Only Leah heard the whispered word. Tears began to stream down the little girl's face. Leah tried to pick Molly up but the little girl shoved her away.

Jake's head was lowered and he was listening intently to Nellie. Their voices were low and they seemed unaware of everyone around them.

Distressed by Molly's tears and her refusal to be comforted, Leah called out, "Jake."

It might have been the urgency in Leah's tone, or maybe he'd been aware of her the whole time, but for whichever reason, Jake looked up. His eyes connected with hers and he tilted his head sideways as if to silently ask, what?

She motioned toward Molly.

His long legs had him standing before them in an instant. He knelt down in front of his niece. "Molly, what's wrong?"

Her little hand shook as she pointed at Nellie and whispered once more, "Mama?"

She'd spoken! Her gaze moved to Jake. Jake knelt and stared at the child, the expression on his face revealed her own surprise and wonder.

Molly had finally spoken.

Get 2 Books FREE!

Harlequin Reader Service,
a leading publisher of inspirational romance fiction, presents

Love Inspired HISTORICAL

A series of historical love stories that will lift your spirits and warm your soul!

FREE BOOKS!
Get two free books by acclaimed, inspirational authors!

FREE GIFTS!
Get two exciting surprise gifts absolutely free!

2 FREE BOOKS

▲ To get your 2 free books and 2 free gifts, affix this peel-off sticker to the reply card and mail it today!

Love Inspired HISTORICAL

W

e'd like to send you two free like the one you are enjoying now. Your two free books have a combined price of over $10, but they are yours to keep absolutely FREE! We'll even send you two wonderful surprise gifts. You can't lose!

Each of your **FREE** books is filled with storical periods from biblical times to World War II.

GET 2 FREE BOOKS!

Chapter Eleven

How could he have been so stupid? Why hadn't he realized the impact seeing her mother's twin sister, Nellie, would have on Molly? Seeing her had thrown him for a loop, as well. He'd never even thought about Nellie arriving in Colorado. She looked so much like Sally that at first he'd been fooled, as well. But when she began talking, Jake remembered how different from each other the twin sisters had been.

Feeling like a heel, Jake tried to turn Molly so that she would look at him. She refused. Molly only had eyes for her mother's twin.

"I want my mama!" Molly wailed as she tried to pull away from Jake. Her little arms reached for Nellie.

For a brief moment, Jake saw Nellie's face soften. But as if she realized she was about to give in to caring emotions, Nellie's features hardened and she snapped, "Mama? Hardly." Nellie walked toward them. She flicked her hair back over her shoulder with a manicured hand. Ignoring Molly, she walked on by them. "Did someone say something about eating? I'm starved. Marshall, bring my bags."

Jake's heart went out to Molly. The little girl's face was filled with hurt and confusion. She finally turned her face to him.

"I'm sorry little one. She's not your mama." Jake held her little face in his hands. "Nellie is your mama's sister, like I'm your daddy's brother."

He was startled when she jerked her face from him and rushed into Leah's open arms. Jake heard the sobs tear from her small broken heart. His gaze moved to Leah's.

Leah held fast to the child and patted her back. "It's all right, Molly. You'll be all right, I'm here." Her troubled eyes searched his. "I'd like to take her to our room."

Jake knew she was asking his permission. He nodded, unsure why she felt she needed to ask. "If you need me, call down the stairs. I'll stay inside."

She nodded and carried Molly into the house.

Jake turned to see the man Nellie had referred to as Marshall struggling to carry five large suitcases.

"Women can be a handful sometimes, can't they?" Marshall set the cases down.

Jake didn't comment on Marshall's statement, instead he said, "Here, let me take some of those for you." Jake wondered what Marshall's relationship was with Nellie but didn't ask as he picked up two of the cases. What were they doing here? Jake knew better than to ask. In the mood Nellie was in, he wouldn't get an answer anyway. He'd wait—Nellie would tell him why she was here soon enough.

"Thank you." Marshall grabbed the other two. He

looked over his shoulder. "I'll come back for those, Mr. Edwards. There's no need for you to have to lug them in."

The stagecoach driver answered, "I got them. Let's get inside where it's warm and there's sure to be hot food for our bellies."

Jake led the way to the house. He wanted to know more about this Marshall fellow but now wasn't the time. When he stepped through the door he heard Nellie attempting to give orders to Agnes.

"Shouldn't you have the place settings out already?" Nellie asked. She was sitting in Leah's usual place.

"You're welcome to help, if the way I'm preparing the table isn't up to your standards." There was an edge to Agnes's voice that indicated Nellie had gotten off on the wrong foot with the older woman.

Nellie ignored her. "Jake, come sit by me. I want to hear all about your new life." She patted the chair where she expected him to sit.

"How long are you staying?" he asked, instead of doing as she bid.

Marshall answered, "A couple of days." He looked to Mr. Edwards for confirmation. "That's when the next stage to Denver will be coming through, right?"

Mr. Edwards nodded. "Yep, if she don't run into Indians or some other kind of trouble."

Jake slipped into the chair beside the stage driver. He knew about the earlier attacks but wanted to see what the stagecoach driver might add and asked, "What other kind of trouble?"

Agnes set a bowl of hot rolls on the table and turned to leave again.

The older gentleman grabbed one of the rolls and tore into it with his fingers. "Attacks. Mostly happens at night. Can't tell who the enemies are, so we've gotten to where, if we travel, it's during the day."

Jake thought about that for a moment. He glanced at Nellie, who seemed to be absorbed in looking the place over. "What's the purpose of the attacks?"

"Well, so far we've lost horses, and every so often a passenger will lose money and jewels." Edwards took a big bite of the bread and sighed. "I declare, Mrs. Frontz, you make the best grub on our route."

The older woman set ham and beans out on the table. "Thank you, Mr. Edwards. That's mighty kind of you to say."

Jake noticed she hadn't brought out any plates or bowls. He couldn't help wondering if she intentionally left them till last just to irritate Nellie. As Agnes started back to the kitchen, Jake rose. "I'll help you finish setting the table," he offered, following her into the kitchen.

In a hushed voice, Agnes hissed, "That has to be the rudest woman I've had the displeasure of meeting in quite a while. I hope she's no kin of yours." She handed him a stack of bowls.

"No, but she was my brother's sister-in-law." He gathered up a handful of spoons.

"Oh, I'm sorry. I'll try to abide her." Agnes patted his arm. She scooped up another plate with ham slices on it.

Jake opened the door and allowed her to pass in front of him. His gaze moved up the stairs and he wondered how Leah and Molly were doing. Even before he set the bowls and silver down, he'd made up his mind to go check on them. He walked to the stairs.

"Jake, where are you going?" Nellie pouted from the table. "I was hoping we'd get a chance to catch up."

He turned to face her. "I don't know if you noticed, Nellie, but my niece is pretty upset and my fiancée is trying to comfort her. I'm going to go check on my family." Jake had already had about all he could stand of Nellie, and to think he had two more days of listening to her whine and be rude.

As he climbed the stairs he realized he'd referred to Leah as his fiancée and family. Why had he done so? Was he trying to prove to Nellie that Sally's up and marrying his brother hadn't bothered him as much as she probably thought? Or had he begun to think of Leah as family?

Jake stopped just outside the bedroom door. He heard voices from inside and it suddenly dawned on him that Molly was speaking.

"Leah, are you going to be my new mommy?"

He leaned forward and listened for Leah's response.

"Molly, I can never take your ma's place but I do want to be like a mother to you."

"Why?"

"Because I love you as if you were my daughter."

"Why?"

"Well, I never had a mother, and when I met you you'd just lost yours. I guess I felt a kinship with you. We seemed to belong together, and over the past few months I believe we've started to love each other, too."

"I love you, Leah. But I don't think I will love my aunt."

Silence filled the space. Jake chanced glancing into the room. Leah had her back to him and was facing the window. He could see that she held Molly in her arms.

Leah spoke again. "Don't you remember your aunt Nellie?"

"No, Ma didn't like her. It was a long time ago but I 'member Ma told her never to come back to the farm." The top of Molly's head rubbed against Leah's shoulder.

"I'm sorry to hear that." Leah rested her head against Molly's. "But you know what?"

"What?"

A smile filled Leah's voice. "I'm glad your aunt came today."

"Why?"

"Because she reminded you how to talk." Leah hugged the little girl close.

Molly looked over Leah's shoulder. "Hi, Uncle Jake."

Leah turned to face him. "I didn't hear you come in." Her voice was soft and she radiated love and warmth.

Jake felt sure the emotions were for Molly and not him, but they still left Leah with a soft glow about her face. He couldn't help comparing her to Nellie. Where his brother's sister-in-law was rude, Leah was kind. Nellie had a striking beauty that soon turned cold; Leah had an inner beauty that sent off warmth and love to those around her. Of the two, he'd choose Leah's beauty over Nellie's any day.

He knelt down and held his arms out to Molly.

She climbed out of Leah's lap and hurried to him. "Leah's going to be my new ma," Molly announced as she hugged him around the neck.

Leah stood facing them. Jake held Molly close and mouthed, "Thank you" to Leah.

She offered a sweet, sad smile.

Without thinking, Jake stood, picking up Molly, and then he held his arm out to Leah. He watched as she slowly walked toward him. When she stepped into his embrace, Jake knew this truly was his family.

He still didn't trust it would last, but for now he was content. Jake inhaled Leah's sweet fragrance. He refused to fall in love with her. Jake reminded himself that his heart couldn't stand another breaking, but he would always cherish this moment.

Leah dreaded the moment when Jake would quit reading for the night and they'd all be spending another evening in Nellie's company. Her husband, Marshall, was a kind man who followed Nellie around like a dog on a leash. It really was sad watching the way she ordered him around.

Jake sat with Molly on his lap. He finished reading about Noah and the flood. The little girl had listened quietly. At times her eyes had grown big but she'd held her questions until he finished and shut the Bible.

Molly laid her hand on his cheek and asked, "How did that Noah man get them animals to go on the big boat?"

Jake grinned at her. "Noah had lots of help from God."

"Oh, so God made them go on?"

He nodded. "Yep." Jake grinned, knowing another question would soon pop out of his niece's mouth. She'd been asking questions or talking non-stop since the moment she'd started talking.

Her little face twisted as another question worked its way through her mind. "How come the bigger animals didn't eat the littler ones?" she finally asked as she patted the stubble on his cheek.

"Well, I believe God shut their mouths and wouldn't let them," Jake answered. He looked about the room at everyone. Each person nodded their agreement except Nellie.

Agnes darned a pair of socks; Ike worked on a length of rope. Leah wasn't sure what Ike was doing, or was going to do with the rope, but his fingers worked the threads. Mr. Frontz sat with a catalog of some sort in his hands. Leah didn't think he was really reading it but was listening to the soft conversations going on around them.

"That book isn't real. You know that, right?" Nellie asked as she pulled at the lace on her dress.

Jake shook his head. "I believe the Bible is real, Nellie." There was a warning tone in his voice that she simply ignored.

"Oh, really? Well, I have the same questions that Molly does. How can it be real? I mean, you expect us to believe that every animal came by twos." She laughed bitterly.

For the first time, Leah looked beyond the hateful words, the cruel looks and the mean-spirited actions of the young woman. She saw Nellie now as a scared, confused woman. "What makes you think it isn't real?" Leah asked in a soft tone.

"How can it be? The stories are just that, stories. There is no God." Nellie stood up and walked to the fireplace.

Its crackles and pops were the only sound in the room for several moments.

Jake's jaw worked. The pony express riders looked uneasily at one another.

Mr. Frontz yawned. "I believe we will be retiring now." He stood, took Agnes's hand and they left the room.

"'Night," the three riders said in unison as they each picked up their belongings and headed for the front door.

Leah watched them leave. She saw the anger in Jake's gaze as he stared at Nellie. The young woman seemed unaware of his emotions.

"Perhaps we should retire, too." Marshall stood and held his hand out to Nellie.

Nellie continued to stare into the flames. "You go on, I'll be up later."

He dropped his head, and like an obedient servant, Marshall followed the Frontzs up the stairs.

"Jake? Would you tuck Molly in for me tonight?" Leah turned to face him. She wanted to talk to Nellie alone.

Molly laid her head down on Jake's shoulder. Her thumb had worked its way into her mouth.

His gaze searched hers, then he nodded.

"Thank you." Leah waited until they were up the stairs. She heard the bedroom doors shut behind Marshall and then Jake and Molly.

Leah moved to sit on the chair by the fireplace.

From this vantage point she could see Nellie's face. "Why do you think there is no God?" she asked.

A tear slid down Nellie's face. "How can there be?" Misery filled her voice.

"What do you mean?" Leah wanted to understand. She felt she needed to understand the emotions that Nellie was going through.

"If there was a God, He would have spared my sister and her husband. I begged Him not to take them. But what happened? Sally died first." She slapped her hand against her leg. "I bet you didn't know that twins can sense things about each other, did you?"

Leah shook her head.

"I knew the moment my sister became ill. I begged God not to take her like He had our parents. I asked Him to let me arrive in time to help her." A sob caught in her throat. "But did He?" She slapped her leg again. "No, and do you know why?" Nellie didn't give Leah a chance to answer. "I do. It's because He doesn't exist."

"You don't believe that, Nellie. You are angry and hurting."

Nellie spun to face Leah. Anger radiated from her very being. "How can you know what I believe or don't believe?"

"You prayed. Nonbelievers don't pray to a God they don't believe in," Leah answered in a quiet voice.

"No, I quit believing the day Sally died." Nellie allowed the tears to fall down her chin. A sob caught in her throat, and she turned back to the fireplace. "After our parents died, Sally asked me to take Molly in should something happen to her and John." Silence hung between them.

Leah wanted to allow Nellie the opportunity to let her past hurts work their way out of the grieving woman. She remembered being told once that it was best to listen when someone hurting is talking because it could help them heal.

Nellie sighed heavily and turned back to face Leah. "That's why I'm here. I am going to take Molly away from Jake. I'm going to remove all this foolishness of a God who cares for her from her memories. She's still young and can be taught differently."

The mother bear arose in Leah. She stood to her full height and said, "I know you are hurting, Nellie and I can respect that, but rest assured, Molly is not going with you."

Nellie laughed. "Oh, and are you going to stop me? You have no legal claim to that little girl up there. I do. You're not even related, I am." She pushed past Leah and walked to the foot of the stairs.

Leah said a silent prayer for help. She couldn't, wouldn't let Nellie have Molly. "Nellie, I'm going to prove that there is a God."

She turned at the foot of the stairs, and a wobbly simper twitched at Nellie's lips. "Really? How?"

Leah knew she couldn't do anything but she had a God who could. "I'm going to pray and ask God to keep you from taking that child from her uncle. I'm also going to ask Him to help you find your way back to the God who loves you."

Nellie shook her head. "Pray all you want, Leah. We'll see if there is a God who loves you enough to answer your prayers. Don't be surprised when I ride out of here tomorrow with Molly by my side."

* * *

Jake walked down the stairs slowly. He stopped right behind Nellie. Keeping his voice much calmer than he felt, Jake said, "You aren't taking Molly anywhere, Nellie."

She spun around looking wild-eyed. "How dare you sneak up on me!"

When had Nellie become such a dramatic personality? He remembered her being sweet and quiet, like Sally. "I walked down the stairs, Nellie. That's hardly sneaking up on you. Now, what makes you think I'll let you take Molly away?"

Steely green eyes glared up at him. "You don't have a choice. My sister asked me to take care of Molly and I intend to do just that. I'd thought about letting you and Leah keep her, but after tonight, listening to all this talk about God and reading the Bible, well, she's better off living with me and knowing the truth. There is no God." It sounded as if she were trying to convince herself more than him.

"Aunt Nellie?"

Jake turned to find Molly standing at the top of the stairs. Her hair was down and the light from the bedroom shone behind her, giving the little girl an angelic appearance.

"God is real." Molly held on to the railing as she walked down the stairs.

Nellie's voice softened as she watched Molly's descent. "Honey, you are mistaken."

"No, I'm not. The night Mama died. I prayed and talked to God. I know Mommy is in heaven. She's waiting for us all to get there." Molly took Nellie's hand in hers. "I feel her in here." She pressed Nellie's hand against her heart.

Tears rolled down Nellie's face. She hugged Molly to her and wept.

Marshall came down the stairs, brushed past Jake and hurried to his wife's side. He gently pulled her into his arms. "Come along, dear."

Nellie released Molly and offered her a gentle smile. "Thank you, Molly. I feel her in here, too." She laid her hand against her own heart, then Nellie allowed her husband to lead her up the stairs.

The next morning, Jake entered the house long before anyone else was usually awake. He'd tossed and turned all night. Nellie could still insist on taking Molly and that worried him. His hand moved to the letter in his shirt pocket. If he had to, Jake would use it to keep the little girl with him. He loved Molly as much as he could love anyone and he wasn't about to let her go.

Nellie and Marshall came out of the kitchen. She wore a deep green robe that picked up the color in her eyes. A gasp tore from her throat when she saw him. "Oh, I wasn't expecting anyone else up this early." Her hand went to her neck.

"Good morning, Nellie, Marshall." He stood staring at her. She looked so much like Sally that for a moment Jake allowed himself just to stare at her.

Marshall carried the coffeepot and two cups in his hands. "I made coffee, if you'd like a cup," he offered.

Jake took a deep breath. "I believe I will. Please, stay down here. I'd like to talk for a few minutes."

When they nodded their acceptance of his invitation, Jake pulled out a chair and sat down.

"Give me just a moment and I'll get another cup." Marshall set the coffeepot and the other two mugs down and then hurried back into the kitchen.

Jake tried to get control of his emotions. The last thing he wanted was bad blood between himself and Nellie. Molly needed her aunt as much as she needed him. Family was important; he just wished he'd realized it sooner and had made peace with his brother and Sally.

Nellie sat down at the end of the table when Marshall returned. Marshall poured her coffee and then gave a cup to Jake.

She cupped the coffee between her palms. "I think I know what you are going to say, Jake, and you are right."

Her words took him by surprise. "What am I right about?" He slipped into the chair beside her.

"Marshall and I have been talking and we believe Molly should stay with you and Leah." Nellie offered a soft smile before taking a sip from her coffee.

Jake wasn't sure what to say. He'd been prepared to fight for the little girl. His gaze moved to Nellie's face. Was it his imagination or had it softened during the night?

"Marshall assures me that I was wrong in so many ways." She shook her head. "And thanks to Molly I feel differently about so many things, but change isn't going to happen overnight. Marshall and I prayed together last night for the first time in a long time." She reached out and took her husband's hand. "But I think I'll need many more prayer sessions to become the woman I want to be. I still don't understand why God would take Sally, but I'm trying."

Jake wasn't sure what to say. He took a sip from his coffee and nodded, understanding Nellie's words. Hadn't he behaved much the same way when he'd first learned of John and Sally's marriage? He'd wanted to blame God but with time realized John and Sally had been the ones to hurt him, not God.

Marshall patted the top of her hand. Nellie looked into her coffee. "I don't know how this man has stood by me over the last year. I've been mean and rude to him so much but he still put up with me."

"What about God? Do you still think He's not real?" Jake had to know. If there was some way he could convince Nellie of the one true God, he wanted to do it.

She smiled. "I always knew He was real. I just didn't want to trust Him anymore. As strange as it sounds, after Sally died, I didn't think He loved me anymore." Her voice caught in her throat.

"That doesn't sound strange at all." Jake set his cup down. "Right after Sally and John married I lost my way for a while, too. I guess it's human nature, but I am so glad God can forgive us and keep on loving us."

She patted his hand. "Yeah, me, too."

He released her hand. "You are always welcome to visit Molly."

"Thank you, Jake."

They talked for a few more minutes and then he finished his coffee and carried the cups and coffeepot back to the kitchen. When he returned to the table, they were gone. He assumed they'd returned to their room.

His thoughts turned to Marshall as he headed out to start his morning chores. Nellie's husband had stuck by her as she worked through the grief. He'd put up with her abusive behavior and still seemed to love her.

Nellie had gone from the bitter woman of yesterday to the sweet woman that he remembered Sally being. Spending time with Nellie reminded him of what he'd lost by trusting Sally. She'd seemed sweet and loving, but at the same time Sally had been in love with his brother. Would he ever be able to take down the wall around his own heart? Leah's faced floated in his mind. As much as he was growing to care for her, Jake still had his doubts.

Chapter Twelve

Two weeks later, Leah grinned at Agnes. "I think it looks very festive around here." She looked at the banister covered with greenery that seemed to flow down the stairs. Decorative Christmas ornaments hung about the room on boughs of green and red garland.

"What are your plans for that?" Agnes pointed to the Christmas wreath they had just finished making.

"Hang it on the kitchen door, of course." Leah glanced up the stairs. "Would you mind listening for Molly while I do it?"

Agnes stood. "Not at all. I think I have some candles we can place in the windows. I'll go look up in the attic." She headed upstairs.

Leah picked up the wreath and headed for the door. She hummed a Christmas carol under her breath. It was hard to believe that the holiday was only a week away. The sun shone and filled the house with light when she opened the door.

Laying the wreath against the wall beside the door, Leah decided to go in search of a hammer and nail.

The sun glinting off the white landscape created

a brightness that was almost blinding. Shielding her eyes against the glare, Leah followed the packed snow path to the barn.

She pulled the door open and slipped inside. The scent of warm hay and horses greeted her. It took Leah's eyes a moment to adjust to the change in lighting.

Jake sat on a barrel just inside the door, applying oil to one of the saddles. When it was clear that Molly wasn't with her, he asked, "Is Molly all right?"

Leah turned to face him. "Molly's fine. She's napping."

He laid the oil rag to the side. "Then what brings you out to the barn?" Jake smiled.

"Agnes and I are decorating for Christmas and I was going to hang a wreath on the kitchen door, only I don't have a nail." She smiled back at him.

Jake walked to a small shelf and dug in a bag. He pulled out a couple of nails, then reached up and took a hammer from one of the many hooks. "These should do it." He walked back and handed them to her.

"Thanks."

"You're going to need a ladder, also." Jake walked to a corner of the barn and returned a few moments later. "Ready?"

"You're going to help me?" Leah asked. He'd spent very little time with her since Nellie had left. She was both happy and nervous.

He held the barn door open. "Yep."

Leah nodded and headed back up the snow-packed path to the house. "I'm not sure we need the step ladder."

"Maybe not, but we'll have it just in case." His

boots crunched along behind her. "How have you been?"

The question took her by surprise. He'd seen her while reading to Molly at night and during meals. "Good."

Jake followed her up the steps and into the house. He set the ladder against the kitchen wall. "Where did you want to put the wreath?" he asked, facing the closed door.

Leah walked up to the door. She held the nails and hammer in her left hand. Using her right hand, she reached up above her head and pointed. She looked over her shoulder at him. "Right about here. What do you think?"

He nodded. "That looks like a good place." Jake moved up behind her. "Keep your hand where you want the nail." He reached down and took the nails and hammer from her other hand.

She could feel the warmth of his chest behind her. Leah faced the door and inhaled. He smelled of hay and warmth. She felt his hand cover hers.

"Okay, you can move now. I think I have it."

Leah moved off to the side. Her heart beat against her chest.

Jake placed the nail against the wood but before hammering it in he asked, "Does this look about right?"

She tried to focus on the job at hand. "It looks about right."

Jake hammered the nail in and picked up the wreath. He slipped it onto the nail. "You were right, we didn't need the ladder." He stepped back to admire his work.

They stood side by side, staring at the wreath. She didn't know what more to say. He'd put up the wreath, nothing more needed to be done.

"I'm sorry I haven't been around to help out with Molly," Jake continued. "Seeing Nellie took me back a few years and I needed to think through some things."

"Want to talk about it?" Leah didn't know why she'd asked him that, but now that the words were out she hoped he would.

He turned to face her. "Did Nellie tell you anything about our past?"

Leah realized that maybe she didn't want to hear this. Nellie hadn't said anything on the subject. Leah knew that Molly was her niece and that Molly's mother had been Nellie's twin sister, but not once had they discussed Jake. Leah shook her head.

Jake took a deep breath. "Then I should tell you. As you already know, Nellie had a twin sister, Sally."

"Yes, she did mention that Molly's mother was her sister," Leah said.

"Did she mention that Sally was engaged to me before she married my brother?" Hurt filled his voice.

"No." Leah didn't say any more. She wanted to give Jake the chance to pour out what he felt he needed to say.

"She and I were to be married. On the morning of our wedding, my brother, John, and Sally got married and then came out to the ranch and told me." He stared deeply into her eyes.

Leah saw the betrayal in his eyes. "Oh, Jake. I am so sorry."

Jake brushed a strand of hair off her forehead. "Thank you, but that was over five years ago."

It was her turn to nod. "True, but I can see that you are still hurting."

He seemed to ignore her last comment. "Seeing Nellie again brought back some old memories. I just needed time to sort through my thoughts."

"And did you?"

Jake looked deeply into her eyes. "Do you remember me telling you that our marriage would be in name only?"

All Leah could do was nod. She'd lost her means of speech as she tried to figure out where he was going with this conversation.

"Well, Sally and John's betrayal is the reason. I haven't worked through the hurt, Leah." He paused. "I'm not sure I ever will."

Leah didn't know how to respond. She'd known he'd never love her and now she knew why. If Sally hadn't broken his heart and his brother hadn't betrayed him, would Jake have taken a chance on loving her?

That cruel voice she'd heard in her head since childhood answered, *No, he wouldn't have*, reminding Leah that her parents had abandoned her. Her parents hadn't loved her enough to keep her. Even if he could have grown to love her, there was always the chance he'd desert her much like her parents had.

Jake saw the hurt drift across Leah's face. He hadn't meant to hurt her, but she needed to know why he couldn't allow his heart to be broken again. "I'm sorry, Leah. If you want to call off the wedding, I understand."

She reached up and touched his face. A wobbly

smile filled her lips. "I still want to marry you, Jake." Her soft fingers warmed his cold cheek. "Since you are being honest with me, let me assure you that I am not looking for love. I simply want to be with Molly and have a place to call home."

He knew there was more to her story. There was an old saying that the eyes were mirrors of the soul. Leah's eyes were filled with hurt. She could no more hide it than he could, apparently. They made quite the pair. Jake allowed her to see his true feelings and knew his eyes reflected his unhappiness and mistrust of love. Why didn't Leah want his love? The question filtered through his mind. Had she been hurt, too? He couldn't stop the word from leaving his lips. "Why?"

Her hand slid from his jaw. "Why, what?"

"Why aren't you looking for love?" he pressed, wanting and dreading to hear her answer.

Leah folded her arms over her chest. "I'm not lovable." She didn't dare tell him that people who loved her in the past had abandoned her for strangers to raise. Who would want to marry someone whose parents hadn't cared enough about her to keep her with them? He'd leave her, too, and Leah didn't think she could take that kind of rejection.

How could she say that? Didn't she realize it wasn't true? Molly loved her. Agnes valued her friendship and even he cared deeply for her.

"What makes you think you are unlovable?" Jake wanted to reach out and touch her as she had him but didn't trust himself not to pull her into his arms and offer her the comfort she deserved.

She opened her mouth to answer but at that moment the sound of the stagecoach rolling up in front of the house stopped her. Leah offered him a sweet smile. "Looks like it's time to get to work. Thank you for helping me with the wreath."

Leah entered the house, leaving Jake on the porch, confused by the emotions washing over him.

Leah walked into the kitchen aware that she'd almost told Jake about her parents leaving her on the porch steps of the orphanage and how she had always been the child who was overlooked when people wanted children. The last thing she needed was his pity. It was a good thing the arrival of the stage had interrupted them.

Agnes turned from the stove. "Heard the coach drive up. How many passengers are there this time?"

Leah sighed. She'd been so rattled by Jake that she hadn't stuck around to count. "I'll be right back." She hurried to look out the front window.

Two men and a woman stepped down from the stage. She recognized Nellie, but Marshall wasn't with the pretty young woman. The men both wore business suits; one of them looked to be clutching a Bible against his chest. Jake walked down the steps to greet them.

She returned to the kitchen and answered Agnes, "Three, two men and Nellie."

Agnes turned with a frown. "Molly's aunt?"

Leah nodded. She crossed to the sideboard and poured hot coffee into four mugs, one for each passenger and the driver. Placing them on a tray, her mind tried to grasp the reason Nellie had returned. The other woman had been gone almost two weeks, why return now? Had she changed her mind about taking Molly from them?

The sound of boots stomping at the front door had Leah hurrying into the main room. Agnes followed, carrying four dessert plates with sliced apple pie on them. They set each member of the stage party a place at the table. The men immediately sat down but Nellie hurried over to them.

She gave them each a hug and then turned to Leah with a big grin. "Guess what I found?" she asked with a twinkle in her eye.

Molly came down the stairs looking sleepy. "What?" she asked, before Leah could get the word out.

Jake followed the men in, carrying a small bag that Leah assumed was Nellie's. "I believe your aunt wanted Leah to ask that." He scooped up his niece with one arm.

Molly giggled.

All eyes turned to Leah. "All right, what?" she asked.

"A preacher."

Leah felt her mouth flop open. A preacher? Her eyes darted to Jake and then the two passengers. "Really?"

The one who held a Bible laid his hand on the book and answered, "Really."

Nellie swept into a chair. "Right before I left, Jake asked me to see if I could find a preacher to marry the two of you. Well, I met Reverend Rice and Mr. Slade yesterday on our way to Denver and I convinced him to come back with me here. Isn't that so, Reverend?"

The preacher swallowed a lump of pie before answering. "Yes, Mrs. Crane can be most persuasive."

Nellie giggled. "Yes, I can."

Jake walked over to Leah. "What do you say? Shall we get married?"

Molly grinned at her and nodded her head. "Yes, let's be a family." She clapped her hands at the idea.

Leah's throat closed up. She'd so wanted a Christmas wedding. One week before Christmas wasn't that far from Christmas Eve, the day she'd always dreamed of getting married, like the couple who'd stopped at the orphanage. Their Christmas Eve wedding had seemed perfect and they'd seemed so happy. She looked about the room. It was decorated for Christmas. Leah nodded.

Agnes laid a hand on Leah's shoulder. "This is kind of sudden, Jake. A girl needs time to prepare for her wedding."

Jake's warm brown eyes softened as they searched her face. "I agree. Leah, do you still want a Christmas wedding?"

Had he seen her disappointment at the proposal of an earlier wedding? "Yes, but I can't ask Reverend Rice to wait a whole week."

The preacher thumped his Bible on the table. "Of course you can, young lady! Every bride should get a say on when she will say her vows. They are for life, you know."

"I know, but Parson John won't be coming back until spring, so even if we wait for him it won't be a Christmas wedding." Leah offered what she hoped was a gracious smile.

He nodded and then looked to Agnes. "That pie

was really something, Mrs. Frontz. Mr. Porter told me I had a treat waiting for me." The reverend laid his fork down. "Do you serve pie often?"

Mr. Frontz and two of the express riders entered the house. Leah knew she should go pour the men some hot coffee but her legs refused to move. Unsure where the conversation was going, Leah waited for Agnes's response.

Jake set Molly down.

The little girl climbed up into her aunt's lap. Nellie immediately began spooning pie into Molly's mouth. Leah wanted to protest that pie would ruin the child's dinner but didn't trust her voice to say anything.

The other three men sat down at the table. They looked from the preacher to Agnes and back again.

Mr. Frontz nodded to Mr. Slade, who returned the gesture. Tension filled the room as if everyone expected something wonderful or strange to happen.

"Every day. But it's not always apple. Sometimes it's peach or cherry. Pretty much whatever I preserved the year before. Why do you ask?" She arched an eyebrow at him and a gleam filled her eyes.

He tilted his chair back and grinned. "Well, as long as your parson is out of town, I could stick around and provide the Christmas service. That is, if you don't mind my staying here and eating up all your pie."

"You mean, have the services here for a couple of weeks?"

Everyone in the room remained silent. The preacher looked to Leah. "Well, I believe I could be persuaded to stay for a few weeks, if I can stay here and enjoy that pie every day." His gray eyes rose to meet Leah's and Jake's. "Might even be willing to do a Christmas Eve wedding."

Joy leaped in Leah's chest. God had just answered her prayers. She smiled and felt like clapping her hands the way Molly did when she became excited.

Jake draped his arm about her shoulder. "We'd be honored if you'd say the blessing over our wedding." Then he leaned close to Leah's ear and whispered for everyone to hear, "And you, my pretty bride, better learn how to bake pies. I have a feeling the reverend will be expecting a slice of payment every day."

The room erupted with laughter and talking all at once. It was a joyous occasion for them all. For Leah, it was a dream come true.

Chapter Thirteen

Leah walked into the general store holding Molly's hand. Jake followed close behind. She smiled down at the little girl and said, "We are here for you, Miss Molly. Look around and tell me and Uncle Jake what you'd like for Christmas."

"Just remember, we aren't going to buy you anything today," Jake reminded her with a pat on the head.

Molly looked about the store with wide eyes. She released Leah's hand and walked to the toys, her head held high and her little shoulders back.

Leah leaned over and whispered up to Jake, "What did you say to her at the house?" She continued watching the girl walk about the store in a dignified manner. It was so unusual for the child, who practically ran everywhere.

He bent down and whispered back, "That only good little girls who don't run in the store get presents on Christmas morning."

Now, why hadn't she thought of that? Leah grinned. "Very wise counsel," she teased.

"Be sure and get whatever you want or need," he whispered against her ear.

A shiver ran down Leah's spine. "Thank you." She stepped away from him, moving to the fabric. She was just giddy about the upcoming wedding, Leah told herself. Happiness enveloped her at the thought. She couldn't believe they'd be getting married in two short weeks.

Her gaze moved to her groom. Jake knelt down beside Molly. The two of them were looking into a glass case. Leah studied the two most important people in her life. Their faces were the same shape, and Molly's little nose mirrored Jake's exactly. She looked to see what they studied so intently. A beautiful porcelain doll sat in the center of the shelf.

Leah turned back to the fabric. She'd thought Agnes might like a pot holder for Christmas. It wouldn't take much fabric, Leah reasoned, as she ran her hands over brown and yellow calico fabric.

She'd never given anyone a gift before and was looking forward to doing so. In the orphanage, Christmas was just another day. Leah assumed the caretakers did the best they could for the children, but even their best wasn't much.

"I see you've found something you like," Jake spoke behind her.

Leah jumped. How long had he been standing there watching her? She cleared her throat. "Yes, I'm thinking I'd like to get a little bit of this fabric so that I can make Agnes two pot holders." To avoid his gaze, she looked about for Molly.

The little girl stood at the counter picking out a

piece of candy. Leah took a deep breath and returned her attention to Jake.

He laid his hand on her shoulder. "That's nice. Which two colors do you want?"

Unnerved by his closeness, she pointed out the yellow and brown prints. "I think those two would be best." She was thankful her voice came out strong instead of quivery, the way her insides felt.

Jake picked up both bolts and stood with them under his arm. "Would you mind making Molly a couple of new dresses?"

Her gaze moved to the little girl. Molly's dress looked worn at the hem and a little too short. "I would be happy to," Leah answered. She searched the table of fabrics once more.

"I like the pink with yellow flowers," Jake offered, reaching for the bolt.

"Me, too. And maybe the blue with green swirls?" Leah asked, also reaching toward the material.

Their hands touched and a shimmer of feelings ricocheted through Leah. She felt color fill her face and turned away. She knew her feelings for Jake were changing; Leah also knew she needed to rein in those emotions. The last thing she needed was Jake getting cold feet and leaving her right before their wedding day. "Uh, I'll get the needles and thread while you take care of the fabric." Leah hurried to the sewing notions.

A little while later, they left the store with two boxes, one filled with fabric and sewing notions, the other with food staples for Agnes. Leah couldn't believe what all Jake had bought.

Jake had seen Leah looking at the tin of cocoa

and had placed it in the pile of supplies, along with an extra pound of sugar. He'd also bought a lot more fabric than she'd expected.

All sorts of sewing ideas whipped through her mind. She would be making two dresses for Molly, a set of pot holders for Agnes and with the scraps that were left over, Leah could add them to other sewing scraps and make a nine-patch quilt.

Molly ran ahead of them. She'd asked for a spinning top, new clothes for her rag doll, a child's tea set and a box full of barnyard animals.

Leah noticed that Jake had been quiet since they'd left the store. "Did I spend too much?" she asked, praying that wasn't the reason for his silence.

"No. Why do you ask?"

She looked down at the slushy snow at their feet. "You seem thoughtful." Thoughtful wasn't really the word she'd been seeking but it sounded nicer than quiet. Besides, a man was allowed a moment of silence, so that would have seemed odd to say.

"Oh, I'm sorry. I was just thinking about Molly and her list of Christmas wishes." He turned his gaze on her. "And it got me to thinking, what would you like for Christmas, Leah?"

No one had ever asked her what she wanted. The question took Leah by surprise and she stared at him blankly. In the orphanage everyone got a bag of hard candy and an orange for Christmas. Nothing more.

If he thought her behavior strange, Jake didn't let on. "Maybe something for the house? Or a piece of jewelry? A book?" he hinted.

"I haven't given any thought to receiving a gift," Leah admitted.

Jake laughed. "Well, think about it and let me know if you come up with something."

Something white sped toward Jake. It hit his coat with a splat. His wide eyes revealed that the snowball had taken him completely by surprise.

Childish laughter filled the chilly air. "I got you! I got you!" Molly squealed.

Jake set the box he was carrying down and bent to scoop up some snow. "Now it's my turn!" he called back to his niece.

Molly took off running. Jake followed. Leah shook her head. Then it dawned on her she should join the fun. She sat her box on top of Jake's and scooped up the moist snow.

The little girl came running at her. "Save me, Leah! Uncle Jake's gonna hit me with a snowball!"

Leah hid her snowball behind her back and as soon as Molly and Jake sped past her, she let it fly. The cold wet snow hit him right between the shoulder blades.

He spun around and growled like a cranky old bear. "Oh, an ambush. Two against one."

Molly had already armed herself and let fly her snowball. It flew past Jake and hit Leah in the chest.

"Oops." Molly bent down and began forming another ball.

Leah ran from Jake. She heard him catching up with her and squealed as she made a mad dart to the side.

"You better run! This snowball has your name written all over it!" Jake called.

Molly chased after him and tossed her snow as hard as she could. It hit Jake in the shoulder.

Watching Jake and his niece playing made Leah

aware that soon she would have a husband and child of her own. They would have many years of playing. She'd never dreamed of having a real family. One that played and loved deeply. Thank you, Father, for bringing Molly and Jake into my life.

Jake pretended to roar like a wild animal and whirled around to chase his niece. The snowball he carried was turning into a puddle in his hand. He watched Molly's stocking hat fly off her head. Silky stands of blond hair flew out behind her. She squealed in delight at his pursuit.

Another wet glob hit him in the back of the head. Jake turned and tossed his snowball at Leah, making sure to miss her. She laughed and ran away again. Jake chased her. He loved the way her laughter flowed behind her and into his ears.

She jumped over something but he was too close to jump, too.

Jake felt his feet start to go out from under him as he hit the icy patch. In an attempt to keep from falling backward, he lunged forward.

Leah chose that moment to bend over for more snow ammo.

He couldn't stop. Jake knew they were going to collide. With all the thought he could muster, he grabbed Leah around the waist, twisted her around and then flipped just before the cold, hard ground collided with his back.

Leah landed on his stomach and chest with a loud whoosh. Her hat flew off her head and her hair fell forward, creating a curtain about their faces.

Without thought, Jake kissed her.

The sensation of their lips meeting knocked all the air from his body. His eyes flew open and he looked into her face.

Molly's laughing face was mere inches from theirs. The little girl had landed on top of Leah. Leah was sandwiched between uncle and niece like ham on rye.

Leah looked down at him with laughing sky-blue eyes. The joy of snowball fighting had taken all the seriousness from her face. She appeared younger, more carefree than he'd ever seen her.

"Uncle Jake? Are you all right?" Seriousness filled his young niece's voice.

He groaned as if in great pain. Both Leah and Molly leaned forward to look at him. Jake wrapped his arms around them both and quickly rolled. He kept his weight from crushing them as they squealed in surprise.

Jake pushed himself up and then reached down to grasp Leah's hand. She gave it to him with a grin. Was she thinking about the kiss? Or was she simply acting as if it hadn't happened?

Molly whimpered. "Uncle Jake, you got me all wet from the snow."

Leah turned and helped the little girl up. "I think all this fun has put me in the mood for hot chocolate. Does anyone else want a cup?"

The little girl immediately began hopping up and down. "I do! I do!" She raced ahead once more, unaware that she'd lost her hat.

Jake found both Molly's and Leah's hats. He handed Leah hers. Expecting her to place it on her head, Jake was surprised when she set it in the bag full of fabric.

Together they walked on to the house. Leah carried the fabrics and sewing notions. Her cheeks were rosy from the cold air. It had been fun seeing the carefree side of her. She'd lost some of the caution that always seemed to shroud her.

He held the door open for her and once she was inside he glanced at the clock. Time had passed faster than he'd realized. Jake set the food by the door. "I'll be right back. We have a rider coming in about twenty minutes. I need to prepare his horse."

Leah offered him a sweet smile. "Do you want hot cocoa or hot apple cider?"

"The cocoa will be fine." Jake closed the door behind them, shutting out the cold air. Molly stuck her head out the kitchen door. "Hurry, Leah. Agnes already has the milk heating for our cocoa." She darted back around the door.

Jake shook his head. "That child is demanding, now that she can talk." He turned to leave, feeling foolish for hanging around after he'd plainly stated he had work needing to be done.

Leah's soft laughter followed him back out the door. What was he thinking, playing out in the snow when he had a job to do? Jake's thoughts turned to the fun they'd had and he smiled.

He entered the barn and headed straight for Lightning's stall. The mustang would be raring to go. It was funny how the horses sensed when it was their time to take the trail with a rider.

Cole stood in the stall with Lightning. "Hope you don't mind, but I thought I'd go ahead and get him ready." He grinned at Jake.

The teasing grin on Cole's face put Jake on his

guard. "Now, why would you go and do a thing like that?" Jake leaned against the door to the stall.

"To help out a friend?" Cole tightened the cinch on the saddle.

"Well, in that case I don't mind at all." Jake pushed away from the door. "Want a cup of hot chocolate before you ride out?" he asked, giving the young man a slap on the back.

"Hot chocolate? Really?" Joy leaped in Cole's eyes.

Jake noted it and mentally decided a small tin of hot chocolate would be Cole's Christmas gift from him. He grinned at the young man. "Come on, and if we hurry you can have a cup before the next rider arrives."

Cole led the way back inside. "Ya know, I'll be happy to stay here, play snowball fights and drink hot chocolate with Miss Hollister and Molly. Want to trade places?"

Jake laughed. "Not on your life." There was a time he would have gladly become a pony express rider, if he hadn't been too large for the job, but not now. For the first time in his life, he had a family and something to stick around for. Being a pony express rider was just too dangerous for a family man.

He stopped suddenly and turned in a slow circle. When had he started thinking of himself as a family man? Was it when he'd learned Molly was his niece? Or the day Leah had said she'd marry him?

Leah stood at the washbasin pretending to ignore the little girl beside her. Over the past couple of days, she had allowed Molly to play alone outside in the afternoons beside the house. Leah kept a close eye on the little girl and wanted to make sure she was always safe. Today she was having fun, playing with the child even though she felt more tired than she had since her arrival at the home station.

Molly pulled on Leah's skirt to get her attention. "Leah? Please, I want to go play in the snow," she begged.

"I suppose so, but only for a little while. Stay close to the house and the snowman. As soon as I get these dishes done I'll come get you for your nap." Leah realized she was talking to empty air because Molly had already grabbed her coat and mittens and headed out the back door.

She should have put her hat on, too, but seeing as she wouldn't be out there that long, Leah decided to let her go and returned to scrubbing the last pot. She found her mind wandering to the upcoming wedding.

Both excited and a little nervous, Leah had taken her dress out and hung it beside the mirror in her room. She hoped that the wrinkles would fall out on their own and she wouldn't have to iron it. The dress seemed to shimmer in the morning light when the sun came through the window.

Agnes entered the kitchen. "Thank you for doing those for me. You know, you really do too much." She pulled a clean mug out of the cupboard. "When you get done with those, why don't you sit down and have a cup of tea with me. I'd like to talk to you for a few minutes before we have to get busy again."

Leah dried the pot and put it away. She picked up the washbasin and carried the dirty water to the back door. "Do you mind if I dump this first and then put

Molly down for her nap? That way we can talk in peace."

"That will be fine." Agnes sat down at the table. She poured hot tea from the teapot.

It had become a daily ritual for them to sit down for a few minutes while Molly napped. "Good." Leah pushed the door open and carefully walked to the edge of the house where they tossed out dirty dish water. She noted that the hot water melted what little snow had accumulated there. Then Leah headed to the other side of the house where Molly would be playing.

Just before she rounded the corner, Leah heard the little girl talking to someone. Thinking Molly was playing make-believe she didn't give it much thought. Then a low grunting sound answered the little girl.

Leah became instantly alert. What on earth was Molly playing with? Maybe a dog? Or had she come into contact with a black bear? She'd heard one of the express riders talking about bears being in the area. But weren't they hibernating now?

Leah hurried around the corner of the house and saw a little boy. Had he made that noise? Well, maybe they were pretending he was a dog or a bear.

His dark eyes widened and then he ran. Leah could tell from his clothes and darker skin that he was an Indian child. Probably no more than six years old.

"Molly, who was that?" Leah asked, trying her best to be calm. Her gaze searched the trees that the little boy had disappeared into.

The little girl shrugged. "I don't know. He doesn't talk very good."

He probably spoke better than Molly, only in his own language. Leah didn't press the issue, but asked,

"Have you played with him before?" She took Molly's hand and began walking toward the house.

"No." Realizing that Leah was taking her inside, Molly pulled her arm. "I don't want to take my nap."

"I know, sweetie, but if you don't rest, you will be cranky for the rest of the day." Leah held fast to Molly's hand and helped her up the back stairs.

When they got to the kitchen Molly pleaded with Agnes. "Miss Agnes, please tell Leah I'm too big for naps." Despite her words, Molly yawned.

"Nope, you need your rest." Agnes took a sip of her tea. "Besides the sooner you go down, the sooner you can get up."

Leah had no more trouble out of the little girl. Once they were upstairs, Molly took off her shoes and climbed into the bed they shared. "I still don't like naps," she complained.

"I know." Leah handed the rag doll to Molly.

"Thanks." She cuddled the doll close and within a few minutes was fast asleep.

Leah would have liked to crawl in bed with her. She stifled a yawn and shut the door. She and Agnes had been working doubly hard the past few days to keep the house clean in order to make a good impression on Mr. Slade, the pony express division agent.

Mr. Slade had kept all the men busy and Leah had seen very little of Jake, other than meals and their nightly Bible reading with Molly. Her thoughts went to the little Indian boy. Molly said she'd never talked to him before. Should she mention the boy to Jake? With Mr. Slade about, everyone seemed a little higher strung. Maybe now wasn't the best time to mention the child. After all, he was probably no older than six, so what harm could he do?

She walked into the kitchen. Once more Leah yawned.

"Maybe Molly isn't the only one who needs a nap." Agnes motioned for Leah to join her at the table.

She did as she was bid. A hot cup of tea sat before her. She inhaled its rich fragrance before answering. "No, I'd rather stay up with the grown-ups." She smiled over her cup.

Agnes laughed. "Not me. If I could, I'd take an afternoon nap, too."

Leah took a sip from her tea. "Mmm, this is good." She set the cup back down. "What did you want to talk to me about?"

"Well, your wedding is coming up soon and we haven't discussed what type of flowers you will be carrying, what kind of cake I should bake or discussed your wedding dress." Agnes stood up and went to the cookie jar.

While Agnes put cookies on a plate, Leah said, "I'm not sure I'll be carrying flowers. After all it is the dead of winter. Where would we get them?"

Agnes set the plate on the table. "I've thought of that. Maybe we could get some plastic ones from the general store here or in Julesburg." She picked up a sugar cookie and munched around the edges of it.

Leah didn't like the idea of fake flowers. She shook her head. This wasn't a real marriage, but she would like for everything about the ceremony to be real.

"No?" Agnes said, breaking the cookie in half.

Again Leah shook her head. "No, if I can't have real flowers, I don't think I want any."

Agnes reached out and patted her hand. "I understand. Well, what about the wedding cake? What flavor would you like?"

Leah drew a blank. She had no idea what Jake's favorite flavor of cake might be. Was that something other brides knew about their future husbands? Or did she simply make the decision and not worry about what he'd prefer? "I'm not sure about that either. What is normally served at weddings?" Leah asked, praying Agnes wouldn't realize how little she knew about Jake and his preferences.

"My wedding cake was simple. One layer, more like a loaf than a cake, but everyone seemed to enjoy it." Agnes set her cup down.

Leah leaned forward. "Do we have the ingredients for it?"

"I believe so." Agnes went to the cupboard and pulled out a cookbook. "My mother wrote the recipe in here for me." Agnes returned to the table and flipped through the pages of the book. "Here it is. Let's see, we'll need one pound of butter, one of sugar, ten eggs, half a pint of brandy, a glass of wine, three nutmegs, a tablespoonful of mace, one pound of flour, two of currants, one of stoned raisins and half a pound of citron."

"I'm not sure about the alcohol in it, Agnes. What about Molly?" Leah shook her head.

Agnes waved her hand. "Oh, that cooks out. It will be perfectly safe for everyone to eat." She looked up and grinned. "Please let me make the cake for you, Leah."

"You're sure it will cook out?"

Agnes nodded. "I promise…"

She looked so happy that Leah didn't have the heart to take this from her. "Then I'll be most appreciative if you will make the cake for us."

"Good. Now that that's settled, we need to start thinking about a wedding dress." Agnes shut her recipe book.

Leah smiled. "I already have a wedding dress. I thought I would be marrying Thomas, so I brought my wedding dress with me." She didn't tell Agnes that she'd worked several days for the local seamstress to get it.

"Well, then, I guess that's settled." Agnes sighed. "I suppose I better check on the lamb stew." Agnes stood up and walked to the large pot sitting on the stove.

Leah carried their cups to the washbasin. Setting them down, she glanced at Agnes. The older woman had her graying hair pulled up into a bun at the back of her neck.

Agnes stirred the stew and glanced over at her.

"Thank you, Agnes. I'm glad you will be by my side during the wedding."

Tears filled the older woman's eyes. "I'm glad to be able to help."

Before she started bawling, Leah smiled and left the kitchen. For the first time in her life, she felt as if another woman really cared about her. Was it possible that she finally had people in her life who could love her? Care what happened to her?

Chapter Fourteen

Jake hummed as he left the barn and headed up to the house. He couldn't help but wonder what wonderful concoction Leah had baked today. She had a knack for creating pies and cakes that filled his senses long before he arrived at the table.

Since Leah's arrival they'd added two wooden rockers to the front porch. Right now, the preacher sat in one of them. His voice drifted across the yard. "Let me guess. The smell of peach cobbler has you coming to the house early tonight." He grinned to soften the words.

Jake laughed. "You better believe it."

"I envy you, young man."

Jake took the steps two at a time and then joined the preacher. "How so?" he asked, taking a seat and inhaling the sweet scent of sugar and cinnamon.

Reverend Rice rocked gently. "You get a new bride for Christmas who can cook and has a soft heart for old men."

What did he mean by that? Was he calling himself old? "What old men would that be, Reverend?"

Gentle laughter spilled from the preacher. "Myself, of course."

Jake looked at him. "You, sir, are not that old."

The reverend patted the Bible on his lap. "Yeah, I am. But enough about me. I'm curious, young man. What are you going to do after the telegraph lines run this way and the pony express has run its course?" His gray eyes searched Jake's.

"Well, I'll have to talk to Leah but I'm thinking I'd like to start a horse ranch." He looked out across the snow-covered yard.

"That's a fine plan." Reverend Rice nodded. "Any idea where you might start this ranch?"

Jake leaned his arms on his thighs. "Well, I'd have to sell my place in Texas then we could stay here in Colorado, but if we do I think I'd like to move into the mountains."

"It's mighty pretty up in the mountains."

The sorrow in the preacher's voice had Jake asking, "Why do you ask?"

His gray eyes looked deeply into Jake's. "After your wedding, I think I'll retire and find a cabin somewhere. I'd like to just rest."

"I didn't realize that preachers retired." Jake muttered it more to himself than to the preacher.

Reverend Rice stood. "Everyone retires at some time or another." He walked to the door. "It's a good thing that you are young and can have several young sons to leave that horse ranch to when you retire." He opened the door. "You coming?"

"No, I think I'll sit here for a moment longer," Jake answered. He'd not thought of what would happen to the ranch once he died. Retirement had never entered his mind, but if a preacher could retire, well, it bore thinking about.

"Don't wait too long. That cobbler will be about ready to eat and I'd hate for Will to get it all before you get a shot at it." Rice laughed and went inside.

Jake blew on his hands to warm them. His marriage to Leah was to be a marriage of convenience, nothing more. But one didn't acquire sons without making the marriage real.

He'd not given any thought as to why people had children. Sitting on the porch in the cold, his mind began to count off the reasons. Sons to take over the farm or ranch, daughters to help their mother in her old age, and what man didn't want a legacy of some sort? Molly could take over the farm and help Leah, but would his niece want to? Would Molly marry someday and move away, leaving his life's work to another?

And then there was Leah. Who would take care of her in her old age, should he die? Sadness enveloped him. By offering Leah a marriage of convenience had he sentenced them both to a life of loneliness?

The stagecoach arrived with three passengers. Leah scooped cookies onto a plate and picked up the coffeepot. She didn't know where Agnes and Molly were, but she knew what needed to be done.

Two women and a man entered the house, shivering.

Offering a bright smile, she greeted them. "Please, come on inside. I have hot coffee and cookies ready." Leah laid the plate on the table and set the coffeepot beside it. "Give me a moment and I'll have cups for you."

"Oh, thank you, my dear." The older of the two women hurried to the table. She looked longingly at the fireplace and around the warm room.

Leah hurried back into the kitchen and grabbed dessert plates and five mugs. She placed them on a tray and carried it all back into the main room. Most of the time only men traveled through, so the arrival of two women set her heart to pounding with joy.

When she reentered the room, Leah said, "I'm Leah Hollister. I hope you have had a good trip so far." She'd heard Agnes introduce herself in that manner many times.

"It's nice to meet you, Miss Hollister. I'm Christina Watts, friends and family call me Chrissy, and this is my daughter, Savannah Watts." She smiled and continued with the introductions. "This is my son, Michael."

"It's nice to meet you all. Please help yourself to refreshments." Leah poured them each a cup of coffee.

"Oh, thank you, dear." Mrs. Watts took the mug Leah offered her with a smile.

Once everyone had filled their plate, Leah said, "We can always move closer to the fireplace, if you ladies would like to."

As they walked, Leah observed how quiet Savannah and her brother Michael were. Neither said anything while their mother talked as if she hadn't had a living soul to talk to in weeks.

"This has been the worst trip ever," Christina Watts said as she plopped down on the settee. "Besides being bitterly cold, we had that bunch of Indians chasing us, and we'd no more than escaped from them when a group of men tried to rob the stage. Can you believe that?"

Leah drew up a wooden chair from the dining table. "Really?"

Mrs. Watts waved her hand. "I imagine it's because the weather is a little better this way. It's cold, but the icy rain and snow no longer plague us. As long as it was snowing, we had no trouble at all."

Mr. Edwards's feet pounded on the rug by the door. He carried three large suitcases and two smaller ones tucked under his arm. "Thanks for your help, young man," he growled at Michael Watts before dropping their suitcases in a pile beside the door and leaving.

"Oh, dear, son. I do believe you should have offered to help the driver with our baggage." Mrs. Watts looked at her son.

Michael shrugged his shoulders and bit into a cookie.

Mrs. Watts refocused her attention on Leah. "The luggage is inside now, so I guess no harm was done."

The sound of the stagecoach leaving didn't stop the three of them from eating the cookies as if they hadn't had a decent meal in weeks.

Leah frowned. Why hadn't Michael helped the stagecoach driver? Was he lazy? Slow in the brain? Or just unthoughtful? Leah studied the young man.

Michael looked to be somewhere between twenty and twenty-five. He was tall with a slim body, brown hair and blue eyes, but nothing special to look at. A smirk pulled at his lips when he caught her looking at him. With the back of his hand he wiped at the cookie crumbs on his lips.

Leah quickly looked away. She didn't want his attentions. Next, she focused on Savannah. The girl looked much like her brother—tall, slender, blue eyes and brown hair, but her nose leaned to the right as if it had once been broken. She kept her head down and didn't make eye contact.

"I declare, I hope you have a couple of rooms for us. I think I could sleep a week," Mrs. Watts said. "Are the beds on this floor? Or upstairs?"

Something didn't feel right. Normally passengers didn't ask where they'd be sleeping. It was times like these that Agnes wished South Platte had a hotel or even a boarding house for visitors to stay in. Most were just happy to have a clean bed and only stayed overnight. Except for the pony express superintendent, Jack Slade. According to Agnes, he stayed a few days, did his inspection and then moved on to the next pony express home station.

And then there was the way the two adult children looked back and forth at each other. Almost as if they were sharing a secret. Mrs. Watts stood, looking up the stairs. She'd already scanned the room they were in, seeming to take in everything at once.

"Mrs. Frontz will be back in a bit. You can ask her about the rooms." Leah felt Michael's gaze upon her. She turned to find him staring and licking his lips. He truly was disgusting in his overdramatization of the action. Leah stood. "Please enjoy the coffee and cookies. If you will excuse me, I need to go check on lunch." She made a hasty exit, not waiting for Mrs. Watts's permission to be excused.

When she got to the kitchen door, Leah looked back. Christina Watts and her children were huddled together talking in low tones. That feeling that something wasn't right crept up her spine and into her hair.

She went to the oven and pulled out the last two loaves of bread. The warm fragrance soothed her frazzled nerves. Maybe she was overreacting to the Watts family.

Agnes came through the back door. "Did you take care of our boarders?" she asked as she hung up her coat.

"I gave them coffee and a plate of cookies to tide them over until lunch. Where's Molly?" Leah placed the bread on cooling racks.

"She's with Jake. The child loves horses almost as much as he does." Agnes smiled. She came farther into the room and stopped. Her gaze searched Leah's face. "What's wrong?"

Leah shook her head. "I can't say anything is wrong. I just have a strange feeling about Mrs. Watts and her grown children."

"What kind of strange feeling?"

She lowered her voice. "I can't describe it."

Agnes grinned. "Honey, you've been out of sorts ever since we started planning this wedding. Could it be you're just on edge because of that?"

Leah didn't think so, but didn't want to alarm the woman. After all, she could be wrong about the Wattses. "Maybe." She moved to the pot of beans on the stove and lifted the lid to stir them. "Oh, before I forget, Mrs. Watts is asking about rooms."

"I'll take care of that." Agnes left the kitchen. Leah heard her introducing herself and telling them about the rooms that were available to the stage passengers.

Leah felt the need to find Jake. She didn't know

why but knew she wanted him close. Crossing the room, she reached for the coat Agnes had just taken off but stopped short. If the Watts were a threat to the station, it wasn't wise to leave Agnes in the house alone with them. She took a deep breath and went back into the main room.

"The rooms are straight up these stairs." Their feet pounded on the steps as they climbed the steps. "The third floor is mine and Mr. Frontz's quarters. Leah and Molly's room is right here."

Leah felt her throat tighten. She wished Agnes hadn't shared that bit of information. Normally it didn't bother her, but she didn't like the uneasy feelings the Watts family brought out in her.

"Mrs. Watts, your room is right here beside Leah's. Mr. Watt, I'll give you the room next to your mother and sister."

Leah heard the bedroom doors open. She knew Agnes was waiting to see if they were satisfied with the accommodations. A sense of unease continued to plague Leah. Fearing for Agnes, she mounted the stairs.

At the top, she heard Mrs. Watts say, "Oh, they are lovely and will do nicely. After the places we've stayed in, these will be more than sufficient for our needs."

"I'm glad to hear that. Lunch is at twelve. Dinner is at five sharp. The price of the rooms is…"

Mrs. Watts interrupted her. "Who is staying in the room next to Michael's?" Her voice sounded sharp, as if she believed Agnes had withheld valuable information from her.

In a tight tone, Agnes answered, "That would be Reverend Rice."

"Did you hear that, children? We are staying under the same roof as a preacher."

Leah watched as both Michael and Savannah nodded their heads. A hard glint entered Michael's eyes and she wondered what he could have against preachers. Or did he know Reverend Rice?

For the first time, Leah heard Savannah speak. "Who will be bringing up our bags?"

"Since the men are all busy right now, perhaps you and your brother can bring them up." Agnes smiled. "I'm sure your mother would appreciate you doing so."

Both Michael and Savannah scowled.

"Thank you for that suggestion, Mrs. Frontz. I'm sure my children will be happy to fetch the luggage." Mrs. Watts's voice sounded anything but pleased.

"Well, if that will be all. We will see you at lunch, should you choose to eat with us." Agnes walked to the stairs with her head held high and her gaze straight ahead. Her anger must have blinded her to the fact that she'd forgotten to tell them the cost of their rooms.

Leah followed the older woman back down the stairs.

Once they were both in the kitchen, Agnes hissed, "I see what you mean by them. Mama Watts tries to let on that they are just regular boarders but there is something that I can't put my finger on." Fire blazed from her eyes. "And did you hear the way they implied we should bring them their bags?"

Leah nodded. She heard a commotion on the stairs and eased the kitchen door open to peek out. Michael was juggling with the big bags and Savannah walked in front of him holding the two smaller ones. "Well, I'm glad you didn't give in. Michael and Savannah are carrying them up now."

Agnes gave an unladylike snort. "With the way they behave, what do you think? Do you think they are wealthy? That could account for their high-handed rudeness."

"If they are, they don't dress the part. Savannah's dress is about a half inch too short for her. Michael's boots are scuffed and worn. Mrs. Watts might have money, but if she does, she doesn't use it to buy her children decent clothes." She slipped onto a stool beside the table.

Agnes stared out the kitchen window. "Would you do me a favor?"

"Sure, anything. Just ask." Leah stood, waiting for orders. She expected Agnes to ask her to clean.

"Thanks." Agnes moved to the cupboard and pulled out her picnic basket.

Leah watched as she loaded it with chicken and cheese, a mason jar full of beans and half a loaf of bread. She added a jug of apple cider. Since apple cider was Molly's and Jake's choice of drink, Leah knew the basket was for them. When she was finished adding a napkin filled with cookies, she handed the basket to Leah. "Please take this and go have a picnic with your soon-to-be family."

"I won't leave you in the house with them." Leah pulled her chin up and dared Agnes to argue with her eyes.

Agnes nodded. "I agree. I'm going to slip out with you." Both women put on their coats and left the house using the back door. "The thought of Molly around those people gives me the willies. You go get Molly and Jake, I'm going to go get Mr. Frontz and make him come to the house with me."

Leah nodded. When Agnes started to walk toward one of the outbuildings, she followed.

Agnes stopped. "Now, where do you think you're going?" she demanded.

"With you."

"Why?"

Was she correct in her suspicions? That Agnes hadn't planned on getting her husband but on slipping back to the house alone? "I'd like to ask Mr. Frontz a question before I go have lunch."

"What sort of question?" Agnes asked suspiciously.

"You'll hear it when he does." Leah pushed onward toward the building Agnes had been going to.

Agnes called after her, "You know, I just remembered Charles said he was going to be working on the north fence." She turned and stomped off in that direction.

So she had been right! Leah grinned and followed.

Mr. Frontz looked up when he saw both women coming toward him. His gray brows drew together. "What are you two doing out here?"

"It seems we have questions of our own," Agnes snapped back at him.

His eyes softened. "I'm sorry. That didn't come out the way I intended."

The tension in her face relaxed. "We have new boarders."

He leaned against a fence post. "Anyone I know?"

"Christina, Michael and Savannah Watts."

Mr. Frontz pushed his hat back and scratched his head. "Never heard of them. Have you, Ike?"

The pony express rider shook his head. He nailed in the wire and straightened.

"Didn't think so." Agnes chewed on her lip. "I need to be getting back to the house and would like your company." She looked up into her husband's eyes.

Whatever Mr. Frontz saw within hers had him agreeing. "Ike, take the supplies back to the tool shed."

"Yes, sir," Ike answered.

Mr. Frontz turned to Leah. "What's with the picnic basket?"

"Agnes wants to keep Molly away from our boarders as much as possible," Leah answered, falling into step with them.

He frowned. "Got yourself a funny feeling about this group, do you, Aggs?"

Leah could tell Agnes was too much of a lady to voice her objections of the Watts in front of others. A slight nod of her head was the only answer she was willing to give.

"Before I forget, it seems Miss Leah has a question for you, too," Agnes announced with a triumphant grin.

The older man turned his head and looked down on her. "What can I do for you, Miss Hollister?"

"I don't have a papa to give me away at the wedding and I was hoping you might like the honor, sir." Leah hadn't planned on asking him like this but she guessed now was as good a time as any. Her palms began to sweat as she waited for him to answer.

Mr. Frontz stopped walking. He turned and took

her hands in his. "Well, since I don't have a daughter to give away at her wedding, I'd be honored to give you to Jake Bridges. But I want you to know, I don't take this chore lightly."

Leah stared up at him. "I don't understand, sir."

"Me and the missus have grown fond of you in the short time you've been here and well…" He paused, then released one of her hands and rubbed the back of his neck. "What I'm trying to say is, if I give you away then that will make us family. Jake Bridges will answer to me if he harms one hair on your head." His eyes misted up.

Leah found she had a lump in her throat. "Thank you, sir."

He released her other hand and nodded. "Let's get you ladies out of the cold."

Agnes beamed as they walked back toward the home station. Leah felt as if someone were squeezing her heart. If she understood Mr. Frontz correctly, he'd just adopted her as a daughter. No one had ever made her feel like family before. She'd always been just another mouth to feed or someone to take care of the younger children in the orphanage.

Was this what it felt like to be loved?

Later that evening, Leah handed Jake a small bag with Molly's things in it. "Are you sure you want her to stay overnight?" she asked for the tenth time.

"If Agnes thought she was in danger and wouldn't even let her eat with those people, of course I want her to stay overnight." He took the bag from her hand.

Leah nodded. The idea had been his, and since Jake was Molly's uncle, Leah really couldn't say no.

Not that she wanted to put the child in danger but this would be the first time they'd been separated since their journey began. Sadness filled her. She looked to the little girl.

Molly seemed thrilled with the idea of having a sleepover at Uncle Jake's house. She held her rag doll and smiled, showing all her baby teeth.

"All right. I'll bring breakfast over in the morning. But who's going to take care of the horses in the morning?"

"Ike said he'd take care of things until I got to the barn." Jake smiled at her. "Stop worrying, Leah. Everything is under control."

It didn't feel that way to Leah. She offered him what she hoped was an unworried-looking smile. "All right." Leah knelt down in front of Molly. "Promise you'll be a good girl and go to sleep when Uncle Jake tells you to. Promise?"

Molly drew an *X* across her little chest. "I promise." Then she grabbed her uncle's hand and began tugging on him.

"Leah? Will you be all right?" Jake asked. Concern filled his chocolate-brown eyes.

She nodded. "I'll be fine. For the first time in a long time, I'll get to sleep without little feet in my back."

Jake chuckled at that. "All right. We'll see you in the morning." He waved goodbye as he and Molly rounded the corner to go to the old homestead.

Leah climbed the stairs. Her lamp cast shadows on the walls. Everyone had gone to bed. The house seemed quiet. Probably because Molly wasn't in it, she thought.

Once in her room, an uneasy feeling crept up her spine. Now that she was inside, Leah was thankful Molly would be with Jake tonight. She put her light down on the side table and locked the door to her room.

Leah prepared for bed. The sheets were cool against her overheated body. It felt odd having a whole bed to herself; for as long as she could remember Leah had to share with one child or another. That was just the way it went when you were raised in an orphanage. Her eyes drifted shut and she felt her body relax into the mattress. Leah inhaled but stopped midway when she heard a creaking sound drifting from the stairs. She sat straight up. Was there someone moving about the house?

Leah swallowed and looked toward her bedroom door. A light flickered through the crack at the bottom. She pushed the covers back and on shaky legs walked to the door.

Through the wall she heard Mrs. Watts hiss. "Come on, Michael! Get away from there. We have a lot to do and not a lot of time to do it in."

His boots thudded against the wooden floor as he walked away. She exhaled. What were they doing? What could she do to stop them?

She rested her back against the door. If they were downstairs, maybe she could make it up to the third floor and warn Mr. Frontz. Taking a deep breath, Leah unlocked the door. Her hands trembled as she eased it open.

Darkness filled the hallway. For a moment, Leah's legs refused to move. She said a silent prayer for strength and released the air in her lungs. Trying not to make any noise, she started for the staircase that led to the Frontzs' living quarters.

Leah placed her hand on the banister and started up the stairs.

A crash below and a man's yell had her turning around on the stairs. More crashing sounded. Leah looked up the stairs. She couldn't see anything but darkness. With her heart pounding in her chest she wondered why Mr. Frontz or Agnes hadn't come down.

Leah started back down the stairs. She heard the preacher come out of his room and run down the first flight of stairs. Just when she decided to follow, Leah felt something hard and cold push against her ribs. Paralyzed with fear, Leah recognized the object in her side as a gun.

"If you don't scream, I might let you live," Savannah's voice whispered against her ear. "Is there another way out of here?" she asked, pressing the firearm harder into Leah's side.

Leah fought the panic that screamed in her ears. "I don't think so." She was surprised that her voice didn't shake.

"Then I guess we'll have to take the long way."

"The long way?" Leah parroted.

Savannah grabbed Leah by her hair and yanked. "Just walk," she demanded.

Leah stifled a cry of pain. Tiny ants danced about her scalp where Savannah held her head in place. When they got to the next flight of stairs, Savannah pulled her back into the deep shadows.

Michael Watts sat on the floor with his hands

bound behind him. His angry voice drifted up the stairs. "You won't get away with this."

Jake and Mr. Frontz stood looking down at him. The preacher was carrying a chair from the dinner table toward them. "Where are your mother and sister?" Mr. Frontz demanded.

What was Jake doing at the home station? Why wasn't he at the cabin with Molly? Her thoughts turned to the little girl. Anger swept over her at the thought of the Watts family hurting the little girl. Reason settled in. Jake wouldn't be here if Molly needed him.

Ike staggered into the house. Blood ran down the side of his face. Still hidden in the shadows upstairs, Leah thought she might be sick on Savannah's shoes.

Mr. Frontz pulled the young rider inside and placed him in the wooden chair the preacher held. "What happened, son?"

Ike touched the side of his head and held his hand over the wound that was bleeding. "I'm sorry, boss. Mrs. Watts hit me from behind. She must have known I was there."

"Where is she now?" Jake asked, looking up the stairs.

Michael laughed. "Ma is long gone."

Did Jake realize she was still up there? Leah wondered. Did he know about Savannah? Or at least speculate that Savannah might be holding her captive?

Savannah yanked Leah's head back. "Don't even think about doing anything. I'll put a bullet in him and then you," Savannah hissed in her ear.

Leah's head exploded in pain. Savannah wrapped

her fist tighter in her loose hair. Tears pooled in Leah's eyes. She listened as Jake spoke again.

"Mr. Frontz, let's get Mr. Watts on a horse and headed to the sheriff in Julesburg. Reverend, would you help Ike into the kitchen and wait with him there for Agnes?" Jake patted Ike on the shoulder as the reverend proceeded to help him up. "I'm sure she'll be able to make you feel right as rain in no time. We'll send her back from my place on our way to Julesburg."

Jake's back was to the stairs but Leah felt sure he'd just signaled something to Mr. Frontz. Savannah pulled her back farther into the shadows as if she'd sensed it, too.

Agnes was at the homestead? Taking care of Molly? Slowly Leah realized that they had all acted together to set a trap for the Watts family. Why hadn't they included her in their plans? Had they thought her an outsider? Tears pooled in her eyes. She'd foolishly thought they counted her as family.

"Come on, Watts, time for you to meet our local law." Mr. Frontz pulled Michael to his feet.

Michael came up sputtering, "When Ma gets back with my uncle you will be sorry."

Mr. Frontz ignored Michael and opened the front door. Jake followed them out. A click signaled that the door had been firmly closed. Leah felt truly abandoned. Ike and the reverend were in the kitchen and the other men had just left, leaving her alone with a crazy woman. A gun-toting crazy woman, Leah mentally added.

Savannah laughed. "Well, they made that easy, didn't they?"

Leah didn't answer. Anger at Savannah boiled in her gut. How was she going to get out of this mess alive? Would Savannah really shoot her?

After several moments, Savannah shoved Leah down the stairs, making sure to keep one hand securely tangled in Leah's hair and the other on the gun pushed firmly into Leah's side. "Let me go, Savannah. I'll only slow you up," Leah said with a confidence she didn't feel.

A sharp jerk and pain sickened her stomach. Leah gasped for air. Anger and fear warred for Leah's attention, not to mention the ache she felt every time Savannah pulled her hair and scalp.

"Not on your life and keep your jaw shut," Savannah hissed in her ear. "We're going to the barn where you'll saddle one of those pretty little horses for me. If you do it right, I might not shoot you." Savannah jerked her head back again for good measure.

They stood in front of the door. Savannah stopped Leah and pressed the side of her face against it. A few minutes later the sound of two horses riding away met their ears. Savannah shoved Leah hard into the wood. "Hurry up and get that door open. I don't want those dimwits in the kitchen stumbling out here."

Jake growled behind her. "Too late, Miss. The dimwits have returned. Now release Miss Hollister."

Leah felt the cold metal leave her side. She started to move away but Savannah still held her securely by the hair. The feel of Savannah's knuckles bunching up against her scalp had Leah grabbing her hand.

Mr. Frontz stepped into Savannah's line of vision. He held a rifle aimed at her head. "I believe you've been asked to let her go."

Savannah's hand relaxed. She straightened her fingers.

Leah used those actions to move out of her grasp.

Chapter Fifteen

Jake flinched inwardly when Leah's tear-filled eyes glared at him and Mr. Frontz before she headed up the stairs.

Unsure what he'd done, Jake turned to watch her go. Leah held her head high and her shoulders back. Would she break down and cry once she got to her room? He hoped not.

Mr. Frontz tightened the knot in the rope he'd tied Savannah's hands with. "Come on, Jake. Let's get Miss Watts and her brother to Julesburg. Jack Slade is probably still there. We'll let him deal with these two." The older man's face looked haggard.

Jake followed Mr. Frontz and Savannah out the door. "Well, if you will help me get them to the horses, maybe Will would be willing to go with me to town. I'd feel better knowing you were here protecting Molly and the women."

The older man didn't answer. He seemed to be considering Jake's words. Trying to sound casual, Jake added, "I know Will has been wanting to see a girl there and I have a Christmas gift for Leah that I'd like to pick up."

"Then I guess I'll stay." Mr. Frontz grinned across at Jake. "Besides, Will wasn't too happy to be kept out of the action. He'll regain a little of his dignity by taking these two in, and if that isn't reason enough I'm sure he'll be happy to get away from Agnes's fussing." Mr. Frontz chuckled at the thought.

It dawned on Jake that Leah may have felt the same way as Will. They hadn't told her or the reverend that they suspected the Watts family of being up to no good or about the traps they'd set. Now he realized that it could have gotten Leah killed. He'd have to explain tomorrow that the only reason they had been excluded was because he and Mr. Frontz had been trying to protect them.

They arrived at the barn. Michael lay in the corner, hands and feet tied, mouth gagged. He was tied up tighter than a Sunday turkey. His eyes flashed to his sister's and hardened.

Mr. Frontz shoved Savannah to the ground and proceeded to tie her feet up. She kicked her legs at him.

Jake shoved the gun in her direction. "I wouldn't do that if I were you, miss. This gun might go off." He knew he'd never shoot a woman, unless she was truly a threat. But Savannah's eyes widened in fear just as he'd hoped.

Once she was also tied up and gagged, Jake handed the gun to the older man. "I'll toss her on the horse."

She wiggled and grunted but Mr. Frontz shoved the gun in her direction again. Savannah stopped moving and became dead weight.

"Thanks," Jake said as he put her belly down across the saddle and began securing her onto the horse.

Once Savannah was in place and he was sure she wouldn't fall from the mustang, Jake went to get Michael. He looked down at the young man with derision. What caused a man to turn to a life of crime? Michael had already confessed that they had intended to steal the horses and he'd blamed his mother.

Will came running into the barn. "Aw, man, I missed it all." He slapped his floppy brown hat against his leg.

Agnes followed with a sleeping Molly against her shoulder.

"What are you two doing here?" Mr. Frontz demanded.

Jake noted that the older man hid his true weariness behind a mask of toughness. Jake motioned for Will to join him. "You take his feet and I'll take his head."

"I was worried," Agnes admitted softly. Her eyes held her husband's.

Charles Frontz nodded. His face relaxed. A sigh tore from his body, proof that he couldn't stay angry with his wife. "Everyone is all right. Mrs. Watts escaped but these two didn't." He hooked a thumb over his shoulder indicating Savannah and Michael.

"What are we going to do about their mother?" Agnes whispered.

"We'll let Mr. Slade's men hunt for her. She's a horse thief now, so I'm sure a warrant will be issued for her arrest." Mr. Frontz moved to his wife's side and placed an arm around her waist.

"And Leah?" Agnes's gaze searched the barn as if she expected her to be there.

Mr. Frontz tugged his wife close. "She's all right, too. I'll tell you all about it once we get to the house."

Jake and Will slung Michael over a horse. Air whooshed from his lungs, giving Jake a small degree of satisfaction. He looked to his niece. She continued to sleep peacefully against Agnes. What was he going to do about her?

As if she'd read his mind, Agnes asked, "Jake, do you mind if this little lamb stays the night with us in our quarters?"

"Thank you. That will be very helpful," he answered, tying Michael to the horse.

Agnes had yet another question. "What are you going to do with those two?" She frowned.

"We're taking them to Julesburg. We should be back before Ike rides out in the morning." Jake turned to look at Mr. Frontz, remembering that his young friend Ike had been hurt. "Do you think he'll be able to ride tomorrow?"

"What's wrong with Ike?" Will asked, a look of concern covering his face.

"Mrs. Watts snuck up on him. Took a nasty blow to the head," Jake answered.

Agnes gasped. "Where is he?"

Mr. Frontz patted her back. "The reverend is seeing to him at the house."

"Then I need to get in there." Agnes pulled out of her husband's embrace and started to leave the barn.

"Agnes." Mr. Frontz's strong voice pulled her to a stop. "Hold up, woman." Sure she wasn't leaving, he turned back to Jake. "You two be careful. I want you back here before nine in the morning. Understood?"

Both Jake and Will answered, "Yes, sir."

"Good." The older man rejoined his wife.

Will's young voice called after him. "Sir, if Ike can't make his run in the morning, I'll be happy to do it for him."

"We'll see," Mr. Frontz answered. "Agnes, let me have the child. If I know you, you're in a big hurry to go check on your boy." With that, he gently pulled Molly away from Agnes and settled her against his own shoulder.

Molly continued sleeping. She curled an arm around his neck. As soon as Agnes was sure her ward was in good hands, she marched from the barn at a fast pace. Mr. Frontz patted Molly's back and ambled behind his wife.

Jake walked to his horse's stall and pulled him out. "That was nice of you to offer to take Ike's run tomorrow, Will." He proceeded to saddle the gelding.

Will saddled his horse, also. "Ike would do it for me." There was worry in the young man's voice.

It was true. In just a few months, the pony express riders, Will, Cole and Ike, had formed a brotherly bond. There were several other riders that came through the South Platte home station but none of them were as close as those three.

Jake and Will rode in silence and at a fast pace to Julesburg. Jake's thoughts were on Leah and what had almost happened to her tonight. His heart had leaped in his chest when he'd seen her held like that, with a gun pressed into her side. For the first time in a long time, Jake realized he'd allowed a woman to come close to breaking down the wall around his heart. How was he going to keep her out? They were to be married on Christmas Eve. Would she hurt him the way Sally and John had?

He glanced across at Will. The lad had a smile on his face a mile long. It didn't take a genius to know he was thinking about the girl in Julesburg who had stolen his heart. The young man trusted too easily.

Off-key music was their welcome into Julesburg. A piano played, men shouted and shady characters hid in the shadows. Jake tugged on Michael's horse's reins and trotted farther into town with his prisoners. Will followed.

An old building at the end of town was their destination. Jake simply wanted to get the Wattses in jail and find a place to sleep. He knew he'd stay at the Julesburg home station with the other pony express riders. He might be making his bed on the floor, but at least it was a fairly safe place to spend the night.

The town of Julesburg really had no law but it did have one man, Jack Slade. Jake knew he stayed in the old building at the edge of town. He led the way and tied up their horses in front of the building. Making sure to stomp his boots on the wooden porch, Jake climbed the short steps and banged on the door.

"You better have a good reason for waking me up," a deep voice called.

"Mr. Slade, it's Jake Bridges."

The door opened and Slade stood with his shirt and boots off. His hair was disheveled and he smelled of whisky. "What do you want, Jake?"

"I have a couple of horse thieves here. Thought you might know what to do with them," he answered.

Jack pushed past him and jerked first Savannah's head up by the hair and then did the same to Michael. He spit in the dirt. "They tried to steal express mounts?" He directed his question to Jake.

"Sure did."

Slade grunted. "Take them out back and shoot them."

Jake grinned. "No, sir."

"You disobeying an order, boy?" Slade swaggered toward him.

Jake didn't want a fight but he also had no intention of killing the Watts siblings. "Yep."

Slade's booming laughter filled the night air. "I figured you would." He walked toward Jake and passed him.

Jake motioned for Will to stay put. He noticed the boy had lost the grin that had stretched his lips the whole trip. Taking a deep breath, Jake followed the superintendent, Slade, into the building.

"Well, since you won't shoot them, bring them in," Jack ordered from the army cot he'd fallen onto. He waved his arm toward the far corner of the room and said, "Put them over there."

Jake turned and saw that Will was already down and untying Savannah. He moved to Michael and did the same. Together they carried their captives inside, first Savannah and then Michael.

Tears streamed down Savannah's face. Somewhere along the trail she'd lost her mean attitude. Had she just realized that stealing horses was a hanging offence? Michael scooted closer to his sister as if to offer comfort.

Deep snores filled the room along with the scent of stale whiskey. Slade had passed out on the cot.

"Now what?" Will asked.

Jake looked to Slade. "We leave them."

"Do you think he'll remember why they're here in the morning?"

Once more he thought about the price for stealing horses. Slade wasn't known for his mercy toward horse thieves. For a moment, Jake felt pity for the Watts siblings. But he couldn't have them loose stealing from innocent people or the pony express. He sighed. "I'll leave him a note."

Will nodded.

Jake went to the small desk that sat against the wall. He found a wanted poster and turned it over. Next he moved to the stove and pulled out a piece of cold coal. Flipping the paper over Jake wrote, *Horse thieves from the South Platte station.* He noticed a nail in the wall above Michael's head. Walking over, he stuck the paper on it so that Slade would be sure to see it in the morning.

"Can we go now?" Will asked impatiently.

Tiredness pulled at Jake's shoulder. "Yep, let's put the horses in the corral by the pony express station and then hit the hay."

Will looked disappointed. Jake slapped him on the back as they headed out the door. "Get up early enough in the morning and you can see that gal of yours before we head home."

"I'd like to see her tonight," Will grumbled under his breath.

Jake nodded. "You are a grown man, Will. I can't tell you what to do but I can remind you that you've volunteered for Ike's run tomorrow. Besides, I don't think her Papa would appreciate you knocking on their door at this time of night."

As expected, Will's shoulders came up. His duty and common sense overruled his desire to see the girl. "You're right. I'll need a good night's sleep to make that run. Ike said the Indians are getting braver. I'll need to be alert to ride through the canyon."

Being a pony express rider wasn't for the faint of heart. Jake and Will entered the station. They went straight to the riders' room and bedded down. One other young man was there, and his soft snores told them he was already sound asleep.

Jake lay in his blanket for several long minutes. Was Leah sleeping? Trembling in her room with fear? Or so angry at being left out of their plan that she couldn't sleep?

Leah hadn't been able to sleep. She was angry. Not just at Jake, but at everyone, with the exception of Molly. They had all known what they planned to do about the Watts family but they hadn't told her. Didn't they realize that not knowing would be more dangerous than knowing? Surely they knew she'd come out of her room at the first sign of trouble. Maybe they didn't care about her as much as she cared about them. What had she been thinking? That maybe they were becoming her family? That they cared about her? She'd allowed those thoughts and questions to plague her all night until they had festered into an ugly sore on her heart.

When she got downstairs, Molly and Agnes were already in the kitchen and Agnes was making breakfast for the men. "After last night, I thought you might sleep in this morning," Agnes said by way of greeting.

Leah didn't have an answer. Her head hurt from the thinking and the hair pulling of the night before. "Do you have any headache powder?" she asked, walking into the room.

Molly stopped playing with her doll and searched Leah's face. "Are you sick?" she asked, laying her baby down and coming across the room to give Leah a hug. Worry etched the child's face.

She hugged the little girl back. Would Molly always be frightened when someone had a headache or a sniffle? "No, I'm not sick. I just have a headache this morning," Leah assured the child.

"Look in the cupboard where I keep the spices," Agnes answered.

Picking up a mug, Leah poured herself a cup of coffee and found the medicine. After taking it, she looked about the kitchen.

Automatically she set about doing her part to get breakfast on the table. She placed the plates and poured coffee for the men. As soon as she'd done all she could to help Agnes, Leah excused herself and stepped out onto the front porch with the intention of sitting quietly and letting the headache powder work.

"Good morning, Miss Hollister."

She turned to see Reverend Rice sitting in one of the two chairs. "Good morning."

"Would you care to join me?"

Leah walked to the empty chair and sat down. "Thank you. I'd be happy to." She realized that her voice was coming out in a whisper instead of a normal tone.

"Are you feeling all right, child?" he asked, pushing off and setting the rocker into motion.

Was she feeling all right? That was a tricky question. No, she wasn't all right. She felt hurt, betrayed and unloved. Who could be all right feeling like that? "I have a headache," she answered, resting her head on the wood of the chair back.

"I'm sorry to hear that. It's my understanding that you had a rough night." The creaking of his chair did nothing to help her head.

Had he heard her pacing in her room last night? Or had someone else told him about her abduction? Probably the latter, at least she hoped it was not the pacing. "I'm sorry if I disturbed you last night." The reflection of sun on the bright snow caused shooting pains between her temples. Leah closed her eyes to shut out the brilliance.

"Not at all. I couldn't sleep either after that dreadful business with the Wattses."

Leah continued to keep her eyes shut. The darkness seemed to be helping her aching head. Why couldn't he sleep? Had being a part of the scheme to catch the Watts family kept him up? Only one way to find out. "If you don't mind my asking, what kept you awake?"

He stopped rocking. "You might find this silly but I was up asking myself if I am so old that others thought I wouldn't be helpful."

She cracked an eye and looked at him. He was staring across the yard as if seeking answers. "Why would you think such a thing?"

"Why else would I be the last one to know about the trap that had been set for the Wattses last night? I'm a foolish old man who thought he'd be able to help, but learned later the young ones had the situation under control." He sighed and then began rocking again, a frown marring his features.

So, he hadn't known either. Leah got no comfort from the knowledge. She sighed and stood up. "You weren't the only one who was left out of the plan." She left before he could comment on her statement. Just before she reentered the house Leah heard him make a *tsking* noise.

She saw that Agnes had placed the food on the table and Molly was already in her place.

"Oh, good. I'm glad you are here. Would you mind asking the reverend to ring the dinner bell? I'd do it but I need to get the biscuits out of the oven," Agnes said, setting a large plate of bacon on the table.

Leah knew that she couldn't sit and have breakfast with the very people who hadn't confided in her. She didn't think she'd be able to contain her anger. "All right." Leah opened the front door and called, "Reverend, Agnes has asked that you ring the dinner bell."

The rocking stopped. "Be happy to," he said, picking up the stick that they used on the inside of a metal triangle.

"Thank you." Leah closed the door and hurried to the kitchen so she wouldn't be forced to hear the high pitch of the dinner bell as the reverend rang it for all he was worth.

Agnes shut the oven door and smiled at her over her shoulder. "Thank you."

Leah asked herself if she was overreacting to last night. She needed time to think, time to heal from last night's events. "Agnes, do you mind keeping an eye on Molly for a few hours?"

"Not at all. Why don't you get some rest? Mr. Frontz said that Watts woman was pretty rough on you last night." She took the biscuits from the pan and proceeded to put them on a platter.

Leah didn't want to talk about last night. "Thank you. Don't worry if I'm gone most of the day. I didn't sleep last night, so I thought I'd go back to bed and then go over to the general store. I want to get something for Molly for Christmas."

Agnes waved her away. "Take the whole day, child. After what you've been through, a day of rest will do you good."

A lump formed in Leah's throat. She swallowed and then said, "Thank you."

Tears threatened to spill down her face. She hurried from the kitchen and was at the bottom of the stairs when Mr. Frontz, Ike and the reverend entered the house. Leah ducked her head and continued upstairs, she didn't trust her voice to say anything to them. She didn't want them to see her cry, either.

Once in her room, Leah stumbled to the bed. She unbuttoned her shoes and then crawled up on the soft mattress. For the first time since she'd been grabbed by Savannah, Leah allowed herself to weep. As she cried, Leah asked God to help her get over the hurt of being left out.

The sun was high up in the sky when she woke. Sitting up, Leah was glad that her headache was gone. Her scalp still felt tender as she brushed her hair and placed it in a loose bun. She replaced her wrinkled dress with a soft green one. She hadn't been aware of the aches and pains in her body until now.

Once dressed, Leah slipped out the front door. She

heard Molly playing at the side of the house and knew that soon Agnes would come get her for her afternoon nap. Leah hurried away from the home station and walked as fast as she could to the general store.

The little bell over the door rang, alerting the clerk that she'd entered. Leah inhaled the various fragrances that made up the general store.

"Hello, Miss Hollister. What can I help you with today?"

Leah looked up, surprised to see a younger version of the previous store clerk standing behind the counter. How did he know who she was? They'd never met.

He came around the counter and walked the short distance to her with his hand extended. "I'm Lester Perkins. My father and I own the store."

"Nice to meet you, Mr. Perkins." She allowed him to shake her hand. When it became obvious he wasn't going to let it go, she gently pulled it from his grasp. "Where is your father?"

"Pa had to go to Julesburg so I'm running the store today." Pride filled his voice and he balanced on the heels of his shoes.

"Oh, I see." She walked over to the yellow yarn and picked up what she'd come in to buy. The idea had come to her that Molly might like a knitted scarf for Christmas.

"Miss Hollister, may I ask you a personal question?" He walked over to her and took the yarn.

Lester Perkins didn't look much older than the pony express riders. She decided it would be safe to let him ask his question. Leah nodded.

"It may sound strange, but, well, I've been watch-

ing you and I know you don't know me but, well..."
He paused and scuffed the toe of his shoe against the
wooden floor.

The sound of the bell clanking over the door alerted
them that someone had entered the store. Leah's back
was to the new customer and Lester didn't seem to
notice or care that someone else had joined them.

"I was wondering if you love Mr. Bridges," he finally blurted out.

Leah felt like a fish out of water. When he'd said
a personal question, she hadn't expected that. "I really don't think..."

"I know, but I love you and if you don't love him,
you could marry me." Lester laid the yarn down and
grabbed her free hand.

"Really, Mr. Perkins. We just met and I am engaged to Mr. Bridges." She saw the stricken look on
his young face. His neck and cheeks turned red and
he looked down at the wooden floor. Leah tried to
soften her words. "Look, Mr. Perkins, even if you
and I were madly in love, I'd tell you no. I made a
commitment to Jake and I wouldn't break his trust
for anyone, not even you."

The bell over the door clanged again. Leah removed her hand from his. "Would you put my yarn
on Mr. Bridges's account, please?"

At his nod, Leah picked up her yarn and turned
around, expecting to see two other customers in the
store. She was shocked to see there was no one else
there. Leah realized that the clanging bell had indicated that the other customer had left instead of a
second customer arriving as she'd thought earlier.

Leah hurried from the store. Lester Perkins was a

strange young man. She was beginning to wonder if anyone in these parts was normal. Her head began to hurt again so Leah silently prayed. *Lord, please give me the wisdom to be able to read people. I feel so lost.*

Chapter Sixteen

Jake's mind swirled like a Texas tornado. He continued to replay the morning in his mind.

After praying all morning, he had come to the conclusion that Leah needed to know that he'd only been trying to protect her by not including her in the Watts capture. He wasn't sure how he knew, but he knew that she was upset and that being excluded from their plan was the reason.

When she hadn't shown up for lunch, he'd gone to Leah's room to check on her. The door had been open, the bed made, but Leah was nowhere in sight.

After lunch, he and Mr. Frontz were going to a town council meeting at the livery. The men were to discuss the attacks on the stagecoaches and what to do about them. It seemed the Indians were growing more and more hostile about the settlers invading their land. Even so, Jake really didn't want to go to the meeting without first making things right with Leah.

He walked down the stairs. Where could she be? Agnes came out of the kitchen, drying her hands on a dish towel. "Do you know where Leah is, Agnes?"

"If she's not in her room, she's probably over at the general store. Said something about getting a gift for Molly's Christmas. I declare you two are going to spoil that child rotten."

Jake looked behind Agnes, expecting to see his niece but she wasn't there. "Where is Molly?"

"At the side of the house playing. I'm going to go get her in a little bit and put her down for her nap." Agnes wiped off the table.

He nodded. "I guess I should head on over to the meeting." Jake was disappointed that he'd missed Leah. He walked out on the porch and then headed to town.

As he was walking past the general store, Jake saw Leah talking to the Perkins kid. Maybe, he thought, he might have a few moments to talk to her after all.

Entering the store, the bell rang over his head but neither Leah nor the Perkins kid had responded. Her back had been to him and the kid was looking at the ground.

Jake had listened as the boy had proposed to Leah, asking her if she loved him. He'd held his breath, waiting to hear her answer. When she'd said, "'Really, Mr. Perkins. We just met and I am engaged to Mr. Bridges,'" she'd paused, searching the young man's face. Her tone changed to one of kindness. "'Look, Mr. Perkins, even if you and I were madly in love, I'd tell you no. I made a commitment to Jake and I wouldn't break his trust for anyone, not even you.'"

Jake had left as quickly as he'd arrived. Once on the boardwalk, he'd turned to see if either of them had noticed his departure. They hadn't. He darted down the alley between the general store and the restaurant.

His heart pounded in his chest. Jake felt as if his world had just been turned upside down. Leah hadn't said she loved him but she had, without even knowing it, assured him she'd never break his trust. Could he believe her? It wasn't as though she had been forced to say the words.

His thoughts had no choice but to turn to Sally and John. All the signs had been there that the two of them were in love. After all these years, Jake looked back and saw them.

Memories of the day of their betrayal flooded his mind. They'd tried to explain they were in love and had been for some time. They hadn't meant to hurt him. He hadn't listened. For years he'd allowed bitterness to eat at him. How many missed opportunities at happiness had he allowed to pass him by?

The wall around his heart crumbled. He'd known since last night that he loved Leah. Seeing her in such danger had been almost more than he could stand, but he'd tried to pretend she didn't mean more to him than a good friend.

Jake decided to tell her now. He'd have to explain about last night first, but he felt confident he could make her understand. Taking a deep breath, Jake stepped back onto the boardwalk.

"There you are. I've been looking all over for you." Mr. Frontz's long legs carried him toward Jake.

"I have something I need to do at the house. I'll catch the next meeting." Jake started to walk around him.

Mr. Frontz caught him by the forearm. "Oh, no, you don't. If I have to go, you're going, too. It was your idea, after all."

Jake saw Leah enter the house. He sighed. She'd still be there when he got home in a few hours; he'd talk to her then. After all, he had been the one to sign them up for this meeting and it, too, was important. "All right. Let's go."

Leah entered the house. She made her way up-stairs, thinking Molly would already be down for her nap. Not seeing the little girl on their bed, she hid the yarn and went looking for her.

Thinking she might still be in the kitchen with Agnes, Leah looked there first. Agnes sat at the table with her eyes closed.

"Agnes?" Leah looked about the room for Molly. Agnes had probably put Molly down in the Frontzs' bedroom.

The older woman looked up and yawned, looking very relaxed, reaffirming in Leah's mind that Molly was probably sleeping in the Frontzs' quarters. For a moment she looked disoriented. "Leah, how's your headache?"

Leah looked into the face that she'd come to care about. Agnes may not have given birth to her, but she was more like a mother to her than anyone else had ever been. "It's not as bad as it was but I could use a little more powder."

Agnes pushed away from the table. "Can't believe I dozed off like that."

"You were tired." Leah poured coffee into a cup and took the headache remedy. Her stomach growled. A plate of eggs, bacon and a biscuit sat on the back of the stove.

"Thought you might like a bite to eat, so I scrambled you some eggs and added bacon and bread to it. The plate is there on the stove," Agnes said, sitting back down. Again she yawned.

Leah picked up the plate and joined her at the table. It still hurt that they'd not told her their plans the night before, but she'd made the decision not to allow that to bother her anymore. The eggs were warm and tasted wonderful.

"We should have told you what we were going to do last night. I'm sorry you got hurt."

Had the woman read her mind? Leah looked across into Agnes's bright blue eyes. "Why did you leave me out?" Leah asked.

"Jake didn't want you or Molly getting hurt. Charles agreed and, well, I didn't want you getting hurt either, so I went along with them. I'm sorry." Agnes covered her mouth and another yawn.

So they had cared. Leah felt so foolish. She'd been harboring ill feelings all day and for what? When would she ever learn? "It's all right, Agnes. I appreciate that you all wanted me safe, but next time, please tell me so that I won't come blundering out of my room." Leah offered a smile to soften the words.

"We will." Agnes stood. "I think I'll wait on cleaning those rooms and take a nap."

Leah felt a yawn overtake her, too. "Good idea. Is Molly in your room?" she asked.

Agnes stared at her blankly.

Fear gripped Leah. "Agnes, where is Molly?"

It was as if a fog lifted from Agnes's tired mind. "Oh, my stars, I forgot all about her. She's still at the side of the house playing."

Leah didn't want Agnes to see how scared she felt.

"I'll go get her." She darted to the back door. The sky had darkened and the air had turned much colder. Leah ignored the cold.

Agnes ran after her. "I'm sorry, Leah. I'm sure she is okay."

The two women sprinted around the corner of the house, only to find the snowman was the only thing there. The trees didn't conceal anything. Molly was nowhere to be seen.

"I left her right here, playing with her doll. See? She built a snow house for her." Agnes pointed at a pile of snow that resembled a log cabin, if she really tried to envision a snow home.

Panic threatened to choke Leah. Had the child wandered off? "Maybe she went inside and is playing hide-and-seek." Leah started back inside.

She didn't want to believe Molly had left her play area. Every day Molly had been told where she could play and where she couldn't. Leah didn't want to believe Molly would disobey her but deep down felt Molly had done just that.

They searched the house, the barn, the sheds and even double-checked the Frontzs' living quarters. Agnes thought Molly might be hiding up there. "I'm going to check our rooms again. I just feel she's hiding up there. The little one might have fallen asleep and we're just not seeing her." She started for the stairs once more.

"I'll check outside while you look for her upstairs," Leah said, reaching for her coat.

Leah hurried to the side of the house. Snow now drifted steadily from the skies. Winter storms in Colorado were proving to be very unpredictable. But she didn't have time to worry about the weather. Leah walked toward the orchard.

Two sets of footprints led into the trees. She thought about telling Agnes about the footprints but Molly had already been out in the weather too long. Leah headed off into the orchard, calling Molly's name.

Half an hour later, the snow was flying so thick that Leah almost couldn't see her hand in front of her face. Her coat did little to keep the cold out. Still, she pressed onward, praying that Molly was safe.

Her feet felt as if they were two frozen chunks of ice. Darkness began to descend. Leah's teeth chattered as she prayed. *Lord, please help me find Molly. Let her be safe and warm.*

Tiredness engulfed her. Leah wanted to lie down but knew she couldn't. Molly needed her. "Molly!"

The wind whipped her voice away. Ice began to blend with the snow and cut into her frozen body and face. Leah had no idea how long she'd been out looking. She found herself kneeling in the deepening snow. Slapping herself, she fought to stay awake. Her eyes began to drift shut.

A small figure stopped in front of her. "Molly?"

Covered from head to toe in animal skins, an Indian child walked a few feet away and motioned for her to follow. Unsure if she was seeing things or if the figure was real, Leah forced herself to stand. She struggled forward, keeping the walking furs in her line of vision.

Just when she thought she couldn't go on any longer, they came into a small group of trees. The child ran ahead. He entered a tall structure and returned a few minutes later with a woman. The dark-haired woman helped her through a teepee flap.

Warmth immediately enveloped her. Leah saw a fire in the center of the Indian tepee and Molly sitting beside it. She rubbed her eyes. "Molly?"

"Leah!" The little girl ran to her. She wrapped her small arms around Leah's shoulders.

The child she'd been following stood a few feet away. As the skins were removed from his body, Leah recognized the little boy Molly had been playing with earlier. Why hadn't she told Jake about the child? He'd have no idea where to look for them.

Leah felt a hand on her shoulder and looked up. The woman stood beside her holding up a straight dress. She motioned for Leah to remove her wet clothes and put the dress on.

Molly stepped back and watched as Leah tried to use her hands. The little girl tried to help her, but the buttons were too tight for her little fingers to work.

Tears filled Leah's eyes. With cold, numb fingers Leah worked to unbutton her coat. Her fingers wouldn't obey.

The woman said something to the boy in a guttural tone. He turned his back to them. She then gently removed Leah's fingers from the frozen buttons and began undoing her coat. With swift fingers and hands, she removed the rest of Leah's clothing. Then the woman pulled the dress over Leah's head.

She led Leah to a pile of animal skins and motioned for her to sit. Leah's legs did her bidding without any further encouragement. The woman removed Leah's wet boots and stockings. She gently pushed Leah back into the warmth of the furs.

"Molly," Leah called out, as the warmth of the furs pulled her toward sleep.

The little girl hurried to her side. Leah reached up and touched Molly's face. "Let's take a nap." She knew the little girl would probably object.

Molly jerked out of her reach. "No, no nap."

Leah just wanted to hold the little girl close, make sure she was safe. "Please."

"No, no nap." Molly shook her head.

The woman snapped sharply at the girl and motioned for her to do as Leah said.

Molly looked from the Indian woman to Leah. The stern look on the other woman's face seemed to convince her to do as she was told. "All right." Molly crawled into the furs with Leah and allowed her to cuddle close.

Leah looked to the woman. "Thank you," she said over Molly's head.

The woman nodded and offered Leah a small smile.

Warmth from Molly's little body and the furs relaxed her muscles. Leah wasn't sure her feet would ever get warm. She moved them against the soft fur, praying she didn't have frostbite on her toes.

The little boy approached. He held a fur wrapped much like a pillow. Kneeling down on one knee, he placed the pillow at her feet. Leah realized that something hot was wrapped within the fur. Warmth immediately crawled up her legs.

Leah grinned at him. "Thank you. I think I would have died out there if you hadn't found me." She didn't know if he understood her, but the boy bowed his head once to her before returning to the fire.

She pulled Molly close. "How did he know I was out there?" Leah asked.

"We heard you calling. His mama wouldn't let me go to you. But Boy said something to her and she let him."

"Boy?"

"That's what I call him. He can't talk like we do," Molly whispered over her shoulder.

"I'm glad he found me. I was so worried about you. You shouldn't have come here."

Molly's small voice drifted back to her. "I'm sorry. I just wanted to play with him."

Once more, Leah found her gaze moving to the little boy. She grinned. "Boys will get you into trouble every time." Her eyes began to drift shut.

For now, Leah allowed herself to go to sleep. She didn't know what tomorrow would hold and prayed that Jake and the other men would wait until the storm passed before coming after them.

She also prayed that Jake wouldn't be too angry with her for losing Molly. Leah realized that when Jake wasn't around, she missed him more than she'd ever missed anyone in her life. She loved Jake. There was no getting around the fact.

The storm raged against the house. Jake had been out searching for Leah and Molly for over an hour. He'd returned to the house to see if they'd come back or if anyone had found them during his absence. "I'm going out again," he announced.

"Don't be a fool, Jake," Mr. Frontz growled from his place by the fire. He and Agnes sat side by side on the smaller of the two settees.

Cole and Ike had taken possession of the two arm-chairs. The reverend sat on a kitchen chair beside the fireplace, staring into the blaze, looking as miserable as the rest of them felt. His lips moved as he silently prayed.

"Charles, my family is out in that storm. I have to go find them." He'd never used his employer's given name and wasn't sure why he had then. Restless energy spewed from him and Jake began to pace the floor.

"You don't think I know that?" Mr. Frontz ran a hand around the back of his neck. "It won't do us any good if you go looking for them and get lost yourself."

Anguish tore through Jake's words. "I can't lose them."

"I am so sorry, Jake. This is my fault. If I'd-a taken better care of the child…" Agnes buried her face in her husband's shoulder and wept.

Jake cleared his throat. "Not to be disrespectful, but in this matter, I disagree."

She looked up at him. If he didn't know better, he'd have thought Agnes had aged ten years. He offered her the only comfort he had. "Agnes, this is not your fault. It's not anyone's fault. Children wander off all the time. Molly is no different than any other child. But, Lord willing, she will learn from this."

Cole stood slowly. His green eyes looked into Jake's. "I'll go with you. I'm used to riding in this kind of weather and after dark. We'll find them and bring them back." His young voice cracked.

Ike cleared his throat. "I'm able to ride, too, Jake."

It touched Jake's heart that these young men were willing to ride out in the storm to recover his family. But he knew he could not allow them to endanger their lives. This was his job to do. His responsibility. He shook his head. "Thank you, but I can't allow you to do that." Jake picked up his gloves and turned to walk out the door.

"No one is leaving this house tonight." It was an order, not a request. Mr. Frontz moved his wife away from him and walked to the table. He picked up a chair and set it in front of the door. Steely eyes stared at Jake. "Let's all try to rest."

The message came through loud and clear. To leave the house, he'd have to go through his boss. Jake walked back to the big chair beside the fireplace and sat down. He laid his gloves on the side table once more.

Cole slumped back down on the couch. Ike leaned his head back on the cushions and closed his eyes. The reverend continued praying.

Agnes stood. "Good night, boys." She turned and walked up the stairs, her shoulders slumped, her head down.

The reverend stood also. "Please wake me in the morning. I'd like to go on the search party with you."

Jake looked up at him and nodded. "Thank you, Reverend."

He returned Jake's nod with one of his own and then followed Agnes up the stairs. At the bottom he stopped. "Jake, I believe the good Lord is taking care of Leah and Molly. Please try to trust in Him and get some rest tonight," Rice said, and then continued up the stairs.

It was good advice. Jake knew that God was in control but he couldn't stop worrying, just as he couldn't stop breathing at will. He leaned his head back on the cushion and closed his eyes.

They'd all had a rough night the night before. The symphony of snores told him that Cole and Ike had already fallen asleep. Jake continued to keep his eyes closed. He relaxed and his mind willingly scrolled over the scenes of his life since Molly and Leah had entered it.

Molly was as much his child as she had been his brother John's. The little girl had captured his heart the moment her little hand had touched his jaw and her head rested on his shoulder. Her love of horses matched his. Teaching her how to ride on her own had become something he looked forward to. Someday, she'd be running his horse ranch, if she survived tonight.

The sobering thought tore the carefree images of Molly away. He tried to regain that sense of relaxation by focusing on Leah. Her blue eyes sparkled like no other woman's. She never said a cross word and her laughter lifted his spirits. He'd already confessed to himself that she'd stolen his heart. Jake prayed they'd get to have a life together. Once more, sobering thoughts pulled him from the feelings of calm he'd been trying to capture.

Jake listened to the sounds of three people sleeping in the room. Opening one eye just a crack, he looked at his friend Charles.

The man slumped in his chair. His arms were crossed and his chin rested on his chest. Snores whistled through his nose.

It was time. Jake sat up. He waited a moment more and then picked up his gloves. Careful not to make a sound, Jake stood and walked to the kitchen door. He took one last look back before opening the door and leaving his friends sound asleep.

Once out in the dark and cold, Jake headed to the barn. He pulled his horse out and swung into the saddle. For several moments, Jake debated which way to go. Earlier he'd searched in a state of panic; now, with a calmer head, he reasoned out where he should look.

Agnes had said she'd left the child playing on the side of the house by the apple orchard. Would Molly have gone into the trees to play? If he were four, Jake knew he wouldn't have been able to resist the temptation to climb one of the trees. He nudged his horse forward.

No stars or moon filled the sky. Darkness enveloped him like a sickness as he entered the trees. The horse snorted his uneasiness. Jake sighed. He couldn't see and knew it wasn't safe to ride the horse through the snow drifts. Even a small hole could cause the horse to stumble and break a leg, so Jake knew he couldn't chance losing his horse.

He realized he'd have to trust God to keep them safe. Jake leaned forward and patted the animal's neck. "Come on, boy, back to the barn for you." He turned the horse around.

As the animal ambled back to the warmth of the stable, Jake prayed. *Lord, please keep my family safe. Help me to find them at first light. For the first time in a long time, I am giving You my full trust.*

Chapter Seventeen

Leah woke long before the sun came up. She felt stiff but well.

A slight shuffle sounded beside the fire. The woman stood, stirring something in a cooking pot. The little boy sat on a pelt stringing a small bow. It felt funny to think of them as the woman and the boy. Leah knew they had names, but since introductions hadn't been made, she had no idea what they were.

She scooted off the bed of furs and stood up. The borrowed dress felt comfortable as she walked to her hostess. "Good morning," Leah said in a soft tone.

The woman smiled and indicated that she should sit down on one of the many furs about the fire.

Leah did as she was bid. She sat there for several minutes, waiting to see if the woman would talk to her. When it was obvious she wasn't going to speak, Leah said, "I'm Leah Hollister. That's Molly." She pointed to where Molly still slept.

A nod was her answer.

Leah looked about what she now recognized as a tepee. She was amazed at the warmth of the structure. Having never been in one before, she'd assumed they'd be cold except where the fire was, but that simply wasn't true.

Molly walked over to her. The little girl crawled into Leah's lap. She rested her head on Leah's shoulder and stuck her thumb into her mouth.

The woman handed the little boy a small bowl of whatever was in the pot. He took it and began scooping it out with his fingers. She then handed a bowl to Leah.

Molly sat up and dipped her fingers into the bowl. She pulled out a blue grainy-looking substance. The little girl stared at it with a frown.

The woman grunted and motioned that they should eat.

At Leah's nod, Molly stuck her fingers in her mouth and sucked on them. Leah carefully tucked two fingers into the bowl as she'd seen the boy do and lifted the warm substance to her mouth.

It didn't hold much flavor and felt gritty in her mouth. She looked across at the woman who seemed to be watching her every move. Leah smiled across at her. "Thank you, it's good."

Molly pushed the bowl away and settled back against Leah. The woman sat down and seemed to be pleased as she ate her own breakfast. When the boy was done he set his bowl down and picked up the bow again.

Molly pushed away from Leah and went to sit beside him. She reached for the bow but he pulled it away. The little girl looked up at him with a frown. "I just want to see it," she said.

The boy got up and walked to the back of the tepee. He returned with her rag doll and handed it to her.

"Play with your doll, Molly," Leah said. "As soon as it gets light, we need to be heading home."

As if the other woman understood what Leah said, she shook her head and pointed up at the tepee hole.

Leah looked up but could see nothing. No stars, no sun, nothing. "I'm sorry, I don't understand."

The woman set her bowl aside and motioned for Leah to follow her. She undid the tent flap and stuck her head outside, then indicated that Leah do the same.

Leah gasped. It wasn't still night as she'd thought. The sky outside was dark because of the low-hanging clouds that blocked the sun. "Oh, we need to go now. Come, Molly."

A tan arm blocked her passage. The other woman shook her head again.

Panic threatened to overwhelm Leah. Was she being held captive? Why? It dawned on her that they were alone. There were no other tepees outside. Was the woman simply lonely? Taking a deep breath, Leah tried to explain. "You don't understand. Our men are looking for us. We have to go."

A grin touched the woman's lips. She pointed out that Leah was barefooted, in a stranger's dress and that neither she nor Molly was dressed for the snowy outdoors.

"Oh, I see."

The woman dropped her arm and went back to the fire. She picked up the bowls and put them away.

Molly stood, clutching her doll. For the first time,

Leah realized that the little girl wore the same type of dress that she was wearing.

"Come on, Molly, we need to change back into our clothes."

The woman grunted and the boy turned his back on them. She then moved to another part of the tepee, picked up their dry clothes and carried them to Leah.

"Thank you." Leah smiled at her and laid the clothes down. She found Molly's dress and put it within reaching distance. "Come on, sweetie. Let's get your borrowed dress off."

"But I like this dress," Molly protested as she walked over to Leah. She laid her baby down on the soft furs and turned to face Leah.

Leah smiled at her. "I know you do. I like mine, too, but they aren't ours." She pulled the shift over Molly's head and then dropped her own dress into place. Who did the small dress belong to? It didn't look like a little girl lived here.

"This one's scratchy," Molly complained, tugging at the collar. She sat down and began pulling her socks and shoes on.

Leah slipped into her dress, stockings and shoes. Molly was right in the fact that their clothes didn't feel nearly as soft as the woman's had. Her toes were already starting to cramp as she thought about how the snow had gone into her shoes the night before. Leah sighed as she pulled Molly's coat, hat and gloves on and handed her the rag doll.

She then proceeded to pull on her coat. Leah wished she'd taken the time to grab her gloves and hat but in her rush to find Molly, she'd left them behind. She looked around once more. "I guess that's it."

The boy and the woman stood by the flap waiting. They each had on furs from head to toe. Were they going, too?

Leah took Molly's hand and walked toward them.

The woman handed her a pair of what looked like fur-lined boots. "I can't take these," Leah protested, handing them back.

The woman pointed at Leah's shoes and frowned.

"I know. Not the best for walking in snow, are they?" Leah felt Molly release her hand.

"These are so soft, Leah," Molly said. The little boy and Molly were sitting on the floor. He had pulled off her shoes and was putting on a pair of the boots. A big smile covered Molly's face.

Once more the boots were shoved into Leah's hands. They would be much better than walking through the cold snow in her shoes. "All right. Thank you."

A few minutes later, they stood in the winter wonderland.

The little boy and Molly ran ahead. Leah wished the woman could talk to her. She'd love to know what it was like to travel around and live off the land.

The sun reflected off the woman's black hair, which had been braided down the back. Her high cheekbones and square jaw gave her a regal beauty. Almost-black eyes looked back at her. "You are very beautiful," Leah said in a way to explain why she was staring.

The woman looked to where the children played.

Leah didn't take it as a snub. She knew the woman couldn't understand her. Or could she? Every time

Leah or Molly had needed something the woman had responded.

They heard two horses coming before they saw them. Leah assumed it was Jake and Mr. Frontz and began calling, "Over here. We're over here."

The Indian woman looked at her with a raised eyebrow.

"It's the men looking for us," she answered.

Molly screamed as a rider came barreling down on her. Leah's eyes grew wide as Christina Watts jumped from her horse and grabbed the little girl.

Molly kicked and screamed. Her hat fell from her head. She quickly stopped fighting and screaming when Mrs. Watts jerked her arm behind her back and grabbed her by the hair. "I'll break it, child," she warned, giving a sharp pull to Molly's hair.

The anger of a mama bear filled Leah. "Stop!" Leah screamed, trying to run toward the children. The snow pulled at her feet, keeping her from actually running.

The little boy had run but wasn't faster than the other horseback rider. Horror filled her as Leah watched a man scoop the little boy off the ground like a hawk hunting a mouse. The child kicked and was rewarded with a blow to his head.

The Indian woman grabbed her arm. She shook her head hard and motioned that Leah should look back to where Molly and Mrs. Watts stood. Fear and anger knotted inside her. Christina Watts held a small handgun pressed against Molly's temple.

"Well, look what we got here. Miss Leah Hollister."

Leah recognized Isaac Dalton's voice. She turned

and glared at the man who had just knocked the little boy out.

He rode his horse over to Leah. "I'll say these four are just what we need to get Michael and Savannah back, wouldn't you, Christina?"

Mrs. Watts laughed. "The gods must be smiling on us today, Dalton."

"Let the kids go," Leah demanded.

"Or what?" Dalton asked, smiling down at her. He was using the little boy's back to lean on.

Molly whimpered. "Leah, she's hurting me."

A growl emitted from the Indian woman's throat. She took a step toward Molly, only to be rewarded by Christina jerking back on the little girl's hair.

Leah hated that she was helpless. "I know, sweetheart. Just do what she tells you to. Don't fight her."

Tears flowed down Molly's face. "I'll be good."

Christina Watts leaned down and said, "Yes, you will, or I'll give these golden locks of yours a good yank."

Fury almost choked Leah. "Like mother, like daughter."

Mrs. Watts laughed. "No, I'm smarter than my darling girl. I won't get caught."

Dalton chose that moment to bring attention to himself. "Stop pulling the child's hair, Chrissy, and get back on your horse."

"But how am I going to get back up and hold the girl?"

He frowned. "Let the child go, Chrissy. If she runs away, I'll shoot Leah and then I'll shoot the girl. You don't want me to shoot Leah, do you, child?"

Molly shook her head. "I'll be still."

Mrs. Watts let go of Molly's hair. She mounted her horse.

Molly stood in the snow crying.

Dalton leaned forward and looked down at Leah. "You might want to go help her up."

"I don't think so," Leah answered.

He dug his elbow into the little boy's back, forcing a moan. "No?" His intent clear. If she didn't help Molly he'd continue to hurt the boy.

Leah hurried as fast as she could in the deep snow. When she got to Molly, she hugged the little girl to her and whispered, "Uncle Jake is on his way. Just be a good girl and do whatever they tell you to, all right?"

Molly clung to her. "All right."

"Stop your blubbering and hand her up."

Leah looked up at Christina. She now pointed her gun down at them. She looked back at the Indian woman. Dalton had his gun trained on her. Leah picked Molly up. "I'm going to put you in front of Mrs. Watts. Help me out, all right?"

Molly touched Leah's cheek with her hand and nodded. Trust shone from the little girl's eyes. "I love you."

"I love you, too."

"Stop with the sweet talk and get on with it," Mrs. Watts demanded.

Leah handed Molly up.

Christina Watts scooted back in the saddle to make room for the little girl. With Molly's help, the child soon sat in front of her captor.

Resting a hand on Mrs. Watts's thigh, Leah squeezed. "Pull her hair again and when this is over, you'll answer to me."

Something in her eyes caused Mrs. Watts to frown. "Are you saying you'll kill me?"

Cold gripped Leah's heart. She'd do anything to keep Molly safe. Murder? It went against everything she believed in. She didn't answer. She simply stepped back and let the woman draw her own conclusions.

"Time to go, ladies. Hopefully old man Slade hasn't already strung up the kids."

Kids? He thought of Michael and Savannah as kids? Leah called after him, "What about us?"

He looked over his shoulder at her. "If you want to watch the exchange, I suggest you keep up."

Dalton urged his horse forward at a fast pace. It was all Leah and the other woman could do to keep up. But keep up they would. Their children were in danger.

Jake didn't know how long Leah and the Indian woman had been trailing after Dalton and Mrs. Watts before he finally found them. He'd been shocked at the way Dalton called back, taunting Leah as they traveled. To her credit, Leah ignored him and focused on keeping up with Molly.

His first instinct had been to rush in, guns a-blazing, but he'd seen the weapons pointed at Molly and the little boy. Attacking too soon could mean the life of one or both of the children.

To keep out of sight of passersby, Dalton and Mrs. Watts traveled close to the river bank. It was late in the afternoon when the sun came out. Now Jake could clearly see the glint of guns close to the children's heads. Fear for Molly and anger at the way Dalton forced Leah to run after him, warred within Jake's body.

Leah looked as if she were about to collapse from exhaustion. Still, she continued to follow. Her companion glared ahead.

Jake had sensed the brave long before he saw him and his traveling companion. The two men were also following Dalton and Mrs. Watts. From the hardened coldness in the brave's eyes, Jake figured out that the kidnappers had taken the brave's loved ones.

When they arrived in Julesburg, Jake left the water's edge and headed into town. He motioned for the brave to follow. If he were a guessing man, Jake would have to say they were headed to Slade's place to exchange prisoners. Had Savannah and Michael Watts already been hanged? And if so, what would become of the women and children?

Chapter Eighteen

Leah hurt all over. She stopped behind the horse and looked at the old shack Dalton and Mrs. Watts had stopped in front of.

"Slade!" Dalton yelled.

The little boy's dark gaze stayed focused ahead. Molly jerked from the sudden yell, earning her a slap on the head. Leah clenched her fist. To Molly's credit she didn't make a sound.

Leah remembered Mr. Slade as being a quiet man. He stepped out of the building with fire in his eyes. She didn't know if it was because of the guns aimed at the children's foreheads or if he was just angry at being disturbed.

"You're just in time for a double hanging," Slade said, looking up at Dalton.

Dalton leaned forward, pressing the little boy forward with his body. "Yeah, I thought so. That's what I'm here about, Slade."

An old rickety rocker sat on the porch. Slade walked over to it and sat down. He set it to rocking.

"Came to join the lynch mob? Or give yourself up and become a member of the hanging party?"

Leah felt the hair on the back of her neck stand up. A sense told her that Jake was close by. She didn't know how she knew, she just knew.

"Are you crazy?" Mrs. Watts squealed.

"Shut up, Chrissy," Dalton demanded, never taking his eyes from the man on the porch.

From the corner of her eye, Leah saw Jake step out into the open. He stood on the right-hand side of the old building. He motioned for her to come to him. She wanted to run to Jake but wouldn't leave her new friend. Leah grasped the Indian woman's hand and gently pulled.

Big black eyes turned to look at her. Leah indicated with her head that they should slip off to the right. The woman's eyes hardened. She shook her head. With that one look, Leah felt the other woman's loathing. It was clear she thought Leah intended to abandon their children.

"Trust me," Leah mouthed.

Again the woman shook her head. She turned and stared at the backs of Dalton and Mrs. Watts.

"Aw, so you've come for your kin, I see." Slade bobbed his head. "Well, what if I don't give them to you?"

Dalton tapped his gun barrel against the boy's temple. "I think two children are worth more than two horse thieves, don't you?"

What was she going to do? It was clear her friend wasn't going with her. Leah looked toward Jake, but he was gone and in his place was an enormous Indian. She gasped.

Leah felt the woman's hand on her shoulder. A gentle squeeze told her that the Indian woman had seen him, too. She turned to make sure that Dalton and Mrs. Watts hadn't heard her gasp and given Jake and the Indian brave away.

"I suppose so." Slade stood. "Let the kids slide off those horses and I'll give you my prisoners."

Leah inched toward where Jake had stood earlier. The other woman followed. They both kept their gazes locked on the scene before them. She was sure Mr. Slade could see them, but he didn't indicate it.

Leah slipped through the throng of people to Jake. She wanted to hug him and feel safe in his arms, but that wasn't meant to be, and now wasn't really the time. Molly still needed rescuing.

"Stay here and no matter what, do not leave the side of this building," Jake ordered. His gaze focused on Molly.

Anger radiated from him. Leah knew that Isaac Dalton would be sorry he ever threatened Molly's life. She watched as he and the Indian man beside him stepped in front of the building.

By now quite a crowd had gathered. All the focus was on the outlaws and the kids. She prayed it would continue to be that way.

Dalton laughed. "Now, Slade, did you really think I'd agree to that?"

Slade leaned against the porch and pulled a big cigar from his pocket. "Naw, not really, but it was worth a try." He looked about shrewdly at all the men that surrounded the two horses.

"Send out my family. I'm getting impatient," Dalton demanded.

When Slade saw the two men, he answered Dalton's impatient comment with one of his own. "So am I."

At Slade's words, no less than twenty men drew their pistols. The sound of guns cocking had Jake's heart hammering in his chest. He wanted to run to Molly and get her out of the range of fire. His new companion laid a heavy hand on his shoulder.

Dalton's eyes grew round. The sound of Mrs. Watts's gasp would have been comical, if the situation hadn't been so delicate. She tightened her grip on Molly.

Jake knew the moment Molly saw him. A smile radiated from her tired little face. He held her gaze and then demonstrated that he wanted her to bring her elbow back hard against Mrs. Watts's stomach.

Without looking at the Indian, he knew that the man had just shown his son the same action. Fortunately they'd had time to make this short plan with Slade before Dalton and Watts had arrived. So far, everything was going as planned.

Molly looked at the little boy beside her, just as Jake had hoped she would.

The boy nodded at her and then he rammed his small elbow into Dalton's stomach. Before Dalton could react, the boy slid from the horse.

At the same moment, Molly did the same. The two children grabbed each other and ran for their families.

Dalton and Watts were caught. The men moved in swiftly, jerking them from their mounts, but Jake didn't have time to dwell on that. He raced toward the kids.

Molly jumped into his arms. The smile on her face assured him that she wasn't hurt as he'd feared. "Papa! Did you see me? I did what you said!"

He hugged her close. Did she think he was John? Had the terror of the day addled her mind? Jake pulled her back and kissed her forehead. Slowly he turned to where he knew Leah would be waiting beside the building.

She hadn't listened to him. Leah stood watching them come toward her. A smile touched her pretty lips. Hair hung about her shoulders and she looked tired, yet happy.

Then her expression changed to horror. "Jake, get down!"

He instinctively did as she screamed.

Not so Leah. Jake watched as she gasped. Her hand covered her heart. Big blue eyes widened and held his as a red stain seeped under her fingers.

"Leah!" Molly screamed.

The sound of commotion behind him couldn't pull Jake's eyes from the woman he loved. It all seemed to be happening in slow motion. She glanced down at the blood on her hand. Then Leah dropped to her knees. Her eyes returned to his and she offered a weak smile. "I should have listened to you," she said, then fell forward.

He caught her just before she hit the ground. Jake turned her over slowly. Her pretty eyes were closed now and he feared the worse.

The Indian woman knelt beside him. She jerked open Leah's coat and dress revealing a bullet hole in her left shoulder. Next she cut the hem of her dress and used the fur to press against the gaping wound.

Her soulful eyes met his, and he felt the dull ache of foreboding.

The Indian woman's husband stood behind her. He held both Molly and his son's hands within his own, but he tipped his head at Jake. "My name is Gray Hills. This is my woman, Nightfall, and my son, Soaring Eagle. The evil man and woman are inside. Take your woman to the medicine man."

The woman nodded her agreement.

Tears spilled down Molly's cheeks. Jake felt his composure slip. The two most precious people in his life needed him in different ways. He had to choose which one needed him most at the moment. The knowledge twisted inside him.

Jake prayed Molly wouldn't revert back to her silent world. "Molly, she's going to be all right. Let's take her to the doctor."

Again Gray Hills spoke. "We will care for the little ones." Even though his statement was firm, there was a question in his eyes.

Jake knew he'd rather Molly not see Leah like this. He nodded and lifted her in his arms. "Stay with Gray Hills, Molly. I'll be back." The crowd parted as Jake made his way to the doctor's home. With each step he felt the nauseating sinking of despair. He prayed for her not to die. He felt her shudder as she drew in a deep breath. Terrible regrets assailed him. He'd never told her he loved her; now he may not get the chance.

The next morning, Leah awoke. She tried to push up off the mattress that seemed to be attached to her back. It proved to be difficult with her left arm in a sling.

"Lie still, Miss Hollister," a woman's voice said off to her right. "I'll help you up, if that's what you really want to do."

Leah turned her head and saw an older woman. She'd seen her many times during the night. For a moment Leah wished the stranger was Agnes.

Her shoulder burned and her mouth felt as if someone had stuffed it with cotton balls. Leah remembered being given a bitter drink before drifting off to sleep and wondered if that was why she felt so thirsty now. Her shoulder burned and her mouth felt as if someone had stuffed it with cotton balls. "May I have a drink?"

"Of course, dear." The woman poured water into a glass from the basin beside the table. "I'm Elsie Capshaw. I assisted my husband, Dr. Capshaw, in digging that bullet out." She handed the glass to Leah then slid an arm under her shoulder and propped her up just slightly.

Leah remembered that when she woke up the first time it had been to excruciating pain. Several people were holding her down and the doctor was working to get the bullet out of her shoulder. She heard him say, "Got it. Good thing it wasn't in there very deep." Never in her life had she felt such pain. She'd passed out. Pushing the horrible thought away, Leah drank deeply from the water and then handed the glass back. "I want to sit up, please."

"Are you sure, dear?"

Leah nodded. "Where's Molly?" She also wanted to ask about Jake, but since they weren't married yet, wasn't sure it was appropriate.

Mrs. Capshaw helped Leah sit on the side of the bed. "She's in the sitting room with Jake. I hope you don't mind, but I loaned you one of my blouses and a skirt to replace your dress," she said.

"Thank you. I'll return it the first chance I get." Leah looked longingly toward the door. All she wanted was to see that Molly was safe and for Jake to hug her and tell her everything would be fine.

"Don't you fret none about giving it back." She brought Leah's borrowed boots over and slipped them onto her bare feet. "I assume you'd like to get out there with your family. The doctor says you can travel whenever you feel up to it, but he wants you to take this powder if you're in pain. And don't be surprised if you're sleepy after taking it." She handed Leah a bag with several small paper envelopes inside. "Just put it in some water and drink it down."

Leah nodded. Her left arm still burned, but the pain wasn't so bad. She felt sure she was still under the influence of the powders she'd taken earlier.

Mrs. Capshaw opened the door and Leah followed her out of the doctor's office and into the waiting room where Jake and Molly sat. Jake reclined in a big fluffy chair, his eyes closed, with Molly sleeping on his lap. Both were pure delight to her eyes. She'd never wanted to hug two people more in her life.

When she'd seen Christina Watts aim the gun at Jake's back, she'd thought both Molly and Jake were going to die. Panic such as she'd never known had welled up in her throat, almost choking her. She was thankful her scream had caused him to fall to his knees. It had all happened so fast, she couldn't believe she'd been shot. Then she'd seen the blood on her hand and had watched Jake's eyes widen in horror.

Right now, though, he looked at peace. Had the

doctor told him she would be fine? Or did he always look so relaxed when sleeping? The line over his eyes had smoothed out and he snored softly into Molly's hair.

The little girl opened her eyes first. Leah placed her finger over her lips and knelt down. She extended her right arm and waited for Molly to run into it.

"I was so worried," the little girl whispered loudly as she hugged Leah tight.

She returned her hug. "I'm going to be all right," Leah assured her.

"My turn."

Molly stepped back and looked up at her Uncle Jake. "I was hugging her." She pouted.

"There will be plenty of time for you to hug her later, right now I want to hug her." Jake reached down his hand to help Leah to her feet.

Mrs. Capshaw reached out a hand for Molly. "Why don't you and I go find a cookie to nibble on and let these two talk?"

Molly took her hand. "All right."

As soon as the door closed behind them, Leah took his hand and allowed him to pull her up. She stepped into his embrace. Her heart sang with delight. She felt blissfully happy, fully alive. This was where she belonged. This was where she never wanted to leave. These two people were her heart, her home.

Jake pulled away from her and Leah felt disappointed. Only, he didn't completely release her. "Leah Hollister, I love you more than you'll ever know. Do you remember the day you were in the shop and the Perkins boy said he loved you?"

Leah nodded.

"Well, your loyalty gave me a reason to believe you would never betray me or my emotions for you." He stopped and leaned closer so that they were eye to eye. "I want to get married in more than just name only. I want to love you forever and never let you go. God brought us together and no one will ever pull us apart. I promise."

Leah's heart and mind raced. How had he known that she feared he'd leave her like her parents had? Had God given him the sense that those were the reasons she'd withheld her own confession of love?

"What do you say? Will you marry me for love?"

Tears of happiness streamed down her face. Leah nodded. She forced the word "yes," from her tight throat.

Concern filled his face, "Are you sure? You don't look happy."

Leah laughed and cried at the same time. "Oh, Jake, I was so afraid you'd leave me before the wedding and I never dreamed you would love me like I love you. You've made me so very happy."

When Jake gently pulled her to him again and kissed her lips, Leah knew they would be happy together. What started as a marriage of convenience, God had blessed into a marriage of love.

Epilogue

Leah stood in front of the mirror. Her pale cream-colored wedding dress flowed about her legs and feet. Thanks to Nellie, her brown hair was up in the latest style. Bright blue eyes of excitement were reflected back at her.

She couldn't believe it was true. Today was her wedding day. After all they'd been through, it was finally going to happen.

The house had been decorated specially for a Christmas wedding. The staircase she would soon descend had streams of red, green and white garland strung down its banisters. The windows were snow kissed with frost. Each one held a single candle in its sill. A large cedar tree had been brought down from the mountains and decorated with strings of cranberries and popcorn. Jake had found red and green Christmas plants to place about the sitting room. It was perfect. It was her Christmas wedding.

"You look beautiful," Agnes said, smoothing invisible wrinkles out of her dress.

Leah smiled. "Thank you. I feel beautiful." She twirled around in front of the mirror.

A knock sounded on the door. "Who's there?" Agnes demanded.

Mr. Frontz's voice came through the wood. "It's time to start, ladies."

Agnes opened the door and allowed her husband inside. "I thought Nellie was going to come up and get us."

"She's too busy bossing the men around downstairs," he answered, taking in Leah's reflection in the mirror. "You look wonderful. Almost as pretty as Agnes on our wedding day."

Mr. Frontz cleared his throat. "I'll walk the missus down and wait for you at the bottom of the stairs," he said, never taking his eyes off his wife's face.

"Thank you." Leah watched them leave.

Mr. Frontz pulled the door shut behind them, leaving her in silence. Leah closed her eyes and prayed that God would bless her marriage to Jake. Jake's actions had expressed his love for her more in the past week than anyone else's had in her entire life. He stayed by her side as much as he possibly could, tried to wait on her hand and foot and took care of Molly, allowing Leah time to heal from her gunshot wound. He'd done even more by getting flowers and the tree to the house in the few short days before the wedding.

Molly slipped into the room. "Leah, everyone is waiting."

The little girl, her reason for searching out Jake, stood before her wearing a pretty red-and-white dress. Her hair was pulled up and small ringlets framed her face.

Leah loved her. She still couldn't believe that soon they would be family. A real family. "I know, Molly. I was just thinking about how pretty everything looks downstairs."

Molly walked across the room and took her hand. "You should see Uncle Jake. He's dressed in a real suit."

"He is?" Leah hadn't expected Jake to dress in a suit. At the thought of how handsome her soon-to-be husband must look in a suit, she grabbed Molly's hand and headed to the door.

The sound of the piano was her cue to descend the stairs.

"I'm supposed to go first and throw these flowers in front of you," Molly said, picking up a small wicker basket that held paper flowers.

Leah nodded. She lifted her head high and tried to control her breathing. This was her big day; the day she would start her new life with Jake. Her heart pounded in her chest with joy.

Jake watched as a vision of beauty floated down the stairs. He'd never seen anyone look as lovely in his whole life. Leah smiled at him, and his heart beat double time. He still had a hard time believing that Leah loved him and would soon be his wife.

Little Molly passed Mr. Frontz and began tossing her paper flowers as she walked toward Jake. Jake smiled at his niece. Molly had brought Leah to him. They were a family. When she came to him, Jake felt her small hand enter his larger one but he couldn't seem to pull his gaze from Leah.

Mr. Frontz offered his arm to Jake's beautiful

bride. She placed a lace-covered hand on his arm. Her blue eyes held Jake's. Together Mr. Frontz and Leah walked to where he, Molly and Reverend Rice waited.

Jake gently released Molly's hand so that Mr. Frontz could place Leah's into his.

He only half listened to the wedding vows. His heart beat so loudly in his ears that Jake feared the others would hear it and call a stop to the wedding.

Leah's voice was soft when she vowed to "love and to cherish, until death do us part." She said it with such conviction that Jake's heart felt as if it would explode.

Jake then repeated the same vows. He placed the ring upon Leah's finger and saw that his hand trembled at the simple action. Someone cleared their throat. "You may now kiss your bride."

Leah closed her eyes and leaned toward him. Jake reached out and touched her face before lowering his mouth to hers. She responded with the slightest movement of her lips. He wanted to deepen the kiss but was very much aware of the people around them. Reluctantly he released her.

Jake laid his forehead on hers and whispered, "I love you and I promise you will never be alone again." She needed to hear those words from him and Jake needed to say them. He was now officially Leah's husband. Excitement coursed through him. Without thinking or worrying about those around them, he pulled her into another kiss.

Molly whispered loudly and tugged on his coattail. "Uncle Jake, you need to stop kissing Aunt Leah. It's time to eat cake."

Reluctantly, Jake released his bride's lips. Reverend Rice laughed and then announced, "I present you with Mr. and Mrs. Jake Bridges. May they forever be happy in their new love."

* * * * *

Dear Reader,

Thank you for picking up a copy of *A Pony Express Christmas*. The pony express has always fascinated me. I used actual places and people in this book. Julesburg, Colorado, has moved three times since the pony express and was known as a rowdy town and was a pony express home station. South Platte was a relay station but for the purposes of this book, I made it into a home station, too. Jack Slade and Jules Beni were real people who lived around Julesburg and their history together is very interesting.

I hope you enjoyed reading Jake and Leah's story as much as I enjoyed writing it.

Feel free to visit me on my website and blog at www.rhondagibson.net.

Warmly,
Rhonda Gibson

Questions for Discussion

1. Leah took Molly to her uncle. Would you have done the same?

2. How do you think Leah's life would have been different if Thomas Harris had lived?

3. Have you ever been so grief-stricken that you haven't been able to talk? Or known anyone that has been that way? If it was you, what brought you out of such grief?

4. When Leah arrived in South Platte she didn't believe anyone could love her. Have you ever felt that way? Do you have any friends (as opposed to family members) who have made you feel loved?

5. Jake was dealing with distrust because his brother married his fiancée. Have you ever felt a deep hurt similar to his that has changed your life?

6. It took Jake a long time to realize that his brother and fiancée hadn't meant to hurt him. Have you ever thought someone hurt you on purpose and then discovered that wasn't their intention? How did you react to that realization?

7. Jake had to realize that Leah wouldn't break his heart. He did that by overhearing her tell someone else her true feelings regarding him. Have

you ever overheard someone talking positively about you? How did it make you feel?

8. Molly and Leah were both orphans. Have you ever adopted someone into your family?

9. Do you have people in your life who feel like family but aren't blood relations? If so, who are they? And what makes them so special?

10. Which character in this book did you most connect with? Why?

REQUEST YOUR FREE BOOKS!

2 FREE INSPIRATIONAL NOVELS
PLUS 2
FREE
MYSTERY GIFTS

Love Inspired.
HISTORICAL
INSPIRATIONAL HISTORICAL ROMANCE

YES! Please send me 2 FREE Love Inspired® Historical novels and my 2 FREE mystery gifts (gifts are worth about $10). After receiving them, if I don't wish to receive any more books, I can return the shipping statement marked "cancel." If I don't cancel, I will receive 4 brand-new novels every month and be billed just $4.74 per book in the U.S. or $5.24 per book in Canada. That's a saving of at least 21% off the cover price. It's quite a bargain! Shipping and handling is just 50¢ per book in the U.S. and 75¢ per book in Canada.* I understand that accepting the 2 free books and gifts places me under no obligation to buy anything. I can always return a shipment and cancel at any time. Even if I never buy another book, the two free books and gifts are mine to keep forever.

102/302 IDN F5CN

Name	(PLEASE PRINT)	
Address		Apt. #
City	State/Prov.	Zip/Postal Code

Signature (if under 18, a parent or guardian must sign)

Mail to the **Harlequin®** Reader Service:
IN U.S.A.: P.O. Box 1867, Buffalo, NY 14240-1867
IN CANADA: P.O. Box 609, Fort Erie, Ontario L2A 5X3

Want to try two free books from another series?
Call 1-800-873-8635 or visit www.ReaderService.com.

* Terms and prices subject to change without notice. Prices do not include applicable taxes. Sales tax applicable in N.Y. Canadian residents will be charged applicable taxes. Offer not valid in Quebec. This offer is limited to one order per household. Not valid for current subscribers to Love Inspired Historical books. All orders subject to credit approval. Credit or debit balances in a customer's account(s) may be offset by any other outstanding balance owed by or to the customer. Please allow 4 to 6 weeks for delivery. Offer available while quantities last.

Your Privacy—The Harlequin® Reader Service is committed to protecting your privacy. Our Privacy Policy is available online at www.ReaderService.com or upon request from the Harlequin Reader Service.

We make a portion of our mailing list available to reputable third parties that offer products we believe may interest you. If you prefer that we not exchange your name with third parties, or if you wish to clarify or modify your communication preferences, please visit us at www.ReaderService.com/consumerchoice or write to us at Harlequin Reader Service Preference Service, P.O. Box 9062, Buffalo, NY 14269. Include your complete name and address.

LIH13R

SPECIAL EXCERPT FROM

Love Inspired

Don't miss the conclusion of the
BIG SKY CENTENNIAL *miniseries!*
Here's a sneak peek at HER MONTANA CHRISTMAS
by Arlene James:

"Robin," Ethan said, just before his face appeared in the church belfry's open trapdoor, "come on up. It's perfectly safe."

He reached down a gloved hand as she put a foot on the bottom rung of the wrought-iron ladder.

"How does this thing work?"

"It's very simple. There's a tall pole with a hook on one end. I used it to slide open the trap and then pull down the ladder. When I'm done, I'll use it to push the ladder back up and lift it over the locking mechanism, then slide the trap closed."

"I see."

"Oh, you haven't seen anything yet," he told her, grasping her hand and all but lifting her up the last few rungs to stand next to him on a narrow metal platform. In their bulky coats, they had to stand pressed shoulder to shoulder. "Take a look at this." He swung his arm wide, encompassing the town, the valley beyond and the snow-capped mountains surrounding it all.

"Wow."

"Exactly," he said. "There's a part of Psalms 98 that says, 'Let the rivers clap their hands, let the mountains sing together for joy…' Seeing the view like this, you can almost feel it, can't you? The rivers and mountains praising their Creator."

"I never thought of rivers and mountains praising God," she admitted.

"Scripture speaks many times of nature praising God and testifying to His wonders."

"I can see why," she said reverently.

"So can I," he told her, smiling down at her with those warm brown eyes.

Her breath caught in her throat. But surely she was reading too much into that look. That wasn't appreciation she saw in his gaze. That was just her loneliness seeking connection. Wasn't it? Though she had never felt this sudden, electrical link before, as if something vital and masculine in him reached out and touched something fundamental and feminine in her. She had to be mistaken.

He was a man of God, after all.

Even if she couldn't help thinking of him as just a man.

Will Robin and Ethan find love for Christmas,
or will her secrets stand in their way?
Find out in HER MONTANA CHRISTMAS
by Arlene James, available December 2014 wherever
Love Inspired® books and ebooks are sold.

SPECIAL EXCERPT FROM

Love Inspired
SUSPENSE

*When a woman's young child is abducted, can a man
with a similar tragedy in his past come to the rescue?*

*Read on for a preview of HER CHRISTMAS GUARDIAN
by Shirlee McCoy, the next book in her brand-new
MISSION: RESCUE series.*

"Just tell me what happened to my daughter."

"We don't know. You were alone when we found you."

"I need to go home." Scout jumped up, head spinning,
the room spinning. The knot in her stomach growing until
it was all she could feel. "Maybe she's there."

She knew it was unreasonable, knew it couldn't be
true, but she had to look, had to be sure.

"The police have already been to your house," Boone
said gently. "She's not there."

"She could be hiding. She doesn't like strangers." Her
voice trembled. Her body trembled, every fear she'd ever
had, every nightmare, suddenly real and happening and
completely outside her control.

"Scout." He touched her shoulder, his fingers warm
through thin cotton. She didn't want warmth, though. She
wanted her child.

"Please," she begged. "I have to go home. I have to see
for myself. I have to."

He eyed her for a moment, silent. Solemn. Something
in his eyes that looked like the grief she was feeling, the
horror she was living.

Finally, Boone nodded. "Okay. I'll take you."

Just like that. Simple and easy, as if the request didn't

go against logic. As if she weren't hooked to an IV, shaking from fear and sorrow and pain.

He grabbed a blanket from the foot of the bed and wrapped it around her shoulders then took out his phone and texted someone. She didn't ask who. She was too busy trying to keep the darkness from taking her again. Too busy trying to remember the last moment she'd seen Lucy. Had she been scared? Crying?

Three days.

That was what he had said.

Three days that Lucy had been missing and Scout had been lying in a hospital bed.

Please, God, let her be okay.

She was all Scout had. The only thing that really mattered to her. She had to be okay.

A tear slipped down her cheek. She didn't have the energy to wipe it away. Didn't have the strength to even open her eyes when Boone touched her cheek.

"It's going to be okay," he said quietly, and she wanted to believe him almost as much as she wanted to open her eyes and see her daughter.

"How can it be?"

"Because you ran into the right person the night your daughter was taken," he responded, and he sounded so confident, so certain of the outcome, she looked into his face, his eyes. Saw those things she'd seen before, but something else, too—faith, passion, belief.

Will Boone help Scout find her missing daughter in time for Christmas?
Pick up HER CHRISTMAS GUARDIAN to find out!
Available December 2014
wherever Love Inspired® books and ebooks are sold.

Love Inspired HISTORICAL

Big Sky Daddy
by
LINDA FORD

FOR HIS SON'S SAKE

Caleb Craig will do anything for his son, even ask his
boss's enemy for help. Not only does Lilly Bell tend to his
son's injured puppy, but she offers to rehabilitate little
Teddy's leg. Caleb knows that getting Teddy to walk again is
all that really matters, yet he wonders if maybe Lilly can heal
his brooding heart, as well.

Precocious little Teddy—and his devoted father—steal
Lilly's heart and make her long for a child and husband of her
own. But Lilly learned long ago that trusting a man means
risking heartbreak. Happiness lies within reach—if she seizes
the chance for love and motherhood she never expected…

Montana
Marriages

**Three sisters discover a legacy of love beneath
the Western sky**

*Available December 2014
wherever Love Inspired books
and ebooks are sold.*

Find us on Facebook at
www.Facebook.com/LoveInspiredBooks

LIH28290

An Amish Christmas Journey

by

Patricia Davids

Their Holiday Adventure

Toby Yoder promised to care for his orphaned little sister the rest of her life. After all, the tragedy that took their parents and left her injured was his fault. Now he must make a three-hundred-mile trip from the hospital to the Amish community where they'll settle down. But as they share a hired van with pretty Greta Barkman, an Amish woman with a similar harrowing past, Toby can't bear for the trip to end. Suddenly, there's joy, a rescued cat named Christmas and hope for their journey to continue together forever.

BRIDES OF *Amish Country*

Finding true love in the land of the Plain People

Available December 2014
wherever Love Inspired books
and ebooks are sold.

Find us on Facebook at
www.Facebook.com/LoveInspiredBooks

LI87927